BROTHER IN ARMS

SACRED HEARTS MC
BOOK 10

A.J. DOWNEY

COPYRIGHT

DEDICATION

To everyone on my beta team, I seriously couldn't have pulled this one off without you. Thank you so much for your hard work and dedication. This book is a thousand percent better because of you.

PROLOGUE

R **ush…**

"Harder!" she gasped, and I felt a wicked grin curve my lips.

"Yeah? You want it?" I murmured by her ear and she locked her legs around my hips, digging her nails into my ass, pulling my cock deeper.

"I want it," she affirmed, her breath heavy with the scent of the bourbon she'd drunk.

We were at *The Spot* and feelin' fucking fine. I had her luscious ass backed into a corner, in the alcove by the bathrooms. Her short denim skirt riding high, her thin scrap of panties moved aside, and my cock buried balls deep inside her.

It was a classless hookup, but she'd been all-in, giving me eyes from across the bar for the better part of an hour before I'd left Nox and Arch and wandered over. She moved her hand from my ass and dragged my mouth to hers and *fuck* she tasted amazing; like bourbon and brown sugar. Some kind of alluring concoction of the liquor she'd been knocking back and her lip gloss, and I couldn't get enough.

"You like that?" I demanded and she gasped.

"Yeah." Her voice was breathy with passion and her body gripped mine like a glove. I bowed my head and nipped the side of her neck, pounding into her, her long brown hair done in twin braids gave her this hot, sexy, little-miss-innocent look while her eyes — heavy lidded with passion — told me just what a little minx she was.

She was far from innocent and knew just how to fire me up; she laughed softly and I thrust as deep as I could go, turning the light sound into a deep, guttural moan.

"Tell me your name," I demanded and she smiled a secret little smile.

"No… and don't you dare stop," she muttered by my ear and added gasoline to the burn in my blood even more. I fucked this bitch in the back of the bar, where anyone could happen by and see us, and all I could think was how I wanted *more*. She was both the sun beating down on me and a cool drink of water on the same long hot day, and I was one thirsty son of a bitch.

1

Six weeks later...

R ush...

"Yeah just about everybody in here is out having relationships and shit and I'm just over here like BRRRRAAAP!" I pantomimed twisting down on a throttle to a bunch of laughter and cracking up in the rest of the club's taproom. I grinned and turned around on my barstool and picked up my Bloody Mary, trying like hell to recover from the hard partying of the night before.

Reaver laughed and Hayden snuggled happily in his lap, I watched them in the mirror behind the bar and was both seriously glad for them and super jealous at the same time. Reaver stared his woman in the eyes and addressing me said, "You don't know what you're missing, man."

Problem was that I did. I so did, and it was hard as fuck not to know when Dray was smiling across a table at Everett and Trig was running his hand through Sunshine's hair, dragging her face to his for a long kiss. I rolled my eyes. My time would come eventually, I had to believe that, but at the same time, I wasn't lookin' for it anymore. I'd given that shit up, all it did was land me with a bunch of bitches only in it for themselves.

"Ooooh I do, trust me," I said. "That shit's a bunch of drama that I just *do not need.*"

Just as the words died on my lips the front door to the club swung open and a woman, complete with a fuckin' pantsuit on, walked in like she fuckin' owned the place. All of us froze and I saw Dray stand up, his chair scraping across the concrete floor as he stepped around from the table he was sharing breakfast with Evy at.

The woman looked around in distaste, shook herself, and squared her shoulders more determined than she had a right to be comin' in here with *that* kind of attitude.

Dumb fuck citizen, I thought to myself. Of course, this is what we were gonna get leaving the gate open all the damn time like we were. No one saw the need to roll it closed anymore on a account of there being no imminent threat.

Dragon leaned back in his seat at the table he was sharing with Doc, the Sunday paper spread out over its top, and cocked his jaw, before he could say whatever it was he was going to say, Dray spoke up.

"Aunt Trudy?" he asked and sounded confused as fuck.

The woman tugged on her suit jacket and rolled her head on her neck to ease the tension in it. I took the opportunity with her standing there all awkward and shit to give her a more thorough going over. Her graying dark brown hair was in a perfect French twist, not a piece out of place. Her suit screamed expensive, the cream-colored blouse she had on with it, complete with pussy bow had the look of silk and her pearl earrings were definitely not fake.

She gave Dray a nod and intoned gravely, "Draven."

For half a second when she'd stepped through the door, I thought she might be one of those jewelry dealer people who'd accidently come here lookin' for Dani, but Dragon and Dray's reaction had belayed that real quick. I never expected her to be any kind of *familia* to my president and VP, and not just because she was white.

"What're you doing here?" Dray asked, frowning and I don't think I could really remember a time my VP looked so damn stiff.

"I was actually hoping to speak with José."

Dragon stood up and she turned, going just about as still as a statue. Dragon cleared his throat and said, "Right here, what brings you walkin' through my door?"

"Is there someplace we may speak that is a little more—"

"Nope," Dray interjected. "Anything you've got to say can be said right here or not at all." Dray's temper was sparking.

"Dray." Dragon's voice held a bit of warning in it... a father chiding his son. It just served to stoke Dray's fire just that little bit more, and Evy reached out a hand touching his wrist. He jerked back sharply from her touch. Evy's mouth thinned down into a straight, disapproving line but her eyes held understanding. Dray shot her an apologetic look. Something sure as fuck was going on here, the tension in the room thick enough I wasn't sure even one of Reave's knives would cut through it.

"Please, José. I wouldn't be here if it weren't important," the woman said and the note of pleading in her voice was unmistakable.

Dragon nodded. "This way, we can talk in here."

Data was either still crashed out or not even here, so Dragon led her over to the vacant fishbowl with all its tech and monitors, the black curtains drawn, and slid the sliding glass door closed behind them. The rest of us in the common room exchanged looks.

"*Aunt* Trudy? Does that mean…?" Reaver looked at Dray whose smoldering look was locked on the curtains blocking our view of Dragon and the woman.

"Yeah, that's my mom's sister."

"I vaguely remember seein' her once before, I just can't remember where from," Trigger said, and Dray shrugged, retaking his seat. He reached out a hand across the table, taking up Everett's.

Dray said, "My mom drew that line in the sand when I was like twelve or thirteen. Haven't seen or heard from that side of the family right up until Mom died. Trudy only showed back up right after it happened; screaming and bitching about how it was all our fault. Fuckin' monopolized the shit out of my mom's funeral and then that was the last of her until just now."

"Ah, shit… that's why I couldn't place her. No offense Dray, but I prefer remembering your mamma when she was alive, those funerals passed in a haze of booze and despair; I could hardly remember how to tie my boots."

"Don't blame you, Trig, I don't want to remember it either. I especially don't want to remember how much harder she made it for me and my dad."

"What the fuck does she want now?" Reaver mused aloud, staring down the still black curtains of the fishbowl like they were some kind of traitor for hiding Dray's aunt from our sight.

"Don't fuckin' know, and don't fuckin' care," Dray said and Everett squeezed his hand.

For a lot of minutes, the only sound in the room was the scrape of knives and forks and the click and clink of glasses and mugs against the worn tabletops. Occasionally, it was the rattle of newspaper as Doc flipped through the pages, peering at the print through his half-moon spectacles. I kept sat at the bar and finished sucking down my Bloody

Mary which was a little on the weak side, more vegetable juice than anything… I guess that counted as breakfast, right?

The sliding door slid open and while I tuned in, I didn't look, just going off of what I could catch with my peripheral vision. Dragon poked his shaggy head out and called, "Dray, get in here, boy, I need you."

Dray got up, I watched him in the mirror behind the bar. He went into the fishbowl, expression stormy and just in time for Data to come out the archway back toward the rooms. He squinted against the light in the common room and I had to laugh.

"I'll make you some hair of the dog," I said and dragged myself around the bar to fix him a remedy.

"Thanks," he said and hauled himself up onto the barstool next to mine with a groan.

"Help yourself," I muttered and thrust a chin at the bottle of aspirin on the bar top next to my empty glass. Data grunted and dragged the bottle closer to him, popping the top and chewing four of them. I winced, I couldn't do it. That shit was nasty.

"Tell me why the fuck we should help her, after all the shit she pulled with Mom?" All heads turned toward the fishbowl and Data looked back toward me.

"What the fuck is going on in there?" he asked.

"Tillie's sister, Trudy, showed up, apparently she's lookin' for help with something," Trigger said and Data frowned.

"Yeah, good luck with that," he muttered and reached for the glass I handed him.

"Gatorade would do you better," Doc said without looking.

"Yeah, that's next," Data said after draining half his glass in three long swallows.

Shouting in Spanish emitted from the fishbowl and the slider opened up, the woman stepping out stiffly and more than a little red faced. She slid the door closed behind her and looked up, startled that all eyes in the room were on her. I put my hands on the bar top and leaned on them taking the whole spectacle in.

She squared her shoulders and put on that haughty air of superiority just as the door slid open behind her. Dragon stopped, and she stepped aside lightly to let him out, her pumps clicking smartly as she made the movement. Dragon stepped out and Dray right behind him. Dray looked over everyone in the room, his smoldering look falling on me.

"Rush, help me out. Take a ride with me."

"You got it," I said without hesitation, because when the VP of your club asked you to do something and his family was somehow involved, that's what you did.

We went out front to the line of bikes parked there and each went to our own. Separated by five or six of our brothers' motorcycles, I asked as we geared the rest of the way up to ride, "Can you fill me in on what the fuck I might be walking into?"

Dray's aunt slipped out of the club right behind us and drifted to a ghostly-grey Jaguar idling nearby, pointing down the driveway ready to leave. "Thank you, Draven," she murmured as her driver came around to open the back door.

"Don't thank me yet, Trudy. I said I'd go talk to her and that I'd scope things out; I didn't promise to get me or mine involved."

She nodded, and I swung a leg over my bike, sticking the key in the ignition. I had my helmet on over a bandana tied tight around my hair which was in need of a cut. I took the time to zip up my jacket and pull another bandana around my face. I didn't need any added protein of gnashing any bugs in my teeth and there were a lot of them this time of year. Early summer was pretty good for bug activity in farm country.

"We'll follow you," Dray called out to the driver who shut his aunt into the car. She settled herself and buckled up.

I was getting the impression there was some kind of deal going on with family in the middle, but I still had no idea what was up.

"You armed?" he asked.

"Always."

"Good. Someone's threatening my cousin and her place, we're going to get the full meal deal. After that, Pops and I will figure out our level of involvement."

"Cool." I fired up my bike and yelled, "I'll keep that in mind, thanks for the heads up."

Dray fired up his bike and tying a bandana around his own face called, "Sorry I can't give you more than that right now."

"No worries!" I slid my protective eyewear onto my face and Dray waved a signal at the driver of his aunt's car. The expensive cage pulled smoothly down the gravel drive and headed left out onto the highway. We checked, and finding the coast clear, rode out behind them.

It was warm, the sun beaming down on us and I don't care what you say, when you're in that much black leather and the temp is in the seventies, you start sweating like a motherfucker. Air movement didn't do you a whole lot of good. I unzipped about fifteen minutes into the ride which helped some, but I was still hungover and dehydrated as fuck so by the time we reached the place where Dray's cousin was supposedly at, I couldn't care less that it was some kind of horse farm so long as the southern hospitality thing rang true and there was something cold to drink at the end of the long, hot ride.

The Jag pulled up in front of this natural wood clapboard ranch-style house with an attached barn. The barn was smaller than the place's actual barn which was across the drive from the house and I wondered why in the fuck anyone would want to have a barn attached to the house like that... then it hit me, foals... it would certainly cut down on travel time to and from the main barn.

The wood on the outside of the house and connected barn wasn't local. I'd been here long enough to recognize that. A rich bright wood with a reddish tint, I'd guess cedar without getting up close to it. It was mighty fine workmanship on the outside of the place, the trim around the doors and windows painted a sage green that kept everything looking earthy and natural to a layman's eye. It'd look more natural to me if the clapboards were hand-hewn rather than machined, but that was a personal preference and machining was faster, easier and more cost-effective. Not that it looked like cost-effective ever entered these happy bastards' minds.

The place stank of a rich so high I was immediately uncomfortable, that is, until I saw the help, then I almost felt like I was back in Arizona for a minute. Mostly Mexicans, these were dudes that knew their way around horses and hard work. I could respect that. I'd worked a couple of dude ranches back in Arizona, so I knew the life. Maybe that was one of the reasons I was here. I still didn't know, Dray hadn't had a chance to tell me and I was okay with that. I wished I'd known they'd had horse farms and the like out here, I probably would have applied. Working the garage wasn't my favorite thing to do for work.

We backed the bikes to one side of the porch steps, in front of the ranch house. The driveway was crushed gray gravel that gave up puffs of fine dirt with just about every movement. I grimaced inwardly at the mess it was going to make of the bikes. It was a tossup when it came to what I hated worse, taking time away from my woodshop, or having a dirty bike. The wheels won by virtue of the respect they deserved for giving me such fucking freedom when it came to living such a shitty life.

Before the club, I had no place, no purpose other than making sure my twin and I made it to our eighteenth birthdays. Once we hit that mile-stone, once we aged out of the system, we were both cut loose and cast adrift. It was Grind and Arch back to the rescue giving Nox and me a life again by introducing us to club life.

Even so, living the club life in Arizona was trouble enough, not that I minded. We were sticking it to the man, running guns south across the border. My foster brothers and me, we stayed the fuck out of the coke trade but guns we had no problem with. In fact, I had one of my best friends tucked into the back of my waistband beneath my jacket and cut in a snug little inner pants holster. I never left home without it, fuck the fact that I could be brought up on charges for having a felony assault on my record and carrying.

Dray cut the engine to his bike and I followed suit, immediately going for the chinstrap on my helmet even as his aunt ascended the ranch house's steps beside us. I exchanged a look with my VP and he scowled. Not at me, but the situation. I could tell he wanted to tell me more about what was up, but I could also tell now wasn't the time. He was still figuring shit out too, although he was still leaps and bounds ahead of my ass which was square in the dark. This seemed to be the kind of thing that required that perfect trust between brothers. It was something we didn't always have back in Arizona; Dom liked to play it fast and loose and it was one of the things that had encouraged the rest of us to consider following Grind. His dying just sealed the fuckin' deal.

We, and by 'we' I meant Archer and me, had been getting tired of living dangerously. It wears on a man after a time, and it wore on us that we weren't really fighting for anything worthwhile. There were other ways of making money. Not the fuckin' loads of it we were swimmin' in by running guns, mind you. You pretty much had to work twice or even three times as hard when it was honest, but the cuts from the gun running were getting slimmer and slimmer while Dom's wallet had been getting fatter. When you're taking on more of the risk for less of the reward… yeah.

I should have done what my twin did from the beginning, kept at an honest living and kept out of the game, but fuck, honest livings were hard as fuck to come by with a felony record. Gun runnin' had been, for the most part, easy. Stressful with lookin' over your shoulder every two seconds, but easy.

Dray and I got up after divesting of what gear we could to beat the heat, leaving our jackets laying across the saddles of our machines, our helmets hanging off the handlebars with our sweat-soaked bandanas in the overturned bowls of them. I propped my sunglasses on the top of my head and looked to Dray to see if he might have any more explanation for me. He gave a shake of his head and I nodded, content to ride it out for now and seeing why he was reluctant to start talking — his aunt stepped back out of the front of the house alone but holding a tray with a full pitcher and glasses on it.

"Come up here, Draven. You and your… friend. Sit for a moment, while I have Renaldo find your cousin." The way she said 'friend' dripped with a familiar disdain that the upper-class had for us perceived losers and degenerates.

Dray nodded but didn't look happy about it and I didn't blame him one bit. I already didn't like the bitch and the look on my brother's face spurred me into a bit of action. I bit out "Just what exactly are we doin' here, lady?"

Dray's aunt looked up from where she poured tall glasses of iced tea, a little bit startled. She was careful not to over pour and handing Dray a glass said, "No, I suppose you can't talk much with how loud those vulgar machines are, can you?"

"Trudy," Dray grated out, "you better check your fuckin' prejudice at the door or do I seriously have to already remind you that *you* came to *us* for help?"

Trudy blinked in surprise and was clearly taken aback, yet still all she had to say for her bigoted ass was, *"Language,* Draven!"

"It's Dray, and the only reason I'm sittin' here through your blatant disrespect is because you happen to be my dead momma's sister. Don't you *ever* forget that I fuckin' hate you for what you did when she died! I hate you so deep, I wouldn't piss on you to put you out if you were on fucking fire. Only reason I'm here is for Bales, now answer the man's question. Why the fuck are we here?"

She sank into her seat after handing me a glass of tea, and I inclined my head with a polite, "Thank you, ma'am." I watched the guilt flicker through her deep brown eyes like I knew it would. It always chapped their fuckin' asses when the likes of one of us showed more decorum than they did. Usually it put them into a more cooperative frame before we had to do something nasty... sometimes but not always.

She licked her lips and said, "As I told my nephew and his father, my Richard died around three or four months ago. He left this place to the three of us — myself, my son, and my daughter." I took a sip of my tea, watching my VP smolder across the table from me.

"I'm sorry for your loss," I said automatically, and she smiled a bit ruefully, bowing her head to regain her composure. So her rich husband's death had actually cut pretty deep. I couldn't decide if she started out with money or if she'd been a gold digger who'd eventually fallen in love, but the end result was etched into every line of her face, she *had* loved him and hardcore.

Interesting...

"Yes, well, I sold my portion of this place to my daughter, Bailey. It took everything she had to purchase it from me, but I can't be bothered, not with how vast my husband's holdings were and Bailey has loved this place ever since she was a child and out of all of us, could make the most of it."

"So, what's the problem, then?"

"Philip, my son, has gotten heavily into real estate and development. A developer has purchased several of the neighboring farms and Philip is furious that Bailey, as a two-third's owner of Blue Hills Farm, won't sell."

She looked out over the green pastures and sighed heavily, pursing her lips. "He's just like his father," she said flatly. "I loved Richard, in the beginning, precisely for that part of him, but Philip? Unlike his father, he just doesn't know when to let go. He'd be willing to tear what is left of this family apart over this, and I just don't understand it."

Dray snorted and stared his aunt down. "Just like his Mom," he said coldly and I cringed inwardly. Our VP had a knack for saying shit that cut deeper than deep with as few words as possible and I could tell he scored a hit, his aunt's brown eyes going wider than wide as she tried to stammer out a defense.

Dray just stared her down and wasn't buying any of it, and Trudy, apparently, had learned somewhere along the way where to quit, because she didn't say anything more, just resolutely shut her mouth.

"What else did Uncle Ritchie-Rich do?" Dray demanded and Trudy's nostrils flared, her eyes glassing over with unshed tears.

I didn't say anything, even though that look on a woman just about always hit me right in the feels. Mostly I kept my mouth shut because I didn't fully know or understand their family dynamic. I could tell whatever was there that the wounds ran deep and they didn't need me picking at the scabs, so I just waited them both out. The tension at the little porch table was thick enough Reaver would have a field day carving it up, but finally, Trudy cut to the chase.

"I'm afraid for my daughter, afraid enough that I went to José for help... I realize I haven't been good family to you, Draven, but please, don't hold that against your cousin."

"It's Dray, that's Rush, and you need to use our fuckin' names correctly and stop being so damn snooty."

"Of course, I apologize," she murmured and the way she said it, automatically lowering her gaze and turning her head to the side breaking eye contact... shit, it echoed Sunshine and Dani who had a major history with abuse — domestic, physical, mental, emotional, shit you name it. Dray and I exchanged a look and he raised an eyebrow.

It looked like Uncle Ritchie-Rich may have been ruthless more places than just the boardroom. I arched a brow at Dray, silently asking if this meant he would go easy, and he gave me a flat, unimpressed look back. I knew this lady probably put on a pretty good show, but the way Dray was portraying her, he made her look like Satan or some shit and I just wasn't getting that from her. Of course, with rich people, appearance was fuckin' everything. I knew that.

"Okay, what did you want me to do?" I asked them both.

"I wish to have Bailey hire you. José said that you have experience working with and around horses. We don't know what happened, but recently, a good majority of our staff here quit with no notice."

"What, just handed in their two weeks?" I asked.

"No, they simply stopped showing up for work."

"Do you mind if I inquire as to their legal status?" I asked, looking back over the railing and out over the few people who were in sight working away.

An echoing silence came from Trudy's corner of the porch and I exchanged another look with Dray.

"Yeah, that one didn't exactly take a rocket scientist. I bet a few choice dropped words about INS in the right corners had them running scared. It's a pretty solid and impactful intimidation tactic. Your daughter won't sell, time to make it so she has to kind of a thing."

"I see," she said, and I realized that she hadn't even thought of the immigration angle, that she hadn't even considered that some of her workers were undocumented. She didn't look happy about that. *I* wasn't exactly surprised. There wasn't much in the world that a rich person loved more than fucking money, and they would tend to do just about anything to keep said fucking money right where they wanted it the most – in their pocket.

That typically meant screaming bloody murder about illegals soaking up resources like a sponge across the land, while simultaneously seeking them out to employ them at bargain-basement prices to the point that it ensures they *have* to get on assistance just to make it. It was a vicious circle these people were trapped in and forced to walk… and the path they had to follow was typically painted in red.

"So let me see if I've got this straight," I said, and I was just plain showing off that I was *not* as dumb as she likely believed. "You're low on staff, Bailey's being stubborn, and her brother Philip is the type to get real nasty over this; so you want to kill two birds with one stone. You want to hire a big bad biker who isn't afraid of the pussy real estate developer, so you went to Dragon to see if he had any guys available. Come to find out, you lucked out and one of them, that'd be me, actually has experience working a dude ranch on his resume. Even better, am I right?"

She blinked and nodded slowly; I smiled, and it wasn't friendly. "Well, it's going to cost you, because I don't work for peanuts and I damn sure don't put my ass on the line for the kind of money these guys are working for around here." I gestured to a few of the dudes visibly sweating their asses off in the sun.

"I see," she said plainly.

"Got plenty of guys willin' to work at the shop; I'm pretty sure Blue and Cell would do anything to get off that road crew," Dray supplied.

"Name your price," his aunt said without any hesitation. I thought about it a minute and figured that even if Dray hated the woman, now wasn't a time to get greedy. We were out here because Dragon had sent us out and I knew Dragon. She may be a major pain in the ass, but she was his wife's sister and when it came down to that… pain in the ass or not, she was still *familia* and you didn't dick over family, even if they maybe did deserve it.

I named a figure that was a pretty substantial raise from what I was making at the garage but wasn't so big as to make someone choke on it. In fact, with the relief that washed over Trudy's face, I probably could have stood to go a little higher, but that was okay. The number seemed to please Dray, he knew what I made at the shop being my boss and all. He gave a curt nod in my direction and Trudy said, "Just let me find Bailey and we can finalize things."

I was curious, so I asked, "Dragon and Dray did tell you what I did to lose my job at that ranch, didn't they?" I asked.

Trudy's dark eyes met mine and some of the ruthlessness peeked out, the calculation clear in her eyes. "Yes, and I'm afraid before all is said and done, that that is precisely the kind of man I will need on my daughter's farm."

She saw some kind of writing on the wall when it came to her kid and it wasn't pretty. I filed that away for later and perked up when she looked past me saying, "Here comes Bailey now."

I turned and swear to whatever fucking god there was, my stomach hit the insides of the soles of my boots. Long dark hair was braided in pigtails on either side of a pretty and familiar face. It made her look innocent, but I knew that she was far from it. Innocent girls didn't like to fuck in the back of a bar where anyone could catch 'em.

At least she'd traded out that short denim skirt for jeans and scuffed cowboy boots made for kicking shit around the farm... still, would have been nice to know she was the president's niece *before* I'd stuck my cock in her.

Fuck. My. Life.

What had I just agreed to?

2

Bailey…

"Mother, why are there motorcycles in my driveway and bikers on my porch?" I asked coolly, or at least I hoped it was coolly. My heart was pounding, and I was seriously hoping my face wasn't giving me away, blushing with color. The one biker I didn't know, but we'd gotten awfully familiar, anyway. The way he was looking me up and down, gaze burning, face otherwise shut down and neutral, told me he knew *exactly* who I was.

Crap, crap, crap!

So much for an anonymous one-time hookup, I thought to myself. The other biker was a familiar face and one that I couldn't help but crack a smile.

"Holy *shit*… is that my little cousin Dray-Dray?"

"Bailey Lynn Berling! Language!" my mother cried but Dray and I both just ignored her.

"You're only four years older than me, Bales," Dray said, as if my mother hadn't just admonished my grown ass over the use of a four-letter word.

"Yeah," I said looking him up and down, "but I can see it might as well be forty. When are you going to grow out of this?" I asked waving my hand over him and his friend. My mother's color drained and she looked like she was about to have a stroke. Dray smirked knowing exactly what I was up to, but it was a nasty little smile. Still, what came out of his mouth was, "Never," and he said it with such a fierce conviction I was taken aback.

Go, go, Bailey, with your no filters! You probably could have done without that last one.

"Alright," I said drawing out the word in a sing-song tone. "Not trying to start family world war three. I just worry about you, that's all." Which was totally true, I'd missed Dray, but his father's lifestyle, and apparently his lifestyle now too, had been what'd gotten my aunt killed. I missed her, but I missed Dray, too, and I had no idea what he would be doing here. After my mom had completely lost her shit at my aunt's funeral, I'd pretty much never expected to see my cousin again.

My mother tugged on her jacket and it reminded me of a bird adjusting her ruffled feathers. I never did get her, she was the one forever going on about my aunt Tilly's poor choices and how José Trujillo would be the death of her and then it'd finally happened. So why would she be sitting on my front porch sipping tea with my cousin and one of his biker buddies? It was completely mind-blowing.

"I never thought I'd see this day, that's for sure," I said and Dray snorted, turning to look out over my farm. I mounted the steps and let him admire the view. I'd been doing great with Blue Hills since my dad had died. All despite the road blocks my asshole brother kept throwing up and the fact that Caleb, my father's best friend and the farm's trustee, listened to Philip more often than not rather than the little woman. Never mind that I was the one that was actually here and running the farm.

I'd loved my dad, but he was a good ol' boy and had good ol' boy friends and had raised my brother to be a good ol' boy too. I don't think Caleb or Philip had counted on my mom selling me her portion of the farm, nor do I think that they thought I would have the money to buy her out at fair market value like my father's will stipulated.

Unlike my asshole brother, I'd socked my money away for years. Didn't spend extravagantly and knew the meaning of hard work. My daddy may have paid for everything when I was in college, but I'd still held a job and had saved everything. I'd had enough and then some to buy out my mom, but I *had* had to buy her out and it'd nearly wiped me out to do it.

That *'and then some'* was dwindling fast, too. Every time I went to buy a much-needed piece of equipment for the place, or hire on more staff, I was pretty much caught in a web of resistance between Philip and Caleb.

If I needed it, I would go to Caleb, and Caleb would then call Philip. Philip, who wanted to see this farm fail, would tell Caleb, 'Nah, she doesn't need it,' and Caleb would tell me no. So, I either had to come up with it out of my own pocket or not at all.

It was tougher than I'd like to admit. Mostly because even though I owned two-thirds of the farm, Caleb declared that my salary earned from it remained the same and that what would have been Mom's portion of it go into a trust for the farm. I couldn't even be sure the money wasn't going into Caleb or even Philip's pocket because every time I asked to see the financials, Caleb told me I didn't need to worry my pretty little head over these things.

I dropped into an empty seat at the four-person table and sighed looking from one face to another, and another, until I finally settled on my mother's.

"So, what is this?" I asked.

"I have hired this young man to help you around here," she said, and I choked on the sip of sweet tea I'd started to take.

"Mom! You sold your portion of this place to me, you don't get to make that kind of decision!"

"I know, you do... but Bailey I implore you to please think about this. He has experience."

I looked over my anonymous barroom hookup, eyes drifting to the nametag thing on his vest which read 'Rush' and tried not to think about how I'd read that faded patch over and over as he'd fucked me against that wall. I pressed my thighs a little tighter together under the table and continued to pretend I didn't know him from Adam.

"What's your name?" I asked him, and his eyebrows shot up.

"Rush, what's yours?" he asked, and I knew he just wanted to hear me say it because I wouldn't tell him before.

I smiled and it wasn't terribly friendly. "I'm sure you're used to hearing this from the cops but *I'm* the one asking the questions here."

"Bailey Lynn Berling!" my mother cried and I looked in her direction. The scowl she gave me was top notch and I just *knew* I was going to hear all about it from her later. My mother didn't allow me to be raised with a single rude bone in my body but here I was, killin' it just the same. Still, so confused! My mother swore she would never talk to José, ever again. Had cut him out of our lives completely and Dray right along with him when Aunt Tillie had died; so this was pretty much mind-blowing.

I turned my attention to my biggest mistake in recent history and he grinned at me. It was adorable, too. I kind of hated how hot he was while he nodded and said, "Okay, fair enough..." before he rattled off a rather impressive resume of things he had done at a couple of dude ranches in Arizona. Horse world was a small world and I'd heard of them in passing, however when it came to thoroughbreds and the kinds of horses they dealt with, it was worlds apart… still, a horse is a horse, is a horse.

"Mm-hm," I said and leaned back in my seat, "and why did you leave?"

"Felony conviction, owners were pretty hardcore Christians and didn't take kindly to one of their hands picking up an assault charge. They pretty much made it so I would never find work in the area again."

"I see, and what happened there, with the assault charge?"

"I'd rather leave it in my past if that's okay with you. It was a long time ago."

"More than ten years?"

"Yes."

"How much time did you serve?"

"What's that got to do with anything?"

"You want the job or not?"

He looked out across the driveway to the main barn where Renaldo was leading Starry Eyed Dreamer back into the barn. She was one of the fastest mares and had been, unfortunately, injured into retirement. Her next career was just beginning here though, as a broodmare. We were lucky to have her and had managed to breed her successfully with Three Legged Singin' Night Train around ten months ago and she had around a month or so to go before she dropped her foal.

"I served a little over three years, was supposed to be eight, got out with time off for good behavior."

"How long ago was that?"

"You already asked me that boss lady."

"You don't have the job, yet."

"Bailey…" My gaze flicked to my mother who gave me a withering look to go along with the warning tone in her voice. I ignored it for now, angry at the ambush, and that she would just make decisions after I'd bought her out of her share. I was trying to prove something here. That I could do this, that I could do anything and everything she and Daddy said I never could, but it was going to be kind of hard to pull that off if she was going to meddle like this. Adding to my aggravation was him… Why, out of all the people in the damnable motorcycle club my mother proclaimed was so rotten to the core, did it have to be *him* that had the required experience?

"Why should I hire you?" I asked bluntly, having a hard time reining in my anger. I had a hard time with a lot of the things going on and the feelings that came with them. *Maybe you're just tired of being the perfect angel when no one notices or cares,* I thought to myself, which is pretty much what had led me to letting biker boy over here bang me in the back of that shithole bar in the first place.

"Because, the way I hear it, you ain't got any other options. That, and I could probably do the work of three of your last hands."

"Right, I can let you know by tomorrow," I said, fully intending to fight this one out with my mother but knowing I was likely going to lose. I really did need the help around here, and my mother never did anything without a reason. She probably had a fully stacked deck of cards to play against me. She could be as manipulative as they came.

"Why not now?" he asked.

"She has to get it approved, don't you, Bales?" Dray said, and it was my turn to give him a withering look. Not that it was his fault that apparently my mother had gotten awfully chatty about my business.

"Caleb will approve this," my mother said and I looked her direction.

"He owe you some kind of favor or something?" I blurted, and it was the closest I'd ever come to really lashing out at either one of my parents. *Well if it worked for Philip...* the bitter thought came unbidden.

"Yes."

I knew that tone of voice... that was the tone of voice that said you didn't ask any more questions, you just did what you were told, *or else*. I looked across the table at Dray who was grinning at me and I frowned. I didn't much appreciate being told what to do as a grown adult. Not by the good 'ol boys club, not by my mother, and certainly not by some outlaw motorcycle club.

I didn't want this guy working here, not after having fucked him. That was just asking for a disaster of epic proportions. I would have called him the next day and said no dice, but I could tell; it looked like my mother was going to be adamant. *Damnit.* I did need experienced help around here, and he had experience... plus he was definitely not hard to look at.

"I'll call you tomorrow," I told him after a tense silence and he gave a nod. I really needed to think about this, clearly, without his darkly smiling eyes looking at me, without my cousin's gaze burning a hole through me and definitely *after* I'd had a chance to find out just what my mother was thinking.

"I do believe we've been dismissed, VP," Rush said, and Dray gave a nasty smile. I sighed and tried not to let it show that this was so not how I imagined seeing my cousin for the first time since his mother's funeral.

"I believe you're right, Rush." Dray's expression softened marginally as he looked over my face. I'd never been good at controlling my expression... my mouth, yes, but my face had always been in need of deliverance. I guess that hadn't changed. I was still working on the mouth part, and from the expression on my mother's face, I'd done a bang-up job just now. I was just so epically sick of being *controlled* and *handled*... Leave it to me to wait until the latter half of my twenties to rebel.

The two bikers exchanged a look and got up, going for their bikes. My mother and I watched them gear up and go in tense silence, but anything we needed to say could wait until they were gone. It wasn't polite to throw down with your family in front of company of any sort and I was, at least, willing to keep from being anymore uncivil than I'd been.

I shook my head as their contrails of driveway dust settled back to the ground in their wake and turned on my mother.

"Just what the hell was that?" I demanded.

"That was a mother's worry, Bailey."

I blinked. My mom had never been terribly maternal, we'd pretty much had a nanny for that. I felt my brow crush down in a frown.

"Why the sudden interest?" I demanded bitterly.

I'd never seen the look that crossed my mother's face just then. It immediately made me feel awful, and I would pretty much agree to just about anything to make it go away. She reached a hand across the table and I took it.

"There is a lot I protected my children from. Things you don't know about your father, and for that I am grateful. Still, there are things I apparently couldn't protect you from… Philip especially. I loved your father, flaws and all, but some of his worst traits have manifested in your brother and I fear for you. Bailey… I see things here that you can't. Just let Dray's friend work here… please?"

I felt my own eyes tear up, like every rich family ours held more than a couple of skeletons in its closet. Maybe my mom had paid attention more than I realized. Philip had always been a shit to me growing up, but then he'd gotten into it deep enough with a girl at his school that father had had to step in. I was sent to boarding school shortly after – an all-girls boarding school.

Yeah, I know, crazy, right? My brother gets in trouble and I'm the one that goes to boarding school, but that was my dad's logic for you. Didn't I say, *good ol' boys club?* I'm pretty sure I did.

It was probably one of the best things to have ever happened to me while at the same time, the worst. The best because the school really was fantastic, the worst because I finally felt cast aside for good in favor of an older brother who was just plain awfully behaved.

I slammed the door on painful past truths and looked critically at the present ones. I really didn't want this Rush guy around, I was pretty sure he knew that I knew exactly who he was and that was just a headache I didn't need. One I especially didn't need on top of the daily headache that was preserving my father's legacy, and to some extent, my dream of finally proving myself worthier than the heir apparent, when it came to Blue Hills.

Still, looking at my mother's face, the worry, and the deep knowledge that things were only going to get worse the more I dug my heels… I ended up nodding reluctantly. It didn't feel good. I'd already used him once and that hadn't felt good either. Okay, well, it'd felt amazing; like really amazing, but it couldn't happen again. It never should have happened in the first place.

"Fine," I said, "I'll hire him on a trial basis. Happy?"

"Relieved, my darling girl. I'm relieved." She sat back in her chair and I picked up my glass, drinking more because I had absolutely no idea what else to talk about now.

3

R ush...

I didn't expect her to call the next day. I was pretty much balls deep in putting a new cat on an old Pontiac 6000 when Dray ducked back out of the office and held out the phone yelling, "Hey, Rush! It's for you, man."

I looked down from the undercarriage of the car above me and set my socket wrench aside from where I was putting the heat shield back up over the exhaust. I walked over and took the phone from him and turned my back on my older brother Archer's curious stare.

"This is Rush," I said into the receiver.

"You're hired, you can start tomorrow," a hard female voice that could only be Ms. Bailey Lynn Berling said through the shop's old land line. I gripped the grease-stained beige receiver a little tighter and thought to myself how I'd like to do bad things to her, bad things she begged me to do more of.

"What time?" I asked.

"I thought you'd been in this line of work before," she said, and I wanted to lay a hand on that ass. Pink it right up and knock the condescension right out of her.

"I have," I said.

"Then don't be late," she said tartly and whatever phone she was on clattered and the call ended. She hadn't answered the question, but she had at the same time.

I swore softly, and Dray asked from behind me, "Problem?"

"Nah, I just gotta adjust my schedule… I have to be there early to start work."

"How early?"

"Stupid early." My VP raised an eyebrow and I sighed. "There's the ass crack of dawn early, but this is earlier than that," I said.

"Go back to the club then, rack out. I can finish up."

"Naw, I just have to finish bolting on the heat shield and it'll be good to go. You can call the customer if you want."

"Right."

He ducked back into the office and I finished the last few bolts needed to complete the job and brought the car down off the lift. I didn't hear Archer come up behind me over the hiss of the hydraulics letting the car down and it startled the fuck out of me when he clapped me on the back of my coveralls.

I jumped and cussed him out while he laughed until tears collected at the corners of his eyes.

"What the fuck you want, man?"

"It's a good thing you're doin' for Dragon and Dray's family," he said. "Still, I wouldn't be any kind of brother if I didn't tell you to *be careful,*" we said those two particular words in unison and he knocked his fist playfully into my chin as we said the rest in unison too, *"and call me if you need a hand."*

"You miserable prick," he added.

"Not my first rodeo," I grunted and went around to the driver's side of the POS I was working on.

"Maybe not, but it is your first horse race, and you know how these rich bastards can get crazy when it comes to money. They ain't got a lick of sense with it."

"Yeah, no shit. Should be mandatory each rich fucker comes up like they got nothing so they have some fuckin' sense when they get it."

Archer shook his head. "Wouldn't make a difference, going that road just breeds a whole different set of troubles."

I frowned and nodded. "Ain't that the fuckin' truth?"

"See you around, little brother," he said as I ducked into the crappy cage and pulled it out of my bay. I parked it, left it, and went for the degreaser for my hands. Clean up was a snap once I got my hands clean, just shuck the coveralls and switch out my boots from work to motorcycle and I was good to go. I pulled my cut down off its peg and shrugged into it as I crossed out from under the shaded bay into the full sunlight.

I took a deep breath, and the air outside the shop seemed cleaner and lighter than it had a moment ago, despite the fact that it hadn't really changed. It was the same old mix of metal, grease, and gasoline that was pretty much a part of any automotive place you went. No, the shop hadn't changed, I think I had. It felt like I'd just had one of those phone calls that changed my life.

I was always cut out for working with my hands, I just wasn't cut out for working on cars. I belonged in a natural setting, with wood and growing things. Working with horses was something I'd taken to like a fish to water and losing that had hurt. It was a stupid ass decision, losing my shit on that asshole, but he'd fuckin' hit me first and had disrespected me something fierce before it'd even come to blows. He'd started shit, then hadn't been able to handle it when I'd fuckin' finished it, but still, it'd been my life that'd ended up in the shitter as a result.

Not that *that* was anything unusual to any of my brothers. That's why this lifestyle fit us the best. I swung a leg over my bike and dropped onto the seat, digging through my keys absently before I found the one to start it. I half-assed put my bandana on my head without tying it off and fired her up. I finished tying off the red bandana behind my head, pinning down the errant corner and crammed my helmet on over it, doing up the chinstrap while I listened to my baby chug reassuringly beneath me.

She could be a cranky bitch when she was cold, but she always fired true. I could probably stand to give her a tune up in the next few weeks, but I don't know, sometimes that wasn't so much a necessity as much as it was I liked working on her.

I patted the glossy black skin, veined with blue lightning on her tank and didn't care what anyone thought about me treating my iron horse like she was a real one. She'd gotten me through more than one high-speed chase and had never left me on the side of the road, always giving me ample warning that something was going and needed attention. She was a special kind of ride, and even though she was getting way up there in miles, I wasn't even close to ready to trade her in.

I rode back to the club and ran into my twin comin' out the front door, headed for his cage. No Maren in sight, which probably meant she was at *Soul Fuel* learning her new trade. I still worried about my twin brother. I'd been there, with women lookin' at me for financial stability, but fuck if they weren't in it for an actual relationship. No, they'd been getting their dick of choice on the side the fuckin' ticks. I didn't want Nox to go through the same kind of hurt that I had on that front. He was better than me and deserved far better than that as a result.

I got off my bike and wandered in my brother's direction, the sudden quiet from the cease of my baby's engine filled only by the ticking of her cooling engine and the rustle of the leaves in the slight breeze. I loved those sounds, meant I hadn't gone deaf.

Nox stopped and waited for me to come up to him, his scowl tellin' me plainly he knew I had somethin' on my mind. I did, too, and I needed to get it off my chest. I didn't trust anyone else to spill my guts to than my biological brother, even if all we shared was the same mother and the same womb. We were a scientific anomaly to the nth degree that way. Something like a one in a billion chance. We'd faced every odd since the same way — together.

"What's eating you?" he asked when I got within earshot.

"Got time for a beer with your dumbass twin?" I asked.

"Oh, Lord. What'd you do this time?" he asked.

"Do you have time for a beer or not?"

"Yeah! Yeah, I got time."

We went in through the barroom which was thankfully vacant and picked up a couple beers each. I led my brother through the club and out the back door to the expanse of grass rising up into a plateau of some kind. When this was a juvie, I guess this used to be a running track around a raised ball field of some kind. The track had been paved over making a loop of a driveway to get out to the outbuilding that housed my room and the huge, three-bay shop building that now housed Dani's jeweler's studio and my woodshop.

The bay between them we'd managed to clean out the random stored crap in it and it now stored a bunch of my completed furniture. It'd helped me save on a rented storage locker and I was damn grateful Dragon had let me have so much space to do my thing. He hadn't wanted anything for it, either, but it hadn't stopped me.

Nox and I dragged ourselves up to the top of the little rise and to my completed project up here. I'd built the club an outdoor firepit. A raised circle of bricks instead of the old fifty-five-gallon drum they'd been using. Around it, I'd erected a round pergola framework of timber and then I'd gotten really down and dirty.

I'd built six hanging benches and had affixed them to the framework with solid, industrial, weather-proofed chain. When we had a full house, it still hadn't been quite enough seating, so I'd built some sturdy lawn furniture to sit closer to the fire with some tables between 'em to hold drinks and dead soldiers.

I led my brother to a couple of the chairs now, and we each dropped into one. It didn't look like much, but there was an odd rectangle framework on one side of the pergola with wood neatly stacked underneath and to either side. There were some hook and eyes driven into the top of the rectangle and we had a nice LED TV tucked into one of the empty club rooms that we hung from it and could watch the game from. That'd been Data's idea, and with his technical know-how, if there wasn't rain in the forecast, we typically had it hooked up out here except when no one was home, like now.

Nox used one of the bottle openers I'd installed under the overhang of the arm in front of the lawn chair and cracked his beer. I did likewise and took a long drink.

"Looks like I got that job workin' Dray's cousin's horse farm."

Nox nodded slowly and let that sink in. "You need anything—"

"Shit, I'll call the right people, but it won't be you," I said taking a pull from my own beer. He looked pissed at that and I laughed.

"You're as good as a daddy now." I raised a hand to stop him from getting really pissed, and added, "I meant to Sage, I wasn't trying to take a shot there."

"Better not be, fucker. I'd have to kick your ass again."

"You might still wanna when I tell you this next bit."

"What'd you do now?" he asked, and I could just see his heart sink. I had that effect on my twin sometimes, and every time I did, I felt guilty about it.

"To be fair, I didn't know I was doin' it at the time…"

"Rush…"

"I'm serious!"

"Rush…"

"Alright!" I laughed, he hated it when I kept him in suspense when it was likely to be bad news and I couldn't say I blamed him.

"What'd you do now, you fucker?" he asked, and I finished off my first beer and cracked my second. I needed a bit of the liquid courage.

"That chick I told you about, the one at *The Spot*?"

"You got her pregnant."

"What? Fuck no! Although, this could be arguably worse," I said and Nox blinked and leaned back in his seat.

"No!"

"Yeah, none other than my new fuckin' boss and our president's niece."

"Oh, dude… I'm tellin' you right now, it'd probably be a good idea if you told on yourself before shit gets real."

"You kiddin' me? Dragon might be chill about it, but Dray'd probably try to beat my ass. Seems like he and Bailey might've been tight when they were kids." Nox was looking at me and the look on his face, I had to ask… "What the fuck is that look for?"

"I think, right now, I feel a little like you probably did when Maren and I first started seeing each other." He dropped back in his chair, his back thumping hard against the smooth wood. I blinked and started laughing and couldn't seem to stop. I laughed and laughed while my twin turned bright red and told me to shut up.

"Sucks a little, doesn't it?" I asked, wiping at the corners of my eyes.

"A little."

"Yeah, but here's the thing, she doesn't seem terribly eager to let the cat out of the bag, brother."

"I still say you should tell on yourself before either the P or VP find out on their own."

"I don't know what I'm gonna do yet, except take my happy ass to work and do my job."

"Which is?"

"Knowing little miss rich bitch, probably mucking out stalls and general labor. I'm cool with that, though."

"I'll just bet you are. Ranch life always did suit you best."

"Yeah, here's to no more dumbass mistakes."

"Wasn't a mistake, Rush. You did what any man in his right mind would do. You just had the deck stacked against you from the get go with people and their preconceived fucking notions."

"Yeah, that." I sighed and polished off my second beer. Nox handed me his unopened second and finished off his first.

"I've gotta get back to the house, pick up Sage from school, you know, the usual."

"Yeah, you know I'm happy you got your family, unconventional as it is."

"You know me, man. I march to the beat of my own drum."

"Yeah, you do," I agreed.

My twin got up and patted me on the shoulder, heading down the grassy berm back toward the club. I sat in the Kentucky sunshine and finished my beer before I took my ass inside to shower and go to bed. I had to be up fuckin' early if I was going to show this bitch up. Only thing I hated more than a cheating gold digger was an uppity rich bitch.

I sort of wanted to punch her ticket with the little mind games. I don't think she realized the hot seat she'd put my ass in by not being up front about who she was that night. Thing was, I may not have known who *she* was, but she damn sure knew what *I* was. Now I was gonna show her *who*.

4

B_{ailey...}

"Well, looks like the new guy is late," I mentioned to Renaldo who was getting into the farm truck's driver's seat to take me out to the north pasture. Apparently, there was some new fence damage I needed to see and possibly requisition materials to repair.

"The new gringo you hired yesterday?" he asked.

"Yeah."

He looked at me and gave me one slow, long, blink as if to ask silently, *are you serious?* I raised an eyebrow and cocked my head, a classic 'out with it' gesture and he said, "Actually, he was here early."

"What do you mean, early?"

"Got here about two, drove up to the caretaker's house. I was making coffee and told him where to park his truck."

"You're serious."

"Yes, ma'am. He's already making repairs to that fence. Seems pretty handy with a hammer."

I was fuming, but not at Renaldo. He'd been with this farm for as long as I'd been alive and was as dedicated to it as I was. I was more pissed at the new guy for beating me at my own game, but he was about to find out that when it came to me, you were damned if you did and damned if you didn't. I'd perfected the art from my mother.

Now that I'd had a day or two to think about it, I honestly felt like my mother had played me. She was pretty much the queen when it came to manipulation and I was heartily regretting caving as easily as I had. The more and more I stewed on it, the more I thought that having this guy around was just plain a bad idea. My father had always taught his children that there wasn't anything out there that couldn't be fixed without a little ingenuity and elbow grease so that's just what I was going to do. Figure out a way to make this guy quit.

I was doing fine with the farm; I needed the manpower, sure, but I had some interviews lined up this week. I was sure I could get the help I needed. Even Caleb had to admit we were too short staffed to operate fairly. I mean, there was understaffed and then there was *understaffed*. We were the latter by this point, and I had no idea why. I was at a complete loss and none of the men and women who remained would tell me if they knew anything.

I was hoping Renaldo would say something, but alas, the rest of the ride out to the point in the north pasture was completed in little more than small talk about which horse was exercised where and which stud was coming in to be bred to what mare. There was no such thing as artificial insemination in racing world; it all had to be done the old-fashioned way. Personally, in a world full of technological advances, it was nice that there were some old traditions that still held true.

Renaldo pulled up beside an unfamiliar pickup, dented and old. If vehicles were capable of holding an expression, I'd label this one careworn. I didn't see anyone else around except the new guy, so I guess it was safe to assume that the truck was his. He stood driving a post-hole digger into the sod just a bit inside the old fence line and I scowled. Renaldo hadn't even stopped the truck completely and I already had the door open. I hopped out onto the uneven ground and called out, "Trying to take out my property line?"

"Trying to fix this damn fence," he called back and lifted his clinging white tee shirt off of his chest. He was sweating and the material was nearly transparent and molding to his musculature. I mentally slapped the shit out of myself and tried to focus on why I was really here which was to inspect the damaged fence.

Damaged… yeah, that was one word for it. Several of the fence posts were ripped clean out of the ground while several more of the split-logs had been cut through with a chainsaw, bright sawdust littering the ground like confetti. I gritted my teeth and actively fumed, pulling my cellphone out of my pocket.

My asshole brother picked up on the second ring. "Really, Philip? Now we've moved on to actively trying to sabotage the farm? You selfish prick, why can't you let me have just one thing?" I demanded.

"Bailey, where is this coming from? I have no idea what you're babbling about."

Right. He was too calm and I could just *hear* the grin in his voice.

"Fuck you, Philip. Stay the fuck off my goddamn farm," I seethed.

"*Our* goddamn farm, little sister. Or did you forget that I still own a third of it?"

"I swear to God, you don't stop this I will find a way, come hell or high water, to buy you out, you smug bastard."

"You can try, but just remember, I don't have to sell either." He ended the call on me, the dick. I turned around to find both Renaldo and the new guy both watching me intently.

"What are you looking at?" I snarled at the new guy. He leaned on the fence post digger and swept his golden-brown eyes over me in an appraising look that set my goddamn panties on fire.

"Nothin', ma'am."

You're goddamn right, nothing, I thought to myself and then remembered to ask, "Did you come in early today?"

"Yes, ma'am. Thought I'd give myself the opportunity to get familiar with the place. Didn't want to be late on my first day."

The bastard had the nerve to give me this sexy little smirk and I went to wipe it right off his face with, "Yeah, well the next time you just want to help yourself to overtime – do me a favor and don't. I'm the one who makes that call. Am I clear?"

A muscle in his jaw flexed and he gave a nod. "Crystal, ma'am."

"And don't call me 'ma'am.'"

"Yes, ma'am." He smiled and I wanted to punch him.

"Where did you get this replacement timber?" I demanded, looking at the neat pile on the ground and pieces in the back of his truck.

"Would you believe I just had them in the back of my truck?"

"No."

"It's the truth, I like working with wood. Had a plan to put up some decorative fence line at my twin's girlfriend's place but there seems to be a more immediate need here."

"Oh God, there's two of you?" I demanded. Fuck, which one did I sleep with?

"After a fashion, Nox, that's my twin, doesn't look like me. We just shared the same momma."

I let that pass, I didn't much care for his entire family history except to know who I'd fucked in the back of that cheap ass bar the night I'd gotten wasted. It'd been the night that my brother had pretty much told me that it didn't matter that Mom had just sold me her share of the

39

farm; that I needed to know my place and get on board and just trust that he knew best and sign it over. *Condescending asshole.*

I'd gone out, gotten drunk, and had decided to take the biker for a ride because I knew just how much it would have pissed everyone in my family off. They hated the dirty little family secret, and this guy had been conveniently there at the right time, or wrong time, depending on how you looked at it. The next morning had been a hangover to remember, and the encounter from the night before? God, it was hard to forget. I *still* woke up from dreaming about it, sweat soaked and slick between my thighs.

I realized I was just standing there staring at the guy, both him and Renaldo staring back at me waiting for me to say something. I tore my gaze from the guy's and stared at the split timber resting on the ground nearby.

"How much are you going to want for this?" I demanded.

"Nothin'."

"What? Why?"

"I got it for free off Craigslist, no sense in charging you for it. Should be just enough with what Renaldo says you have stashed to make the repairs here and you're already paying me a wage." He shrugged and I hated him for a moment for upstaging me at my own game.

"How long you think it's going to take you to fix it?"

"Better part of today and tomorrow, I'd guess."

"Fine. The sooner the better. This is one of our most used pastures."

"You got it, boss lady."

Well I guess it was an improvement over ma'am. I jerked my head at Renaldo and with an amused look he came back over to me and the truck after shaking the new guy's hand. We got in and he started it up.

"I like the new guy, he's alright," he stated, and it made me silently fume even more.

"Don't get too used to him," I said. "I'm still not sure *I* like him."

Renaldo chuckled. "Whatever you say, boss lady."

I swear to God, I blushed all the way up to the roots of my hair and Renaldo just sat there and laughed and laughed at my expense. Anyone else and I would have given them every shitty job I could think of around the farm, but not Renaldo. He was my most experienced groom and a former jockey. Not only that, if there were anyone on this farm I considered a friend, he was it... hell, he was almost more family than my actual family.

"Shut up," I mumbled, and he laughed some more.

I think the thing I hated most of all was that Renaldo was right and that I didn't really hate the new guy at all. I just hated who I was when I was around him, which was just about everything my cousin Dray had professed about hating rich people. *Users, full of themselves, and rude as fuck to the people that made them.* It'd been a conversation we'd had when we were teens, one of the last times we'd seen each other before Aunt Tilly was murdered.

It'd hurt having my cousin angry at me, and it'd hurt even more that he'd been right. I'd busted my ass to never be that way again, but here we were and here I was, the same thing he'd professed to hating all those years ago and I couldn't exactly be sorry. If I wanted to keep this farm, then I needed to play by high society rules and the rules were that the game was cutthroat as hell while still holding a thin veneer of civility.

It was exhausting, but this farm had become my whole life and I wasn't going to give it up for some fucking subdivision or amusement park, or some shit to go on it. Instead, I focused on keeping the farm making the kind of money that my father would've been proud of. Of course, it helped a lot that Blue Hills had the sterling reputation that it did. There wasn't much my brother could do to ruin that, not with me holding two-thirds ownership of the place.

"When do you want to move Starry to the little barn?" Renaldo asked and I thought about it.

"Under usual circumstances, I'd say leave her in the main stable another month but I don't think it would be such a bad idea to move her early. She's the only one far enough along to warrant a move though."

The rest of the ride back to the farm proper was mostly planning and making arrangements for our boarder's accommodations. Not all of the horses here were owned by us. Most of them were simply on loan or being boarded by their actual owners.

I sighed and sat back in the seat and worried about not only our missing employees but my mangled fence. I knew he wasn't done. I had the same red warning lights flashing that my mother did. I just didn't know to what extent my brother would be willing to go to on this one to get his way.

It was food for thought… It was definitely food for thought.

5

R ush...

It'd taken me a couple of days to finish repairing the fence and that was with me working my ass off to do it almost double-time compared to what it would have normally taken me. I was in the main barn, stacking the bales of fresh straw that'd come in when she found me again. It'd been a few days since I'd last seen her up close, but it'd never been hard picking her figure out at a distance. It was even nicer up close. What wasn't as nice was the mouth or the rich-bitch attitude Bailey had on her.

Like now, her greeting was a sharp, "What *are* you doing?"

"Stacking these bales, puttin' 'em away, what's it look like I'm doing?"

"That's not your job!" she snapped. "That's the delivery company's job. I pay *them* for that, though to tell you the truth I'm not sure what I'm paying *you* for right now... Jesus!"

"Whoa, easy, slow down." I put down the hay hooks I was using and said, "Looks like your delivery guys got one over on the FNG, I didn't know."

"FNG?" she echoed.

"Fucking New Guy," I supplied, and she covered her face with her hands and shook her head.

"This isn't the dude ranch you came from! You can't talk like that where clients could potentially hear you!"

I raised my eyebrows amused and said, "Darlin', I'm pretty sure you know exactly who and what you hired on the day that you did it, and I'm tellin' you," I stepped into her personal space and dropped my voice real low so only she could hear, "if you wanna ride my dick again, all you have to do is ask. I'm not real fond of you ridin' it any other way."

She looked up at me stricken and a little horrified before the blush of her embarrassment had a chance to set in, which was a boner killer right there. Never quite had *that* reaction after I'd fucked a woman. Couldn't say I much liked it. I stepped back and picked up the hooks and marched past her to the jumbled pile of bales the delivery company had just dropped in the middle of the barn haphazardly. I hooked a fresh one and walked it over to the neat stack against the wall I was making.

"I am your *boss*," she was sputtering. "You can't, you *won't*, talk to me that way or I'll fire your ass!"

Twice in one day, that'd be cute. I was surprised by how much I wanted this job. It was an opportunity to get back some of what I'd lost back when I'd had to go to prison. I had just told her about how I'd been released early, partially for good behavior and partially due to over-crowding. By the same token, in my eyes and the eyes of the state of Arizona, I'd done my bid... even if a bunch of folks didn't think it was fair. She hadn't needed to know all of that. Probably wouldn't have hired me if she'd known, so I'd kept my mouth shut. I'd wanted this fucking job, wanted it bad and now here it was the first week and I stood a chance of losing it because the little rich bitch didn't think I could hack it.

No, because I was letting her get to me, and by extension, letting my mouth get ahead of me… Fuck.

No, again, I could eat some fuckin' crow here. I opened my mouth to apologize, as much as I didn't want to, because I really genuinely liked this place and the people left in it… present company excluded at the moment.

I never got the chance to say anything, though, because a ruckus went up outside. Bailey whipped around to face the barn doors and we both froze, listening for a moment.

"Bailey, wait!" I called out, but she was closer and already striding that direction. I put down the hay hooks and picked up the baseball bat I'd been keeping around and handy while I worked. The other employees of the farm had been talking, and I'd been pretty much accepted as one of them already, once they saw I wasn't afraid to work, so I'd heard the stories.

Men coming to their homes, local thugs, threatening them with deportation or violence if they went back to Blue Hills. Some of 'em had taken the threats seriously, some of 'em didn't, then there were guys, like Renaldo, who knew what loyalty was and whose whole lives revolved around this place. I liked the guy. He'd been born and raised here, a boy of seven kids born to immigrant parents who worked the fields. He'd somehow gotten into horses and had won the genetic lottery being a little dude. It made him perfect for the position of jockey and he was a fearless motherfucker.

I'd liked him instantly, when I figured out he was calling me the gringo because that's what all his people called me. I also liked it that he took a hard line when any of them said something even remotely disrespectful behind Bailey's back. He was always quick to remind them that her being *Jefe* was the only thing keeping the lot of 'em employed, didn't matter if they thought her becoming *Jefe* had turned her into a bitch.

So it was no surprise that he ended up being the primary target for any strong-arm tactics to get people to move on from here. What *was* surprising was that they would do it in the middle of broad daylight, at the farm. I went out into chaos boiling over. Strong-arm local thugs holding Bailey and the rest of the guys left working late aside with sticks and batons. No guns that I could see, but that didn't mean there weren't any in play. I had mine, but I never brought it out unless I was ready to kill a motherfucker which we weren't quite to that point yet, especially considering Bailey was on her cell, and likely with the police while a couple of these assholes were whoopin' the shit out of Renaldo.

I counted five, and I liked my odds with the bat. Still, it was time to nut up or shut up, and I was all about the former. Adrenaline rushed through my veins as I waded in and cracked one of the fuckers kicking Renaldo, who was down on the ground. I took one of his attackers out, bashing him in the side of the knee with a stroke that damn sure broke something. His buddy rounded on me just in time to get the blunt end of my bat in his guts.

His other buddies tried to come to the rescue, one of 'em jumping on my back, an arm across my throat trying to ride me into the dirt. I heard Bailey screaming and yelling and my presence and willingness to go to bat had woken a couple of the other farmhands up out of their stupor. They started to throw down with me, keeping the other two occupied enough for me to take care of the one trying to choke me out.

I flung him over my shoulders and slammed him into the ground. It helped that I hadn't had a shirt on. It was too fuckin' hot in the barn which wasn't air conditioned like the stables, but that was a whole different story for another time. Once I had the happy bastard on his back, he scrambled to his feet. He had a pair of brass knuckles and he made a big show of sliding 'em onto his hand. I quirked an eyebrow like *really dude?*

Bailey screamed something at me like look out, and the dude snarled at her, "Shut up, bitch!"

I told him, "Hey, she ain't your mamma, boy."

It was just the spur to his flank that he needed, because he snarled and lunged. I cracked him right in the fucking face with the bat. I know I broke the fucker's jaw and I know that he lost teeth because at least three of them went flying. The one I'd gut checked scrambled to his feet and yelled, "Fuck man, he's a Sacred Heart!" and my club's reputation, as always around these parts, preceded us because the three of them jumped into one of the two pickups left in the driveway and took off without their unconscious buddies.

Renaldo groaned, and there was no way in hell it was a fair fight. He was just a little guy and these bastards were my size or better. The two farmhands kneeled next to him where he groaned in the dirt and we waited for the distant sirens to get here.

Of course, first thing the cops did was put me in cuffs. I looked to Bailey as they led me past her to sit me down in the back of their patrol car and growled at her, "*That*'s what you hired me for."

She blinked, bewildered while cops and medics swarmed around the farm's drive and I waited for her to either get me out of this situation or to throw me under the bus. Wasn't more than ten minutes before one of the boys in blue, er, brown as was the sheriff's office's uniform, was opening up the back of the patrol car saying, "You do realize you hired a felon, right Ms. Berling?"

"Yes, I believe in second chances. Don't you?" she shot back.

"Still, I can't guarantee these men won't press charges."

I snorted. "Been there before," I muttered as the officer unhooked the cuffs. My shoulders creaked as I brought my hands in front of me and rubbed at my wrists. I sniffed and walked a few paces away to go talk to our guys who were falling over themselves to ask if I was alright. The doors clapped shut on the back of one of the medic busses and I called out to the paramedic going for the driver's seat, "Take him to Mercy General, when you hit the ER, ask for Doc Sim."

47

"Yeah, I know Doc Sim, he's one of the best. We'll make sure your friend is taken care of."

"Alright man, thanks."

The paramedic shut his door, chirped his siren, and pulled out. Renaldo didn't look good. Unconscious and bleeding from his head… fuck, I should have heard that shit going down sooner.

"Where are you going?" Bailey demanded sharply.

"Back to work," I called back. "Straw ain't gonna put itself away."

I left her standing by one of the deputies who told her to let me go, that they'd come find me in the barn if they had any other questions. As soon as I got in there, I hid my gun. Didn't want to be a felon caught carrying, and I was fuckin' lucky that they hadn't had the chance to pat me down to find it in the top of my shitkicker on my right side. I stashed it deep in the hay bales I'd yet to put away and went back to work.

The sharp report of car doors shutting and the crunch of gravel under car tires let me know the cops had taken off. A few minutes later, Bailey slipped back into the barn. I dug out my piece and put it back while she walked toward me. I kept hidden behind the last of the bales and when I straightened, it was with one of the bales on my hooks, so she was none the wiser.

I hauled it over to the wall of straw and got it stacked and when I turned she was in my path, holding out the black leather rectangle that was my wallet. The deputy had lifted it when I was being cuffed, to look me up. I transferred one of the hooks to my other hand and took it from her with a mumbled thanks while she stared up at me with wide brown eyes.

"You just waded in," she said. "There were five of them and they had weapons and you didn't even think about it, you just went in and saved Renaldo."

"Wasn't my first rodeo and those guys were pussies. Local thugs, likely hired by your pissant brother."

She was shaking her head. "One of the men you hurt told the police Renaldo owed them some money before he was taken by the ambulance."

"And you believe that shit?" I huffed a bitter laugh.

"No! It's just... the police did. I don't know what to do."

Yeah, I'll just bet they did, I thought. Out loud I said, "Suck it up, buttercup. It's only going to get worse if you plan to stick this out."

"How would you know?" she asked, scowling.

"It's why I was hired, remember?"

She scrubbed her face with her hands and said, "What, fight fire with fire? Pit criminal against criminal?" She said it with such a huge amount of disdain dripping from her sexy as hell voice, I couldn't help but get fired up but not the way you'd think. She was pissing me the hell off.

"Right, next time you have five guys kicking the shit out of one of your people I'll just stand around with my thumb up my ass like you did. Sound good?"

She scoffed and said, "I called the cops, I'll have you know!"

"Yeah, and what'd they do? Tried to arrest me for saving the day. What were you going to do in the meantime until the cops showed up, huh?"

"I don't know, give them suspect descriptions? License plate numbers?"

"Fucking citizens," I muttered.

"Hey!" she barked. "I didn't ask for this! I didn't even ask for you to be here, so stop being such an asshole!"

"Why, because you've been such a goddamn peach?"

She let fly and I caught her wrist without much effort at all on my part. The hay hooks clattered to the concrete floor and I jerked her off balance, facing her into the bales and pinning the lower half of her body with mine.

"Let me go!" she demanded.

"No dice, buttercup. Your mamma and daddy may not have taught you it's not nice to hit people, but I damn sure will."

"What!?"

I backed off of her, my cock granite in my pants and brought the palm of one hand down squarely on her denim clad ass with an echoing thwack. She fuckin' squealed her indignation and thrust her ass back into me, which she wasn't getting away. I'd moved back in to pin her with my body and I have to say, the curve of her ass fit the curve of the front of my body mighty fine. She wiggled trying to break free and stilled with a gasp when she felt my cock through our clothes.

"Don't worry, I ain't gonna use it unless you ask real nice."

"Let me go," she demanded.

"Not until I'm sure you're not going to hit me again."

"Are you fucking kidding me?" she screeched indignant.

"Nope."

"You son of a bitch!"

"Yeah." I couldn't disagree there. She'd started thrashing and stilled again when I said it.

"What is *wrong* with you?"

"A lot of things, Bailey. Nothing you'd probably understand."

"Why don't you try me?" she asked and it surprised me. She stilled, was out of breath, and tense, but wasn't trying to thrash or hit me again so I eased off some, putting my hands on top of the bales to either side of her hips and leaning over her. She was still pinned between me and the straw, and I could still restrain her if she wanted to take a swing, but she wasn't demanding I back off anymore. If anything, that tight little ass of hers was rubbing up against me in a way that made me wanna lose my mind.

"Bailey, you doing that on purpose?" I asked her.

"Maybe."

"I meant what I said."

"What? I mean, what time?"

"You wanna ride this cock, all you have to do is ask."

"God, why do you have to be so crude?"

"Why you got to be so uptight, and what happened to the hot chick in the bar? If I remember correctly, you were the one who hit on *me*."

"Yeah, that was after something like four shots of bourbon."

"Lightweight," I murmured by her ear and she shuddered.

Yeah, she was definitely turned on. I smiled and whispered, "Undo those jeans and slide them down, take the panties with them." I let my tone carry the command and I felt her go rigid. She swallowed audibly and turned her head. I leaned back just enough so she could see I was serious as a heart attack.

"If I don't?" she whispered quietly.

"Then I let you go, you walk out of this barn, and we can pretend none of this ever happened."

"If I do?"

"Then I bend you over this bale of straw, shove myself in you balls deep, give you the ride of your life and if you want? You walk out of this barn and we can try to pretend none of it ever happened."

She hesitated, her eyes sliding shut, and she swallowed nervously. I bent forward and placed my lips in the hollow behind her ear, planting one light and errant kiss. Her breath left her in a shuddering sigh and her hands moved to the front of her jeans.

Aw yes, option B!

I held still as she slowly worked her hands between herself and the straw bale I held her against. I backed off just enough to allow her some room to work with and wasn't disappointed when she worked her belt free, then the button on her jeans. She unzipped and wriggled her hips in that way only a woman could, and I about lost my mother-fuckin' mind again.

She slid the denim and lace down from the sides and over the ripe, beautiful curve of her ass. I appreciated the view every second it was happening too.

"Your turn," she murmured and there was the girl from the bar. All she'd needed to do was commit.

I undid my belt, button, and zip peeling the flaps of my jeans to either side, sliding the scorching head of my cock up and down against her pussy. The angle was all wrong, so I put my left hand on her right shoulder and did just what I said I was going to do. I slammed her forward, bracing my arm against her back so she couldn't stand upright again. Her hands automatically pressed against the straw and she tested me. It wasn't happening though, not unless she said 'no', not unless she told me to stop.

"What are you waiting for?" she asked, and I was all for having the green light.

I pressed against her opening and filled her up with one long, deep stroke until my balls slapped the rest of her tight little pussy.

She sucked in a sharp breath, her fingers curling into the straw as she held onto the bale and I smiled and told her, "That's right, baby. Hold on tight."

I set a punishing rhythm. Slamming my body into hers until her hips bucked hard against the bale I held her against. I could feel her tight and wet around me and fuck if she didn't fit me like a glove.

I never, not once in a million years, thought I would ever see her again, let alone that I'd ever get the chance to fuck her again, but I was glad we were here, and I was glad this was happening, and I was *really* glad she was as into it as I was. How did I know? The way her ass perked up and she shoved herself back to meet every oncoming thrust I could dish.

She gave a low, quiet, throaty moan and I seriously had to hold on to my shit. I was gonna lose it and come before her if I didn't. I worked myself in and out of her wet heat, searching for that spot that would make her sing, and take her sky high. She cried out and jerked under the hard pin I had her under and I knew I found it. I worked that spot, too. Her breaths coming closer together, faster, her body writhing despite the hold I had on her, her pussy tightening around my shaft. *Fuck that felt so good…*

"That's right, baby. You come for me, you come all over that dick." I kept my voice low, a harsh breathless whisper to spare anyone over-hearing or catching us. Bailey had the same idea, shoving her fist against her mouth as her switch flipped and she shuddered beneath me like she was being electrocuted. I fucking loved it when I took a woman that high and dropped her. Her pussy's rhythmic throbbing and pulling along my cock sent me right over the edge with her.

I spilled inside her and shoved as deep as I could get, pressing our bodies tight together. She went rag doll limp underneath me, and I let up on my punishing grip, dropping both my arms to my sides and tipping my head back to suck in air. My body demanding I breathe and I couldn't disagree.

"Pull out," she demanded after a few false starts and I did, slipping free from her body and watching a spill of my cum follow. *God that was fuckin' hot.*

She jerked up her panties and jeans and swiftly did them up. I blinked and tucked myself back into my pants at a more sedate pace.

"Remember the deal, this never happened," she said curtly and she marched that shapely ass of hers right out of the barn doors.

"Yeah," I muttered to myself, "but we both know it did."

I turned around and leaned against the neatly stacked bales and with my jeans back in place, pressed my hands to my knees and finished catching my breath.

Man, I think I knew how my twin felt now... I was wrecked, and the woman had no idea the kind of affect she had on me. Double damn it, she was just the *wrong* fuckin' kind of woman to get addicted to.

"Fuck," I said to the empty barn then had to repeat it several more times for good measure, "Fuck, fuck, fuck, fuck, fuck it!"

Problem was, I just had, *royally.*

6

B ailey...

Oh my God, I just totally let him fuck me without protection, what was I thinking? I marched straight into the house and went to the kitchen, pouring a good measure of bourbon into a glass. I took a sip just as the first knock landed at my screen door. I turned around and went slowly back to it, hoping and praying it wasn't him, but no dice. He was on the other side of the screen, phone pressed to his ear saying, "Yes ma'am, here she is. Alright now."

He handed me my phone and said jovially, "You left this in the barn, ma'am. I figured you'd want to take the call. It's your mamma. Sorry I answered it for you, but I didn't want it to go to voicemail."

"Thanks," I said and took the phone. None of what was coming out of his mouth was matching the grave intensity that was coming from his eyes. He had me pinned in place with that look just as surely as he'd had me pinned beneath those tree trunks he called arms only moments before.

"Hello?" I said into the phone, and silently he plucked my glass from my hand and downed the remainder of the bourbon inside before he handed it back and walked away.

Oh. My. God.

He was an ass, but he made being one smokin' hot.

"Bailey Lynn Berling, are you listening to me!?" my mother snapped in my ear and I jumped.

"Mom, yeah, sorry you were breaking up," I lied. "Can you repeat what you said?"

"I said, I just heard about Renaldo, is he alright?"

"I don't know, I just finished up with the police. I need to go to the hospital now."

"Are you alright?"

More than alright. Not okay at all... Jesus what was wrong with me!? Fucking biker boy out there while Renaldo was headed to the hospital? God!

"I'm fine," I told her, glad she couldn't see my lying liar face.

"I just knew something like this would happen..." she said and I tuned her out while she went on one of her drama-fueled monologues, just fretting away. I was watching him through the screen on my door. He was loading the farm's truck with mended tack to take it to the stables. His shirt was off, as it'd been in the barn, skin kissed golden by the sun, glistening with sweat, and when he turned around, I had to shudder.

Inked into his back, larger than life, were the same patches that rode on the back of his vest. The Sacred Hearts with that damn, vile heart wrapped in barbed wire. Except underneath, where it should have said 'Kentucky,' like his vest did now, the lettering read 'Arizona.'

He turned back around and inked into the front of his body, low on the ribs was a diamond with a 1% inside it. I didn't know what any of it meant, but I remember Dray telling me once upon a time, when we were still teens, that it all had some sort of meaning to it.

All I could see was the look on the man's face who'd been about to hit Rush over the back with what looked like an axe handle. His eyes had gone wide and he'd cried out about Rush being one of them, a Sacred Heart, and the rest of the men who weren't on the ground had *run...* clearly terrified, not even bothering to try and pick up their friends off the ground that they'd come with. It'd been chilling, making me wonder just what my cousin Dray was into.

"Bailey, are you sure you're alright?" My mother's worried voice pierced the veil of my thoughts and I shook myself as if waking from a dream... a bad one.

"Yeah, Mom... I just... I've never seen anything like it before."

"Like what?" she asked, and the silence following her words was weighted with a held breath.

"He took a bat to those men, the ones hurting Renaldo. He really hurt some of them, like it was nothing."

"It's what they *do*, my darling girl. It's what they do," she said tiredly, and I found myself shaking my head, realized she couldn't see it, and so I sighed.

"I'm going to grab a quick shower and head out to see Renaldo. By the time I get cleaned up and get to the hospital, they might have some answers as to the extent of his injuries. I'll call you later."

"Okay, be careful."

"I promise," I said and ended the call, shoving my phone back into my back pocket where it should have been to begin with. There was no telling if the hospital would even tell me anything, privacy laws being what they were and me not technically being family, but guilt was swamping me now... that Renaldo has so easily slipped from my mind, however briefly, to complete a hot hookup in my barn. *God, you really are turning into the product of your upbringing,* I chided myself and closed my eyes, bowing my head and giving it a little shake to banish the admonishing voice.

When I looked up, he was staring at me, the door to the truck open, one of his large hands on the edge of the truck bed. I had my arms crossed over my chest and was playing with my necklace chain. Something I did when I was uneasy or thinking. I dropped the necklace and tipped my head back, walking away, picking up the empty rocks glass in my hand off the dining room table which was just inside the front door with the way the small, but expensive house was laid out.

I didn't bother with pouring myself any more. Instead, I went straight for the shower off my bedroom and got myself cleaned up. I needed to get an STD test and even though I was already on birth control, I needed a Plan B pill. I still couldn't believe I'd done that. I still didn't know what made me do it...

That's a lie, Bailey. You wanted another one of the amazing orgasms only he's ever been able to give you. You know, just like the one you haven't been able to forget. You wanted him to touch you because watching him beat the shit out of those guys was hot.

I sighed. I couldn't argue with my inner logic on that one, as distasteful and selfish as it was. *What is wrong with me?* I screamed silently at myself.

When I went back out with the keys to my truck in hand, he was gone. I bowed my head and shook it, and jogged down the rest of the steps, taking the path that would lead to the low set of garages to the right and back of the house.

"Going to see Renaldo?"

I jerked my head up. He was standing by his motorcycle, tying a bandana around his head. Thankfully, he had a shirt back on, even if it was one of the white tees that hugged every muscle, his leather vest with the patches on over it.

Admit it, you're jealous you aren't one of those tee shirts.

Shut up, me.

No, you can't make me either…

"Fuck."

He raised an eyebrow and I realized I'd cursed out loud.

"You kiss your mother with that mouth?"

"Ha, ha, very funny; you're one to talk."

He quirked a one-sided smile and said, "Come on, I'll give you a ride."

I rolled my eyes. "My mother would kill me."

"What are you twelve?" he demanded. "Jesus Christ, maybe I was wrong about you."

I jerked back my head and gave him a dirty look. "Oh, yeah?"

"Yeah," he said swinging a leg over the seat and dropping onto it. "Maybe you are some kind of damsel in distress, rich bitch spoiled princess."

I scoffed. "What does that make you? A dirty beast of an asshole biker?"

"You judged first, baby; don't you forget that." He crossed his arms and leaned forward against the glossy black tank of his Harley, the paint job shot through with crackling electricity.

"What happens if I get on the back of your bike?" I asked, remembering what Draven had told me. That everything was steeped in some deep, esoteric, alternate meaning for these guys.

He grinned and said, "I take you for a different kind of ride of your life."

"That's it?"

"That's it."

I shoved my keys into my pocket and came forward. He held out a hand to help me up.

"Ever been on one of these things?" he asked.

"Really, does it look like I've ever been on one?"

"Alright, alright… I just hate repeating information somebody might already know. First thing, hold onto me." He put my hands around his waist, and I swallowed nervously. "I mean it, hold on to me, don't be shy, I just fucked you over a bale of straw in the damn barn, now get closer." I froze.

"I thought we agreed that never happened," I said softly, and I couldn't see his face, but he bowed his head letting it bounce a couple times on his neck.

"Right. Forgive me if I have a hard time immediately erasing something that hot and that satisfying out of my memory banks."

"Right, what else?" I asked in an attempt to change the subject, but the damn seed was planted and growing. *He'd enjoyed it too… couldn't forget just like you can't.*

"Lean with the bike, not against it, when I take turns and try not to shift around too much, okay?"

"Okay."

He handed his helmet over his shoulder and said, "Here put this on." I did and once my arms were back around his waist, he fired up the machine. I jumped at how loud it was and pulled on my big girl panties. Taking a deep breath, I pulled myself tight against his back and did as I was told, leaning with him and the bike as he turned out onto the gravel, following the curve out onto the long drive past the south stables and to the road.

"Think you got a feel for it?" he called over the chug of the motor.

"Yeah!"

"Good, training wheels are off, hang on!"

He punched it, turning out onto the highway and I held myself tight to his body, sheltered from the wind momentarily until I could grow used to it and the *feeling*. Oh my God, it was like how I felt on horseback during jumping competitions. When the horse was moving, muscles coiling and bunching beneath me and taking the jump. It was like that moment where we were both suspended in time, gravity taking over and making the knot of adrenaline in the pit of my stomach rise to the center of my chest. God, it was exactly like that precise moment only a constant feeling.

I suddenly understood the appeal that this held for my aunt and my cousin. I could never understand it before, but now... It was a dangerous drug. One I didn't know if I would be able to immediately put it down. Damn if this guy wasn't a tricky bastard.

We pulled into the lot at Mercy General and he found a space for the motorcycle, tapping me twice on my knee in a dismissive gesture that clearly meant *get off*. I did and he backed the bike carefully into the space. He shut off the engine and I handed him his helmet.

"What'd you think?"

I gave a noncommittal shrug and he chuckled. "It's okay, your highness. Your secret is safe with me."

I frowned at him and he laughed as I walked away and toward the entrance to the hospital. I hit my first roadblock in admitting. "I'm sorry, I can't give out any patient information."

"I know he's here, I would like to know how he's doing."

"All I can confirm is that Mr. Salvador *is* a patient, but he hasn't been assigned a room number yet, you'll just have to come back later."

"Well, I know he's in the emergency room, can I go back there and see him?"

"Are you family?"

"I already told you, I'm his employer. He was hurt at work. Are you serious?"

"Bailey, come here."

Rush's hand closed around my elbow and he drew me away from the unhelpful woman at the reception desk.

"Where are we going?" I demanded.

"The cafeteria. I'm hungry, and you are too. Now shut it."

I felt my jaw fall open. I don't think anyone other than my brother had ever spoken to me in such a way and I wasn't particularly fond of Philip right now, or ever, to be honest. Still, Rush's admonishment to keep quiet held a different flavor than any of Philip's. He had something going on. Philip usually just told me to shut up for the sake of shutting me up. This guy, Rush, however, was leading me toward something.

When we stopped at a table in the cafeteria where a doctor sat with a cup of coffee, a newspaper open in front of his face, I realized that this must be Doc Sim.

"Is this the doctor you told the ambulance crew to take Renaldo to?" I asked.

"That'd be me," the older man said. He sighed and set down his paper looking up at me over half-moon spectacles. I sank into the seat beside him and asked, "Is he okay?"

"Afraid not, honey. I had to put him in a coma. He's got swelling on his brain. Too early to tell."

I took in a deep, deep breath in through my nose and let it out through my mouth. I wanted to cry, but I didn't want to look weak, so I did what Rush had suggested. I sucked it up, bit my lips together and stared at the table top until I was sure my voice wouldn't shake.

"I see," I said and Dr. Sim looked at me sympathetically.

"I wish I had better news, but we're working on freeing up a bed for him now, in the ICU."

"No," I said leaning back. "Thank you for telling me. I was going a little crazy worrying about him."

He nodded. "You got somebody that can stay with you tonight?" he asked, and I shook my head.

"I'll lock the doors; keep the phone nearby. I'll be fine." The doctor looked up over my head and I frowned craning my neck back so I could see Rush. He was just getting through with giving the doctor a nod.

I raised my eyebrows, a silent way of saying, *Oh the hell you will, buddy.* All he did was stare me down until I looked away first, uncomfortably.

"Thanks, Doc," Rush said.

"You betcha," the doctor said and shook out his paper. "Now piss off back to where you come from and let an old man read his paper in peace. First break I've had all day with the mess you sent in here."

"Oh, yeah?" Rush sounded amused.

"Busted that asshole's knee but *real* good. What'd you do, hit him with a bat?"

"Louisville slugger," he affirmed.

"He the one that did your friend?"

"One of 'em."

"Good job."

"Thanks." Rush looked pleased.

For the second time since I'd entered this hospital, my jaw fell open.

"Aren't you under some kind of Hippocratic oath?" I demanded, disbelieving that I was possibly hearing what I was hearing right now.

"Yep, and I didn't do any harm here, sweetheart. I patched 'em both up to the best of my ability. That's what I do. That other fella's jaw ought to be wired shut for a good couple of months or more. No saving the teeth."

"Bet he'll think twice before callin' a lady a bitch."

It was completely mind-blowing, the both of them laughing over what had been done like it was nothing. Like it hadn't been something that'd shaken me to my core. Of course, I could play along to a certain extent but this? This was almost too much. I shook my head and uttered an incredulous, "Wow."

"Don't waste any of yer feelings on those thugs, sweetheart. You just keep worrying about yer friend and his family. He's got a long way to go."

"Yeah," I said faintly. I *was* worried about Renaldo. My heart broke for him and his family and it broke even more that my brother might be behind a thing like this.

"Go on now, before someone sees me talkin' to you that shouldn't."

"Thanks again, Doc."

I walked in silence side by side with Rush all the way back outside to his motorcycle. He looked me over once we got to the bike and asked me, "You just want to go for a ride? Take the long, scenic route home?"

I smoothed my lips together and nodded finally and he didn't press, just said, "Okay, get on."

I, surprisingly, just did what I was told and let the wind move me as the road below us blurred and rushed past as we went over it. He was as good as he promised, taking the long way, winding through foothills and through idyllic tree-lined country roads.

When he pulled down the long drive of Blue Hill's farm, it was nearly dusk, the sun dropping low on the horizon. I got off and thanked him, which I don't think he heard above the bike. I handed him back his helmet and he cocked his head to the side, shutting the machine off.

"I'm going to wait here for one of my other club brothers to come and take night watch. You want I should run back to the club and come back? Crash on your couch?"

I shook my head. "It's okay; no one needs to stay here over night."

"Bullshit. You ain't quittin' and pretty soon they're going to run out of people to target."

"I just wish…"

"What?"

I shook my head again. "Nothing."

What I'd really meant to say was, *I wish I hadn't been such an argumentative bitch. If I hadn't been trying so hard to screw with you maybe one or the both of us would have heard the fight outside sooner. Maybe Renaldo wouldn't be in the hospital like he is…*

"It's not your fault, Bailey," he said after a minute of silence.

I stood up a little straighter and said, "Yeah, yeah it *is* my fault. What's worse? I can't be sorry about it. This place is my *everything* and I can't give it up."

"You shouldn't have to."

I nodded and turned, mounting the steps and going in the front door of my house. Rush was suddenly there, behind me.

"You didn't lock your door. Some great protector I'd be if I didn't check things out."

I rolled my eyes and flung up my hands. "Have at."

He swept the place and nodding, satisfied, went back to the front door. "Lock everything up behind me, and I do mean everything."

"Fine."

He shut the door and I locked it behind him. My heart sank. I have never, not once, had to lock my doors here before. It was a tough feeling made worse by the fact that I was having to lock them because of my own family.

7

R**ush...**

I called Dray, who sent out Data, of all people. I frowned and asked, "You sure you're up for this?"

"What? Hell, no. I'm waiting on Zeb. In the meantime, I've been asked to go over this place and work up its surveillance and security options.

"Ah, makes sense."

"You doin' alright?" he asked and I nodded.

"Yeah, wasn't no thang." Data came up the steps and we clasped hands, arm wrestling style and pulled each other in to tap shoulders.

"Is *she* okay?" he asked low.

"Likes to pretend she's tough, she's handling it." I nodded and worried a little that it wasn't in hers or my best interests to be keeping secrets like that.

"Cool, Zeb should be here any minute, I've got my piece and I ain't afraid to use it. Why don't you go ahead and head back to the club, man? You've probably had a longer day than any of us."

"Yeah, you can get gone when I get here in the morning. I'm glad they paired you off with someone more familiar with hand-to-hand. You'd have to shoot a motherfucker and we don't want blood spilled if we can avoid it."

"Too bad the bad guys disagree," he observed, and I shook my head.

"Sometimes, I miss the days when we brought the pain first."

Data made a face. "I don't. Not around here anyway. It was some bad shit. Dragon used to tear pages from the cartel playbooks on ruthlessness. Reaver was still halfway using back then and his freak was way worse."

I kind of wondered about that and so I asked, "What'd they do?"

"Reaver wanted to see if he could successfully skin a man alive. Turns out they die of shock first, but Dragon? You know he's resourceful and can find a use for anything. The guy who was causing problems? Opened up his front door to get the Sunday paper to find dude's skin nailed to it. Was all over the papers, of course, not like they could prove anything."

"Damn, that *is* some cartel level shit. Actually, I think that may be worse than anything I've heard of the cartels doing." I shuddered.

"I know, right? What's it say that Duracell is in the running for more fucked up than Reaver?"

I barked a laugh. "Hayden's mellowed Reaver's ass out by quite a bit, the way I understand it."

Data looked a little wistful at that and nodded. "Just hope they work their shit out and that they can hang onto each other; it's good to see Reave genuinely happy for once."

"Trouble in paradise?"

"Don't think Hayden's quite forgiven Reave for leaving her like that, all those months her thinkin' he was dead? Not many relationships can come back from that."

I nodded. "I hear you. Anyway, I should get going."

"Yeah, man. See you in the morning."

"Yeah, see you in a few hours."

I went back to the club, the ride only half as good without Bailey's sexy body pressed against my back. I've had women on the back of my bike before, but somehow, this had been different. Maybe it was because our chemistry was off the fucking charts. Things were good the couple of times we'd come together and let all the other shit fall away. I liked who she was when I was in her.

Hell, I decided I liked our little verbal sparring matches after today, too. The heat index on what we'd shared in that barn was *holy shit* and damn if I didn't want more of it. I think our battle of wits just made it that much better, which wasn't that some shit?

I took the bike around the paved track and parked closer to the outbuilding that housed my room. I gave my woodshop a longing glance. I didn't feel right if I went too long without crafting something, and the last time I'd worked with any wood had been to rebuild that fence, which almost didn't count.

When I went through the door at one end of the long hall, all I could think about was Bailey's fine ass and how it fit perfectly inside the curve of my body as I'd pounded that pussy. Yeah, I needed more of her body which meant, I needed to come clean to Dragon and Dray that we'd been doin' the nasty. I didn't want to betray her trust, I meant it, we could try and pretend what happened in the barn didn't... but there was an operative word in there; try.

I don't think either of us could or would forget. The first time in the back of the bar all those weeks ago was seriously supposed to be a one-time thing, but today? Today had been living proof that it wasn't going to be just once, or twice. We were just that damn good together, at least in the bedroom. I didn't know how it would go outside the bedroom, but I was definitely hatching a plan or two as to how to try. The girl could lie with her mouth, but not her face, and those eyes of hers said that all the nastiness she'd been putting up was just some kind of front. She didn't really believe a lot of what she was saying, she was struggling inside with a lot of shit, and she didn't know who she could trust, but she could trust me.

Anyway, it was definitely something that she liked the bike. Maybe it could be a starting point, something I could work with to crack that shell she was trying to hide behind. I shucked out of my clothes and went down the hall to shower, standing under the hot spray to let it relax my muscles. I hadn't come out of that fight completely unscathed. While I'd been lucky and no one had landed any real blows, I'd pulled a thing or two and was starting to stiffen up.

A hot shower, some ibuprofen, and some good sleep and I should be good to go. I went back to my room and racked out, dropping into a deep sleep right off the bat. It felt like I'd just closed my eyes and the alarm was already going off. Still, when I opened them, it wasn't any more than the usual grogginess that accompanied waking up first thing in the morning. I'd slept pretty well.

I pulled on a clean pair of jeans and a fresh tee and sat on the edge of my bed with a big sigh. I bowed my head and pulled on the back of my head to stretch my neck and upper back as much as I could. It was supposed to be my 'day off' but until things had settled, there was no such thing as time off. I thought about it some and decided that after yesterday, I'd earned it and I was gonna have my fuckin' cake and eat it, too. I threw some of my shit together and packed one of my saddlebags after I finished getting dressed.

I rode out to Blue Hills and was surprised to see Bailey was up, sitting with Data on the front porch. I pulled up and backed my bike in line with Zeb's rat bike and Data's resto'ed classic chopper and killed the engine.

"You're up early, boss lady," I called up to the porch softly.

"Haven't slept yet," she called back.

"Been out here long?"

"Figured if I needed coffee, these guys did too."

"Mighty kind of you." I dropped into a seat at the table as I said it.

"It's been known to happen," she shot back with a wry smile.

"Got an extra cup?" I asked.

"Sure." She poured one for me and asked, "You always get here this early?"

"Yep."

"You know starting time isn't until five, I would have thought Renaldo would have told you that."

"You told me not to be late, remember?"

"Right… still, three in the morning is a little excessive, don't you think?"

"A mite, but I like to get here before everyone else. I like the quiet, just me and the horses and hell, half of them or more are asleep, too." I took the coffee she offered and doctored it up to my liking. I turned and asked Data, "Where's Zeb gone to?"

"Foot patrol, don't worry." He lifted a small walkie-talkie and smiled. "Seven-mile range, no interference out here, built them myself."

"Nice."

"Want I should call him in?" Data had a small smile that said he and I needed to talk later, and I wondered just what he'd gotten Bailey to tell him. I gave a nod and he got on the radio.

"Hey, Zeb, reel it in."

The radio crackled and Zeb came over saying "Thanks, bro, I'm buggered."

I chuckled and took another swallow of my coffee. It took Zeb the better part of twenty minutes to get back to us and I called down off the steps, "Man, where the fuck you been?"

"Way out in the wops, I reckon."

"Dude, I have no idea what that means."

"Better yet, be careful where you say that, *wop* is a derogatory name for an Italian person here in the states," Bailey said and then followed up with, "And in New Zealand, 'the wops' is pretty much our rendition of the middle of nowhere or Timbuktu."

"Oh, so BFE."

She looked at me confused and I grinned. "Butt Fuck Egypt, sort of like Fucking New Guy or," and Data picked up with me, "Big Fucking Gun."

The boys and I cracked up hard while Bailey shook her head, knees drawn up to her chest under her cream satin bathrobe, the light spilling from the windows over her and giving her some kind of glow like an angel. It was the first time I'd seen her with her hair down and it made her look softer, less severe. I liked it.

"I always thought BFG was short for *Big Friendly Giant*."

"What the hell is a Big Friendly Giant?" I asked, still laughing.

"It's a children's book, by Roald Dahl! Come on now, it's one of my favorites."

Data got up and stretched, and asked, "Rush, talk to you, bro?"

"Yeah, yeah!" I set my coffee down and got up following him off the porch.

"You guys don't have to go," Bailey said rolling her eyes and Data looked over his shoulder, gaze flicking her up and down.

"It's club business."

She frowned. "What's that supposed to mean?"

"No offense, girl. It means it's none of *yours*. Just the way it is." Zeb shrugged and I wished I knew that trick, how to make a shrug jovial.

We walked across the gravel lot clean out of earshot of our mutterings and I asked, "What's up?"

"She didn't sleep at all," Data said. "This shit's weighing on her."

I grunted and Zeb broke in with, "It's all quiet out there, I think the locals know the club's involved. I don't reckon we're gonna see much action."

"No, it's going to take her douchebag brother a minute or two to think up another intimidation tactic."

"On a personal note, brother, I think she likes you," Data said with a bit of a grin.

"She's the P's niece," I said and he gave me a look like I was a moron.

"She's a grown ass adult."

That right there told me just which way Dragon would sway if it came down to it. Data and the old man seemed to be the closest outside of Doc. The president was still a bit of an enigma to me, but he treated us all fair, which was a lot more than I could always say for Dom, our old chapter's president.

"Thanks, man," I said and I meant it.

"No problem."

We went back over to where Bailey watched us curiously, and I gave parting hugs to my club brothers. They got on their bikes and rode off and I watched 'em go. Taillights fading into the distance before making their left at the two-lane highway out of there.

I finished the climb of the last two steps and dropped back into my seat. Bailey warmed up my coffee, adding more to my mug from the carafe she had on standby.

We sat in a surprisingly comfortable silence for a time until she finally broke first and asked, "You sleep at all last night?"

"Like a fuckin' baby, you?" She shook her head.

"I just kept seeing Renaldo, down on the ground like that…"

"Stop thinking about it."

"I can't."

"It's just going to get tougher."

She sighed and nodded. "That's what I'm afraid of."

"Go get dressed, I'll saddle up a couple of the farm horses. We'll go ride the perimeter. Might make you feel better."

She searched my face and I had to smile. "Just a ride, no ulterior motives here."

"Right," she said and rolled her eyes. She went to slip past me, and I smacked her on her ass. She yelped and jumped just about three feet in surprise, glaring down at me.

"I'm not a saint, Bailey. Don't forget it."

Her eyes fell to my cut and something dark crossed behind them just before her expression became her version of diamond tough. "Hard to," she murmured, and dare I say, that look, combined with her derisive comment hurt a little. I didn't like the deep disappointment that welled up out of the cut her remark left, but it was what it was. Bailey was steeped in years of prejudice where the life was concerned, and chemistry only went so far to bridge that chasm.

She went inside and I got up and went down to the farm's stables. The farm had several horses that weren't thoroughbreds but were still some damn fine animals. One of 'em was Bailey's and had been for several years. A gelding by the name of Boaz. He was a fine animal, a glossy black with a white foreleg to the knee and not a spot of color anywhere else.

When I got to his stall, my heart sank. Something was clearly wrong with him. He was lying on his side, flank heaving.

"Aw, fuck no." I pulled my phone out of my cut and called up Bailey.

"Why are you calling me?"

"Baby, it's Boaz, you need to round up your vet." I stared down at the poor animal and knew, I just knew. "You need to get out here and say goodbye."

8

Bailey…

I knew my brother was an asshole but this? I stood to one side and watched Boaz struggle to breathe. Doc Sanders, the vet for this farm since before I was born, was kneeling at his side; his son had come to assist, following in his father's footsteps when it came to veterinary care. He kneeled back and the first tears I struggled not to let show slid down my face.

"I'm sorry, Bailey, there's nothing I can do. He's too far gone, it's best to end it here."

A hand closed on my shoulder and I shook it off. I pressed my lips together and said the hardest thing I'd ever had to say, "Do it."

I spun on my heel and pushed past Rush. I couldn't watch my best friend die. I'd had Boaz for almost four years. He'd been a college graduation gift from my father because I'd had Arabella since I was twelve and she was just plain getting old. She'd lived out the rest of her days well loved and cared for, passing of old age just last year. This? This was just a waste. Boaz didn't do anything to anybody, and he was such a young horse, too. This had nothing to do with the operation of the farm, nothing to do with taking the farm down. This was to punish *me* for being so stubborn. For ignoring Philip's calls, for deleting the emails without reading them. This was personal, and I couldn't do a fucking thing about it without proof.

"I want a full necropsy," I called back over my shoulder and I couldn't bring myself to look back. I went all the way out to the driveway in front of my house in the early morning light and braced my hands on my knees, taking deep breaths of the cool morning air in an attempt to quell my rage.

"Bailey!" Rush called and I shook my head.

"Not now!" I barked back. "Just get to work."

"Shit, as you wish," he muttered darkly, and I pulled my phone out of my back pocket.

I dialed through a haze and put it to my ear, he picked up on the fourth ring, "Bailey, to what do I owe this –"

I cut him off, "Boaz, really Philip? You killed Boaz. Why? Why goddammit?"

"Slow down, Bailey. What? What now? Boaz? Now wait just a minute, do you really think I would kill your horse? What would that serve?"

"Oh, shut up! You had Renaldo beaten and now this? What kind of a monster are you?"

"You need to watch what you say, little sister. I don't appreciate base-less accusations, now I know you're upset…"

"Upset?" I shouted into the phone, staring at one of the oak trees in my yard. "Oh we are way past upset, Philip. This is *rage*, pure incendiary *rage*. You need to stop. I'm not selling this farm. Not to you, not to anyone, so you just need to knock it off. We aren't kids anymore and I *won't* be bullied!"

"First of all, I didn't do anything to Renaldo, the police said that he owed those men money. Second of all, for you to accuse me of harming one of your animals? You obviously don't know me at all Bales. I would never –"

"Save it, Philip. You would. We both know you would. Your bullshit lies may have worked on Dad, and they may work on Caleb or in the boardroom, but we're family and you don't have either me or Mom, fooled."

I stabbed my finger against the red button on the screen and stood there chest heaving and fought with everything I was not to scream and cry at the injustice of it. It wasn't fair, I couldn't prove anything but I knew, I knew beyond a shadow of a doubt it was Philip and that his time was running out to close this deal with the developer before they moved on to something else. They couldn't make me sell. There wasn't any cause for eminent domain. They could just go fuck themselves and Philip could just go fuck himself right along with them.

"Come on," Rush said tersely, grabbing me by the elbow and towing me along.

"Hey! Let me go!"

"Suck it up, buttercup. We're going. You don't need to be here when they take that horse out."

"Where are we going?" I demanded.

"For that ride, on a different sort of horse," he grated, and I felt my resolve weaken in the face of my want to experience the thrill of the ride at that speed again.

9

R ush...

She followed me, her resistance to the hold I had on her vanishing in an instant and I had to hide my smile. She liked riding, which was good, because when the world went to shit around me, I had only two options, my shop or my bike. The time I spent in my shop, I just couldn't share with anyone. This, though? This I could, and I was surprised to find just how much I enjoyed sharing it with her.

She got on behind me wordlessly and I dug out my spare helmet, which I'd made sure to put with the bike, out of one of the hard-sided saddlebags. She put it on, I put mine on buckling up the chinstrap and fired up the bike. She pulled herself snug against my back and my cock began to stir. I told it to shut it, not that it would listen to me, and pulled out onto the drive and down the long track leading to the road.

I'd shot a text to Dragon telling him what was up, and he assured me he'd have some guys out to the farm to keep an eye on things. I'd told him that what was up with Boaz might not have been an oversight on Data and Zeb's the night before, that if he were poisoned, it could have just as easily happened the day before, there just wasn't any telling.

He'd shot back a 'roger that' and now I was hoping both our phones could go on ignore for a while.

I took her out on the highway, out past the club and up into the hills and this park with hiking and campgrounds. There were these easy gravel hiking trails and shit and she almost yelped when I took us down one on the bike. I didn't give a fuck. I knew what I was doing. I pulled off and into a field and through the long grass, stopping and shutting off the bike. I tapped her knee and she got off saying, "What the hell was *that*?" as I leaned my ride onto its kickstand.

I shrugged with a wry smile and said, "A shortcut."

"God, you all really have *no respect* for people, their property or anything do you?" she demanded.

"Hard to explain, but if you want, I could try." I pulled an old knock-off Navajo blanket out of the same saddlebag her helmet had come out of and laid it out by the bike, flopping down onto it on my back.

She sat down gingerly on the edge, keeping her boots off it. I sighed, she could suit herself.

"Okay, explain; you can start with your tattoos."

I raised an eyebrow. "My tattoos?"

"Yeah, your tattoos."

I plucked a piece of grass and stuck the end in my mouth, chewing thoughtfully. The bright green flavor tinting my taste buds while I thought how to put it into so many words.

I finally gave a shrug and said, "To get 'em you're gonna have to get me."

"Okay, whatever that means…"

I rolled my eyes and sat up, pulling her down so she lay beside me. She wiggled a bit and finally put her head on my chest to stare into the bright blue sky traced with light white clouds with me.

"Why did you join the club?" she asked finally.

"Wasn't no other place for me," I told her.

"How could you think that?"

"You know, not everyone's rich, right?" I laughed when I said it to take any sting out of it.

"I know that." She sounded affronted anyway and it was cute.

"You and me, we couldn't be more different that way," I said with a dying chuckle.

"So, you were poor…"

"No, baby, I was *dirt floor poor.* I was so poor, I couldn't afford the two o's and the r. I was just 'p.'"

She giggled a little at that. "I never looked at myself as rich growing up, I always thought of it as my parent's money. Not Philip, though." She adjusted her head, more up onto my shoulder and snuggled a little closer trying to get comfortable. I gave her a light squeeze in my direction.

"Yeah, but your parents had money growing up. Hell, you *had* parents…"

"Oh, come on, surely you had parents!" she said and I went real quiet.

"You couldn't call 'em that. Me and Nox were wards of the state. Same with Arch and Grind. We all came up under the same roof, but our foster parents weren't parents. Not even close."

"What about your mom?" she asked softly.

"Lot lizard, something our piece of shit foster daddy just loved reminding us about on the regular."

"I don't know what that means," she said quietly and I could tell it bothered her to ask.

"A lot lizard is a hooker at a truck stop. That's how Nox and I came to be the medical marvels we are today."

"Medical marvels?"

"We're twins, but we don't share the same daddy." I let her think about that for a while. Finally, she gave a little startled 'oh!' I nodded. "Yeah."

"So, you have no idea who your fathers are then?"

"Just what they sort of look like and that they drove a truck for a living. That's about it."

"Oh my God, I don't know if I could even imagine such a thing."

"Not gonna sugarcoat shit because I ain't Willy Wonka — there aren't many kids that had it worse than us comin' up. Usually the ones that did, well, they didn't make it."

"I still don't understand what that has to do with joining a motorcycle gang."

"Club."

"Yeah, but –"

"No buts, it's a club, a brotherhood that's given us everything that the life you citizen motherfuckers scorned us for. I'm not gonna lie to you. There was more 'n one time when I was as young as six or seven when I wished our mamma had done the right thing and aborted us before we'd ever come to term."

"That's horrible!" she cried, sitting up and staring down at me aghast.

"That's the truth of it," I said. "These fuckin' red states and their pro-life bullshit. Where are they once kids like me and my brothers are born? Oh yeah, that's right, screamin' in our mom's faces to get a job, and to stop moochin' off their precious system. Well, my mom had a job, the only one she could get to feed her drug habit that she took on to forget how shitty her life was. Only problem was, she was either too high or didn't have access to birth control, and so here I am."

She sat there staring at me, chewing her lip. I hated the pity in her eyes, but it was to be expected. Not a lot of human beings out there could listen to my story and not be moved to pity. The ones that weren't were typically men or women like me who knew what it was like, or the real monsters that people needed to be afraid of but rarely ever saw them for who they were until it was too late. People like my foster parents, real pieces of shit.

"So the club is what? A way to get back at everyone?"

I laughed. "That's right where all you citizens go, right from the get-go, every damn one of you. You're about as smart as you are sexy, Bailey. I need you to use those smarts and think about it."

She blushed and averted her gaze out over the grass to the sound of the nearby river. Finally, her shoulders dropped and she sighed. "A place to belong?" she asked finally.

"Bingo."

"I still don't quite understand."

"My brothers have my back and I have theirs. I'm not just talkin' my twin or my foster brothers. I'm talkin' men like Dragon and Dray. They had family come callin' and by all rights, the way your mamma, and yeah by default even you, have treated 'em, they had every reason to tell y'all to fuck off, but did they?"

"No."

"Did I?"

"No."

"That's the point of the club. We just don't really have time to try and live up to and follow the rules of a society that doesn't give a good goddamn about us. Y'all have your preconceived notions and we could give a fuck less about correcting your ignorant asses."

"Wouldn't it make life easier if you did?"

"Baby, since when has life ever been easy for a man like me?"

She twisted her lips to keep from smiling and picked at the grass by her hip. She looked thoughtful, and finally said, "You know it's not all sunshine and roses on this side of the fence either, don't you?"

I put my hands behind my head and stared at the sky. "There's this saying that comes to mind when you said that just now. 'The grass is always greener on the other side of the fence,'" I said.

"I think everybody knows that saying."

"You know the rest of it?" I asked and glanced her way. She shook her head.

"On a kind of it's fertilized with a bunch of bullshit."

She laughed, a spontaneous sound that wasn't forced but came from genuine surprise. I liked it on her, she hung her head, smiling, her single braid falling over her shoulder and I took in the moment. Long brown hair, the color of a good chestnut wood dark with stain, fell in that braid to just below her breast. Longer than when I'd seen her that first time in the dim light of *The Spot*.

Her skin was lightly sun-kissed. Probably two or three shades darker where she'd tanned than what was underneath her clothes. Her skin smooth and perfect, not battered and scarred like my hide.

She was in her typical work wear of ladies' cowboy boots, light denim boot-cut jeans, and one of those white spaghetti strapped tank top things with the fancy name that escaped me. Over it, she had on one of them white and blue plaid, snap button, ladies fitted blouses with the sleeves rolled up to the elbow.

For a rich bitch, she *worked*. Her hands rough and chapped from handling the horses back on the farm. Her liquid dark eyes were definitely a family trait from her mamma's side. She looked just like the pictures of Dray's mamma I'd seen. Probably enough like her it'd make Dragon shit a brick sideways if he saw her.

I could see why he was so all over Tillie if the stories were half as true as everyone said they were. I was inclined to believe 'em. The man was wrapped around the axle for his woman and it seemed to grow more that way, not less, with every passing year that she'd been gone.

Of course, the rich side of Tillie's family probably never saw it. Never knew anything about the depths any one of us would go. Shit, I was putting even money on the fact Mommy Dearest would have a full-on conniption fit if she saw what her darling daughter was up to with the big, scary, outlaw right now. Good enough to protect her, I'd bet, but so not good enough to fuck her.

I closed my eyes on the vision that was Bailey staring at me curiously, and said, "Any rate, all o' this aside, I'm sorry about your horse. He was a damn fine animal."

"I'm more worried about Renaldo. Boaz hurts, but now I'm afraid people think I care more about my horse than I do my friend."

"The joys of living the socialite life?"

"People judge, it's not mutually exclusive to the rich, you know. Your people do it just as much as mine do if you want to put it in such a way." I jumped when she cuddled to my side, laying her head on my shoulder again. "I'd like to think that people are just people, regardless of their socio-economic status."

I chuckled but kept the thought, *spoken like a true rich girl,* to myself. We were comfortable, and as adorable as she was when she got all pissy pants, I was enjoying this momentary truce. I knew that we couldn't keep this a secret forever and that eventually I was going to get burned, but for now I let myself pretend that this could be something.

10

B ailey...

I drowsed against him, the sun warm and with his arm around me, I felt safe. I mean, kind of hard not to when you'd seen the guy take out five others in a few quick moments. I thought about what he'd told me and realized he'd opened up to me, likely in a way he didn't to many people. I wondered about that. Why he would? Why me of all people? He had that sexy tortured bad boy thing going on now and I wanted to go there. I so wanted to go there, but I was afraid to. Not just because of my mother, I loved her, but honestly her and my father had some seriously skewed views of reality.

I blamed it on the fact that they had both come from money and their relationship and marriage had practically been an arranged one. I know my mother had found love with my father eventually, but I also knew he hadn't made it easy on her. It was one of the most depressing things about being a child of privilege and knowing it. Knowing that pretty much the exact same fate awaited me.

I lost track of how many dates my mother had set me up on with her socialite friend's sons. The ladies from her garden club, and that was laughable all on its own considering not a single one of them would know a hoe from a trowel. Anyway, they would always crow about their son's achievements in this sport or that club and the next thing I knew my Friday night when I was home from school would be all lined up for me with whatever function was the going thing. He'd pick me up at eight in his fancy car that was likely a gift for this or that achievement, birthday, or graduation. Hell, one of them had even gotten a car for beating his first DUI! It was all so ludicrous, awkward, and unbelievable.

"Bailey..." My name startled me coming in that low, almost husky growl from between his lips.

"Yeah?"

"What are you thinking about so hard over there?"

"You'd laugh at me."

"Try me."

Well, he opened up to me...

"When I was thirteen, my brother got himself in trouble with this girl."

Rush chuckled. "Got a girl knocked up, eh?" I think I was silent too long because he jostled me a bit against his shoulder and said, "Bailey, what happened?"

"More like a rape accusation, a bad one. He was sixteen at the time, and as a result, I was sent to boarding school."

"What the fuck is that?" he demanded.

"Um, I think it was my parent's way of protecting me from the fallout. You know the ass backwards way of the Bible belt, the first-born son can do no wrong and women are all basically property to do with what you will. Well, that was kind of how my father ran our house. Mom and I were just ornaments, although, I think he did listen to my mother in private, you know?"

88

"I like my women with a fire inside, so no, I really don't know."

I snorted. "Seems like you're just like my father in some ways, or did you forget what happened in the barn so soon?"

"A deal's a deal. I promised I'd try to forget, but we both know encounters like that, those are the things you *never* forget. Besides, there's a difference between breaking a horse's spirit and taming one."

I rolled my eyes. "Yes, because comparing our sexual encounter to taming a horse is totally making me feel like less of a piece of property or livestock."

He laughed. "Okay, fair point, but I can't think of a better comparison that won't get me into even deeper shit with you, so gimme a break?"

"Just this one time."

"Cool, thanks, and I think you know what I meant."

"I do, I had the choice to walk away."

"But you didn't, why is that?"

I blushed furiously and ran through just about every possibility I could come up with and immediately discarded it, *because you're the only man to make me come like that.* Nope, I didn't need to inflate his ego any worse than it already was. *Because maybe deep down I'm a rebellious little shit and I wanted to stick it to my rich bitch family like my aunt did?* Not only no but hell no, all that would do was reinforce his already poor view of me and my family that all we did was use people.

"Bailey?"

"Honestly?"

"It's the best policy with someone like me," he said frankly.

Ouch, okay...

"Nothing that is going to come out of my mouth is going to sound very flattering," I told him.

"Eh, why don't you let me be the judge of that?"

"The first time, at the bar, I picked you because I was angry at my brother, my mother, and Caleb. They all just made me so…"

"Pissed off?" he supplied.

"Yes, angry. I saw it as an opportunity to get what I wanted which was a good hard –"

"Fuck."

"Yes, thank you; and a way to just stick it to the lot of them at the same time."

"I can appreciate the practicality."

"Really? You're not mad?"

"Naw, I was out lookin' for the same thing sort of. A one-night stand, a one and done. Was a little butt-hurt you wouldn't give me your name, though."

"Wouldn't have been a one and done if I had, now would it?"

He laughed and said, "Fate seemed to have a few other ideas where that was concerned," he agreed.

"Yeah, well…"

"So, let me ask you this? Why round two?"

I groaned. "Were you there for round one?" He laughed, a rich outpouring of sound that did my heart some surprising good.

"I'm not like them, you know. I don't want to be like them."

"I'm kind of getting that," he said. "Making Blue Hills your last stand that you are your own woman and won't do what you're told anymore?"

"Yeah, sort of."

"Welcome to your first step into the life, then. That's part of what this is about. Carving something from nothing, making a life that's better for you going forward and shirking the conventions that 'the man' whoever that is to you, has put on you. It's just one of the reasons people join this life, but it's usually the most popular."

"I don't know about all of that," I said waving a hand ineffectually.

"Sounds to me, you know more than a thing or two about it. Tired of your male relatives and hell, even your mom pigeonholing you as the little woman."

"I think my mom sort of woke up on that front when my dad died."

"Why you think that is?"

"I don't know. I'd have to ask her."

"Why haven't you?"

I thought about that for a little bit and finally said, "I guess I don't want her to hurt, you know? Seem like the thing that would drag up some painful stuff."

"Yeah, I get that."

I lay there and wondered what it would be like if I *did* give it a go, actually *dating* this guy. I mean, we were from *completely* different worlds, not to mention it'd probably devastate my mother. Still, I couldn't help but wonder about a lot of things. Not just what an actual relationship would be like, but all of it. I mean, I already knew the sex would be hot, but what about five, ten, or twenty years from now?

I sat up and stretched, yawning tiredly. It was hot and the sun beating down was uncomfortable. I stared down at him for a moment and twisting my lips in indecision finally blurted out, "I'm hot, I'm going for a swim."

He laughed, and said, "Go on with your bad self." The twinkle in his eyes turned to a spark of desire when I started to lose the clothes, though. When I pulled off my boots, he stood up and pulled his shirt over his head. I paused for a moment and he shrugged.

"Sounds like a good idea to me."

I smiled and stripped the rest of the way down to my bra and panties. Not Rush, though. He apparently didn't wear underwear, so he followed me down the river bank buck naked.

I waded out into the water knee deep and he came in right behind me, hiding the front of himself up against my back crying, "Holy shit, that's cold!"

I laughed, I couldn't help it. "It's river water, which usually comes from snow melt and glacier runoff; of course, it's cold."

"Oh, shit. You totally can't judge because there's gonna be some shrinkage." I threw back my head and laughed for real at that and he wrapped those huge arms around me picking me up and tumbling back into the deeper water. I quickly held my breath as we plunged beneath the surface and both of us came up sputtering.

"Oh my God, I can't believe you did that!" I cried as the shock of the cold water shot through my system.

"That's what you get for preying on one of man's worst fears!"

"Oh, you have got to be kidding me!"

We bantered, we played, and for the first time in a long time despite the horror and sorrow of the last couple of days, I remembered what it was like to relax and really be myself. The real me, not the overcautious and paranoid me that dragged me so far left of center as to be so rude. I wasn't brought up that way. I had seriously been rattled when I'd seen Dray and Rush on my porch.

"Hey, Rush?"

"Mm?"

"Thank you."

"For?"

"Everything you've done so far despite me being a total bitch."

"Like?" I turned in his arms to see the smile I could hear in his voice and I felt one of my own spread across my lips. I twined my arms around his neck and looked him in the eyes. I should have figured he wouldn't make this easy.

"I was raised by a proper southern mamma," I said. "So please accept my formal apology for being so rude the day you showed up at my house with her. Also, my sincerest thanks for providing the fencing material to make my north pasture safe. I wasn't really sure how I was going fix it to make it any kind of usable with everything having to go through Caleb."

Rush's expression changed then, and he searched my face. "What's with that, anyway? You own the place, so I don't get why everything has to go by him."

I sighed, and rested more fully on my elbows, crossing my legs at the ankles behind his back. It felt good, clinging to him, and letting him take the weight for a minute as we bobbed in the river water, his feet firmly planted in its bed. I tried to figure out how to answer the question without insulting his intelligence. I mean, I didn't know how much he knew about how probate and everything else worked.

"Dumb it down for me, Bailey. I'm not stupid, but I have no idea how your world works. Things are a lot simpler in mine and I'd kind of like to keep it that way for now."

I laughed at little and nodded. "You kind of read my mind," I said.

"Not hard, baby. Your face says right what you're thinkin'."

I rolled my eyes. "Tell me about it, I could never get away with *anything* growing up. Philip is the one that got all the talent for lying."

"Don't see it as a bad thing; I don't. Somethin' to be said for an honest face like yours." He reached up and tweaked my nose with a fingertip and I laughed, jerking back from the affectionate move, cold water dripping from my nose.

"Right, so my dad left the farm to all three of us; me, my mother, and Philip."

"But?"

"But he didn't think we were savvy enough to make the business decisions, and so he put a trustee in place to help us."

"And that's Caleb, I follow."

"Right, and Caleb's job is to help oversee the farm's finances and make sure that sound business decisions are being made so that the farm doesn't fall apart."

"So, if your daddy doesn't want the place falling apart or whatever, enough to put his best friend into the mix to make sure things are running right, why wouldn't he put anything in there about the farm not being sold, or whatever?"

"Legally you can't give something to someone and force them to keep it. You can just make it really hard for them to give it up completely. My mom, for example, while she doesn't hate the farm, she never really enjoyed it or was any kind of enthusiastic over it. Not like me and Dad."

"That why she sold her part to you?"

"Yes, but the provision in the will was that she had to sell it for fair market value, which is why it took everything I had to buy her out of it. I wanted it to stay in the family while she was willing to offload her piece to just anybody. We actually had a big fight about it, both ended up crying our eyes out before she realized how much Blue Hills meant to me."

"And Philip?"

I snorted. "God, he hates anything our parents remotely love. He wants to raze the farm to the ground and build some sort of amusement park on the land. Some big developer tried to get my dad to sell it before he died and he said no. Honestly, Blue Hills was just about the only thing Daddy and I agreed on." I sighed. "It's the only thing we really shared. So yeah, I want to keep it. It's the only real link to the good times I had with my dad. Our love of horses."

"Dad sounds like a cold piece."

"Pretty sure he would have been a lot happier if I was the one born a boy instead of Philip."

"Let me guess, your brother's *the* spoiled rich kid of spoiled rich kids?" He bobbed us in the water and I still clung to him, comfortably suspended in his arms.

"Pretty much. He hit his teenage years and it suddenly became all about drugs and partying with his 'friends.'" I took my arms from around his neck just long enough to make air quotes around 'friends' and Rush eyed me critically, his hands automatically drifting to my back to hold me up until I could do it for myself again.

"What about you?"

I snorted. "Too busy trying to stay an A+ student and trying to make my parents notice I existed. Didn't matter, though. Philip still got all the attention."

"The squeaky wheel usually is the one that gets the grease, babe."

"Yeah," I murmured, and tried not to let the hurt show. I lost track of how many achievements of mine my parents missed completely because they were off trying to clean up one of my brother's messes. I seriously just wanted them to *see* me... and now that was too late now that my dad was gone. I shoved down the hurt with a little more anger at my brother and just tried to be grateful that my mom was coming around, as weird as that felt.

I mean, talk about confusing. She hated *everything* biker related. Had railed against it my entire life. Going on about how her sister could do so much better and about how my uncle was a no-good criminal and how he was dragging my cousin Dray down the same path. It was like every foundation I had ever stood on had been thrown into the air and I was falling, falling, falling, with no direction and nowhere to land that wasn't going to obliterate every part of me.

I was grasping at anything to catch myself on, and there was just *nothing.* It was supposed to be Blue Hills… but Philip was intent on taking even *that* from me.

"Why'd you do it?" he asked softly.

"What?"

"Pick me out of every other guy in that bar?"

I put on a brave smile. "Seemed like a really good idea at the time," I tried.

He nodded, and said, "It's okay; you ain't got to tell me right now."

I swallowed hard and nodded and he leaned in, hand grazing the side of my face, drawing me closer. I went and kissed him, because for some reason, kissing him made everything feel like it made sense right now, and it was, at least, something to grab onto.

11

R ush...

Fucking citizens always gotta come around and ruin a good thing. This time it was some old lady and her fuckin' dog. I was getting into her kiss when this batty old bitch starts screaming at us from the riverbank about being ashamed and blah, blah, blah threatening to call the park's services or some shit. All it took was me setting Bailey down where she was safe to stand, and me walking up out of the water in the buff for the bitch to start power walking her fat ass back down the trail.

Bailey followed me out of the water laughing with this bright-eyed expression that made the whole thing worth it. We hurried up and got dressed and passed the woman on our way out the park. I gave her the good ol' one-fingered salute as we went by and took me and Bales the fuck out of there before she could get into any shit.

We rode back to the farm, having no place else to really go and with her energy seriously flagging after more than twenty-four hours of being awake. Dray was sitting on the porch steps fucking around on his phone, one of those fancy black cigarettes that smelled more like incense rather than a proper smoke dangling between his fingertips. He took a drag off it and tucked his phone back into his cut as we pulled up and I tapped Bailey to get off.

He exhaled a cloud of fragrant smoke and grinning said to his cousin, "Look at you all badass! What d' you think?"

Bailey stretched her fingertips to the sky then worked the chinstrap to her brain bucket free and called out, "I think I finally understand the appeal."

"Yeah?" He put his sunglasses on his head and gave me a tight-lipped smile that said I was so getting my ass beat later. Hopefully I could get an explanation in before we had to hurt each other.

"And *you*," he said to me, "takin' my cousin for a ride."

"Oh for God's sakes, Dray-Dray. Give it a rest," Bailey said and rolled her eyes.

"Yeah, Dray-Dray, give it a rest." Dragon got up from the table up on the porch and stubbed his cigarette out on the bottom of his boot before putting it into an empty soda can. I hadn't even realized he was sitting there.

"Jesus Christmas, Bailey Lynn... look at you all grown up," he declared.

He came down the steps to give her a hug and Bailey said softly, "Hi, Uncle José."

"Wish you'd call me Dragon, sweetheart. Only your mamma calls me José and that's only because she knows I don't like it."

"Sorry, Uncle Dragon," Bailey said shyly.

He smiled at her and shook his head. "Lord, child. You are the spittin' image of my Tillie."

"My mom says so, too."

"How're you doin' sweetheart?" Bailey went with him to the porch and they talked softly. She would nod and the mantle of her responsibilities was back, weighing down her shoulders.

Dray stood next to me and growled, "You're seriously fucking my cousin, aren't you, you bastard?"

"One, it's more like *she* fucked *me*... remember the story about the brunette hottie in the back of *The Spot*?" Dray's head jerked back, and a look crossed his face that clearly said he was impressed – with *her*, not me.

"And two?" he demanded.

"You already know I'm a bastard, so why don't you try an insult that isn't actually true?"

He snorted and the ice was broken enough that I figured I was saved from some kind of ass beating to defend his cousin's honor. Not that she needed it. She was pretty fierce, she'd just lost her way some with everything being so overwhelming. Hell, I knew grown ass men who wouldn't be holding their shit together half as good.

"You know if you hurt her, I'm still going to have to kill you, right?"

"That some kind of fucked up blood family clause thing?"

"Yeah."

"Meh, yeah, I could see it," I said and nodded.

"You boys get yer asses up here and let's talk," Dragon called. Dray and I exchanged a look, shrugged and went up to join them.

"Wait, let me get us all something cold to drink, I'm dying," Bailey said and got up. She went into the house and it was just the three of us guys again.

"What do you think happened to the horse?" Dragon asked.

"Poison. I'd bet my fuckin' life on it. What'd your sources say about Renaldo?"

"Now *that* was interesting, turns out he did owe some local loan shark some money, but not enough to warrant a beatdown that fuckin' bad. Bein' a jockey, it stood to reason he'd still played the ponies from time to time."

"So, the local players were legit just trying to get their money?"

"I think it was just a good excuse to cause a little chaos," Dray said.

"Any rate, we ain't gonna have any more problems from the local criminal element," Dragon said.

"Why's that?" I asked.

Dray snorted and smirked. "*They* called *us* fallin' all over themselves to apologize for overstepping."

"Yeah, I know they saw my ink, didn't think it made that much of a difference, though."

"Oh, you bet your ass it did," Dragon said.

"They give up their backer?"

"Yep," Dragon said, pulling a cigarette out of this silver case etched with his namesake etched on it. If I had to guess it was another Dani Broussard original. It matched that silver dragon ponytail holder he had a little too well to be anything else.

"The brother?" I hazarded.

"You guessed it," Dray said.

"Where's that leave us?" I asked.

"Probably nowhere good," Dray muttered darkly.

"We've dealt with this kind of thing before, been a couple a years but it didn't end well for the guy."

"Oh yeah, who was that?"

"Sunshine's ex-douchebag, but somehow I don't think we can employ the same tactic here," Dray said.

"Similar, to be sure, but not same," Dragon agreed.

"I don't know the full scope on that one to agree or disagree," I told them. Dragon looked back over his shoulder into the house and grunted, "Later."

"How much of this you plan on telling Bailey?" I asked quietly but didn't get an answer because she was backing out the screen door with a loaded tray of lemonade this time.

"Here we go," she said and filled four glasses from the big glass pitcher on the tray. She sat down across from Dragon, between me and Dray and sighed out harshly.

"Well, sweetheart, you ain't gonna like this, but I think it's time our man Rush here took up some space on your couch." Dragon took a swallow of the offered lemonade and Bailey looked from Dragon to me.

"I don't know about that," she said shifting uncomfortably and I couldn't say I disagreed. I mean, I wanted her, sure, who wouldn't? But I wanted to do things right – in a way that was a little more familiar to her. The whole pick her up on a Friday or Saturday night for a date kind of thing. Didn't look like that was gonna be in the cards, though, and if it's one thing I did well, it was adapt to survive. I could adapt to this even easier.

"Here I can get to and deal with something faster than if I'm at the club," I said with a shrug.

Bailey's phone started buzzing across the table where she'd put it after pulling it out of her back pocket when she'd gotten to sit down. She picked it up and swiped across the screen with a, "Sorry, have to take this."

"Hello?" she said into it, and immediately an angry voice basically started screaming at her out of the earpiece. She was too far away from me to make anything out except a whole bunch of Charlie Brown's teacher; "Wah wah woh wah wah?"

Dragon, Dray, and I all exchanged a worried look, the 'what now?' etched into all of our faces.

"I understand, Mr. Fairchild, and no, nothing is wrong with any of the horses in the client stables. No, sir… it was only my own horse, Boaz. Yes, thank you, sir. It's very hard, I loved him very much. No, sir, Two Drops in a Bucket is fine.

"I hate that horse," I said out of the side of my mouth quietly to Dray. "We like to call him Two Men Shitting in a Bucket."

Dray had to put his hand over his mouth to keep from laughing, still, he snorted and Bailey scowled at us both, getting up and walking to the opposite end of the porch.

"No, sir, Mr. Fairchild, sir… just a couple of my farm hands talking about a topic unrelated to this one. No one is laughing at the severity of the situation, I assure you."

She paused and listened to whatever the rich SOB on the other end of the line was saying and was nodding along. "As soon as I have the results of the necropsy, I will let everyone know, but I believe that it is far too early to assume that any one of your horses are in any danger. We simply don't know what happened to Boaz and we won't for a while, yet."

Anger flashed across her face and she said, "My brother only holds one-third of this farm and isn't here on a day-to-day basis, like I am. I'm not sure why you would get any of your information from him seeing as we only spoke briefly this morning about the situation. I assure you, everyone's animal is fine and that this was an isolated incident."

Another long pause and her shoulders dropped. "I understand, and that is your right; however, I must remind you that the stud fee has been paid and you are contractually obligated to see the pairing of Two Drops in a Bucket and A Midnight Dreary through.

"I do believe that would be best. Yes, sir. I agree completely. I have men here who will be upgrading our security cameras in the stables. Yes, they're here as we speak. Yes, sir. We already have twenty-four-hour monitoring. Yes, sir. Yes, sir. I absolutely understand. Yes, I *do* know how much Two Drops in a Bucket is worth, if you recall, he *was* bred and born here."

A burst of noise out of the phone loud enough for Bailey to hold the phone away from her ear for a moment, she returned it and said, "Absolutely sir. I am one hundred percent on board with what you are saying, and I don't disagree in the slightest."

A few more words on his end and Bailey turned to us and rolled her eyes. "Alright, now. Bye-bye."

She hung her head and pinched the bridge of her nose. "That man is just like his horse, a royal pain in the ass." She breathed, and I shook my head.

"Does he not realize you have security in the client stables and that's likely why Boaz was targeted?"

"What, you sayin', the farm's stables don't?" Dragon asked.

Bailey shook her head. "I'd been trying to get father to put in security cameras on the rest of the farm for years; we've had the odd vandalized fence but nothing beyond that until now."

"Shit, and your brother's the one that did it. Don't he know how the family thing is supposed to work?" Dragon growled the last and Bailey frowned.

"What do you mean?" she asked and Dray sighed.

"That you have to ask means that you never learned either," he said unhappily.

"So, give her a lesson," I said and both of them looked at me. Dragon nodded and picked up his phone, a few taps and clicks and he put it to his ear.

"Yeah, Data, you busy?" He paused. "Good, come on out to Blue Hills. Bring your truck and all the fixin's. We're gonna see if we can get this trustee to give Bales a little trust to pay for it. If he won't, then I got it." A few more things said on the other end of the line that we couldn't hear then, "Yeah, see you when you get here."

"Get on the horn, girl. See what you can wring out of that rich bastard," Dray said.

Bailey sighed and nodded. She looked exhausted and I shook my head. "I think a nap might be in order first."

"No, Dray's right… I should call Caleb."

"Fine, but you ain't slept since what?"

"Um, I think it's something like thirty-nine hours now," she said with a sigh, looking at the clock on her phone.

"Right, make your call and go try to get some sleep while we handle things 'round here," Dragon ordered, and Bailey opened her mouth to argue. That was rich. "Sweetheart," Dragon interrupted before she could even say anything, "is there anything 'round here that Rush don't know how to do?"

"No, I mean, not that I've seen since he's been here."

"Okay, then. You think the rest of your staff is shit?"

"What? No! My staff is fantastic, well at least the ones I have left." She dropped back into her seat and covered her face with her hands, scrubbing at her eyes which were rimmed red she was so tired.

Dragon perked up and called out in Spanish to one of the passing hands. Jorge stopped and looked up, answering Dragon back with one of his typical smart-ass responses. Dragon put up his hands, laughing, and identified himself as Bailey's uncle by marriage and Jorge nodded. He was much more willing to answer Dragon's questions then. Bailey watched rapt and I could tell she was struggling with the rapid-fire Spanish going back and forth.

She knew it but struggled with it as it wasn't her first or I think even second language. I was a little more up on it as I'd lived with it more back in Arizona. Still, even I was having a little trouble following along. The gist of it was Dragon asking, who was Renaldo's right-hand man. Jorge said that it was another guy who'd taken off because his wife and kids had been threatened with deportation.

He and Dragon went back and forth and finally Dragon asked him point blank, with Renaldo gone, who would be a suitable replacement for him. Who was the most qualified? Jorge took his time thinking about it and Dragon gave him a look, raising an eyebrow waiting him out. Finally, Jorge nodded and committed. "The *Gringo* would be a good choice, but he doesn't know these horses like I do. I can do it." Jorge nodded and made eye contact with my president. "I will do it."

"Good man," Dragon said and pulled a pad of paper out of one of his pockets. He wrote some things down and passed it over the porch railing to him. Bailey looked on mystified at the whole exchange.

Jorge looked over what was written and nodded. He held up the paper and made a great show of putting it some place safe. He turned to Bailey and said, "You're a good *Jefe*, *Senorita* Bailey. Your *papi* would be proud." Bailey's eyes visibly misted but she sniffed and didn't let them spill over.

"Thank you, Jorge," she said, voice thick with emotion.

Jorge nodded and walked back over to the main barn, he paused outside the door and pulled the piece of paper out of his pocket along with his phone and carefully saved the number. He looked up and called to one of the other men and went striding in the dude's direction, handing him the paper and pointing over to where we were sitting rattling some things off at him. The dude listened intently and gave a nod.

"On that note," I said, "I'm going to get out there and pitch in. You get some rest," I told Bailey. She pressed her lips together and nodded, picking up her phone.

I walked away. I hated the arguments she had with this trustee fella, like enough I wanted to reach through the phone and choke the fucker. I had better, more productive things to do with my time around here.

"Hey, Jorge!" I called out. "What d'you want me to do?"

12

B ailey...

I woke up, and by the sounds of the crickets outside, it was night. I sat up and stretched and looked over at the clock. It was just a little after ten P.M., I'd been out for a good long while. I got up and shrugged into my satin robe that I'd carelessly flung over a wingback chair that served more as a decorative accent than any kind of useful in the corner by the door and armoire. I slipped out into the main living area and had a quick look around.

No one out here...

I tried the front porch next and found Rush sitting at the table, booted feet propped on a chair opposite him, an all-purpose carving knife in one hand and a piece of wood in the other. I watched him for a minute, absorbed in what he was doing as he shaped the chunk of stick in his hand with careful strokes. It wasn't the best angle, pressed against the screen, so finally, I hit the latch and opened the door so that I could pass through. The screen door mechanism that closed it automatically made a good old-fashioned ratcheting creak and he looked up from his work.

"Hey," he said softly.

"Hi," I ventured back. "Can I join you?"

He smiled up at me and said, "It's your porch, baby."

"Yes, well, that may be, but if you were enjoying the peace and quiet, far be it from me to intrude. Sometimes it's nice to have some solitude."

"True, but sometimes you can have too much solitude, too."

"Fair point," I said and stepped out onto the porch. I went around to an unoccupied chair and pulled it out, turning it so I could make use of the chair he had his feet propped up on, too. For a full minute, I must have stared at our feet taking up space on the same chair. Mine were bare except for the French pedicure on the toes and the backdrop of his well-worn and many times resoled motorcycle boots made me think that it was almost picture-perfect. We made an odd pair, it was true, but not for the first time I wondered how and if it might work.

"What'cha thinkin'?" he asked quietly, and I turned my head reluctant to pull my gaze from our mismatched feet until the last possible second.

"I was thinking we make an odd sort of pair," I confessed.

"Surprised at how comfortable it is?" he asked.

"Yeah." I smiled and nodded.

"Me too."

"It's nice, being around someone without any expectations."

"Oh, I expect things," he said with a devilish grin.

"Yeah, like what?"

"Sex every day for starters, sometimes more 'n once a day."

"Sounds like a real hardship," I mocked.

"Oh, it'll be hard alright. It's just about always hard when I'm around you." I laughed and he grinned. "Seriously though," he said, "I don't know what it is about the last day with you, but it's been really nice. Thank you for that."

I blinked, surprised and asked, "Have you had dinner yet?" He shook his head. "Well I don't know about you, but I've had a really shitty couple of days. I think this calls for ice cream."

"For dinner?"

"Yep."

"After ten o'clock at night?"

"Yep."

"Well, alright then."

I got up and he followed suit, and we went into the house. I went into the kitchen and brought down two rocks glasses and a couple of bowls while he got into the freezer.

"Your taste in ice cream sucks," he stated, and I looked at him like he was crazy.

He set the carton of pralines 'n cream on the counter and I asked him, "Are you crazy?"

"Certifiable sometimes, sure, but what's that got to do with anything?"

I laughed and was amazed at how easy it was around him. He dished up two bowls and I told him not to forget the caramel sauce. He looked at the jar of it in his hand and I just knew he was thinking all kinds of dirty thoughts about it. He finally set it aside and came over to me where I stood with the bottle of my favorite bourbon in my hand.

"Pour a measure of that for me, would you, baby?" I swallowed hard and wondered if I was ready for this. His voice held that same quality it had in the barn. He was asking without asking and it was oh my God, hot. I uncorked the bottle and poured a finger into each glass.

"Take a sip," he demanded, and I did as I was told, nipples stiffening into peaks, a very definite tingle of arousal between my thighs. "Don't swallow, not yet. Just hold it in your mouth and come over here. Leave the bottle."

I set the bottle on the counter, but he hadn't said anything about the glass, so I brought it with me. I moved slowly across the kitchen until I stood just in front of him. The bourbon, a rich, warm flavor, coating my tongue. The amber liquid in the bottom of my glass just two shades lighter than his eyes which were fixed on my face.

"Swallow," he commanded and I did as I was told. He smiled, a slow, wicked curve of lips and said, "Good girl," his voice low and husky with desire. It was contagious, the desire in his voice sliding through my veins along with the warmth from the Kentucky bourbon I'd just drunk. He bent slowly, waiting for me to push him away but I didn't. His lips met mine, tongue barging its way into my mouth, taking control just like he did with his voice.

I kissed him back, setting the glass aside as his arms swept behind my back and he pulled my body into his. I clung to him, arms around his neck as he straightened, taking me with him, setting me on the cool granite of my kitchen island. He nudged my knees apart and stepped between them, his large rough hands slipping inside my robe and along the satin of my short tank nightgown. He groaned and pulled the robe away, sliding it down my shoulders. I followed along, moving where he posed me, letting him slide the robe away until it puddled around my hips, pinned beneath me where I sat. He never stopped kissing me while he did it and it was incredibly hot, stealing my breath away.

He broke the kiss, both of our chests heaving and stared me in the eyes as he eased the straps of my nightgown off my shoulders, letting the peach satin pool in my lap.

"Don't you move," he growled and I wouldn't dare. He picked up the jar of caramel sauce and twisted off the lid. "Put your hands behind your back, flat on the counter. Lean on them, yes… just like that."

I leaned back casually on my hands but didn't break eye contact, wondering how messy this was going to get. He brought the wide-mouthed jar to one breast and daintily dipped one nipple into it. I closed my eyes at the sensation, probably one of the most sensual I'd ever encountered, gasping as his mouth closed around it, sucking the caramel sauce away. The heat of his mouth combined with the sticky caramel and the velvet of his tongue in such a sensitive place left me arching into him for more. He chuckled against my breast and the vibration of it made me moan.

Oh my God, yes...

The kitchen was silent, save for the faint chirp of crickets from outside and the light smacking noises of Rush's mouth against my skin and I think I died and went to heaven. He pulled back from his handiwork, murmured something about symmetry, and dipped my other nipple just the same. He repeated his worship of my other breast and pulled gently on it with his teeth before returning his mouth to mine. It was a deep, languorous kiss, slower and full of more meaning than any we had ever shared before.

I went for his jeans, fingers finding his belt and deftly loosening it, the leather sighing with relief. I unbuttoned and unzipped his fly carefully, pulling it out and away from his body, the heat of his erection radiating through the cloth and scorching my palm when I gripped it loosely, stroking from root to tip. He moaned into my mouth, and I took a spare second to push his pants the rest of the way out of my way.

He pulled me to the very edge of the counter for better access, shoving my robe and nightgown up, giving a frustrated grunt when he encountered the lace of my panties.

"Rip them off," I begged breathlessly, and he wrapped his fist in the material and gave a hard jerk that lifted my ass up off the granite countertop. The panties partially gave way with a short angry ripping sound, but he had to jerk twice more for them to give the rest of the way. I arched my body and spread my thighs and he dropped the ruin of my underwear to the kitchen floor.

"Put me in, baby. I wanna watch you do it."

Holy shit, that's hot. I'd never had a man make any such kind of request, I'd never had any man like Rush *period.* I stroked him a few times and guided the head of his cock to my pussy, rubbing him up and down the outside of my pussy lips in my gathering wetness. He stared down between my legs, watching me do it, his golden-brown gaze transfixed. As much as what he was seeing turned him on, what I was seeing turned *me* on.

I pressed him to the opening of my vagina with one hand and dug my nails into his ass with the other, pulling him in, my head tipping back and a deep satisfied moan escaping my lips as he slowly filled me. God, he was *perfect.* Not so huge that it was painful when we got rough, but just right for it and I loved that he got rough with me. That he didn't treat me like some dainty princess.

I wrapped my legs around him so he couldn't draw back and out of me too far, and reached up, pulling his face to mine. We kissed and it was one of the longest, deepest kisses I'd ever been a part of.

Then, and only then did he begin to move. He did this slow grinding roll with his hips that'd like to drive me crazy and I went with it, the sensations indescribable. He was winding me up slowly to watch me go, stoking the fire so that when he poured more fuel on it, I would erupt, and I couldn't say I minded one bit. Just the opposite in fact.

"Lay back so I can fuck you right," he demanded finally, just when I thought I was going to lose my mind because while what he was doing felt so good, it wasn't near enough to get me off and he'd reached a holding pattern rather quickly.

I lay back slowly, carefully against the kitchen island and he bent over me, cradling my head so I wouldn't smack it against the granite. When he was sure I wasn't going to give myself a concussion, he straightened up and wrapped his arms around my thighs, dragging my ass practically off the edge of the counter. His hands firmly on my hips, he grinned wicked and wild and said, "Oh God, I wanna watch those glorious tits of yours bounce."

I braced myself, knowing what was coming and he didn't disappoint. He slammed his body into mine to the absolute hilt and I arched, crying out with just how good that felt.

"More!" escaped my mouth and he obliged, setting a dirty, punishing pace that set me on fire from the inside in all the right ways.

"That's! My! Girl!" he said, each word punctuated by a mean thrust that did unimaginable, beautiful things to me.

He fucked me so hard that he would have to pause from time to time and drag me back to the edge of the counter. I closed my eyes, body arching lightly as he filled me and pushed me to the brink. I was riding that fine line where pleasure was pain and pain just added to the pleasure and he knew that he had me; that he played me like a country fiddle.

I opened my eyes to watch him drag the pad of his thumb across his tongue as if to thumb through paperwork. Instead, he thumbed through the curls at the top of my sex, grinning in triumph when he found that hard little kernel of flesh, teasing it gently, surprisingly lightly in counterpoint to the beautiful chaos he was inflicting with his cock.

He shoved into me savagely and stroked over my clit, sparks igniting and catching; the winds of our passions fanning the flames and before I knew what was happening, I was devastated by the ensuing wildfire. My spine bowed so hard just my ass and the crown of my head made contact with the grounding element of the granite stone countertop of my kitchen island. Thankfully, Rush's arms filled the space behind my back, keeping me from breaking. He gathered me up, holding me tightly and gave one final thrust into my pussy while simultaneously pulling my body down onto him and I swear to God, it felt so good, I very nearly blacked out from it.

13

R ush...

I sat on the kitchen floor, back to the cabinets under the sink with Bailey straddling my lap. I'd come so fuckin' hard when she did, but somehow, miraculously, I hadn't lost my hard-on. She was on her knees, the position putting her a head above me but that didn't matter. She was kissing me lazily, rising and falling gently, my cock slicking through her wet, wet, pussy and I was a man who'd died and gone to fucking heaven. I didn't think I could come again so soon, but she was more than welcome to make me try.

She let out this sultry little moan and asked breathily, "You like that?"

"Shit yeah, I like that, baby. You can ride me like this all fuckin' night."

She tipped her head back and leaned back a little, trusting that my hands kneading her ass under the satin band of her fuckin' tiny ass nightie, held her firm. I slid them over her smooth skin, more to her hips and waist to support her and nearly did come at the sensual change in angle. She had me buried in her to the root and it was fuckin' amazing. She rode me slow, and I could tell she was drunk on our lovemaking. I couldn't say I was far behind her, I had the same feeling I got when I was fuckin' flyin' down the highway at breakneck speeds. Like I was lighter than air and let the gods fuckin' take what they would.

Except they weren't taking tonight. Tonight, for the first time in my fucking life, it felt like they were giving me something. I don't think I could ever be so grateful for anything ever again. This was probably the most perfect moment I'd ever been gifted, and I was going to cherish that forever.

I bowed my head and placed my lips against her skin, right between her breasts, a kiss I laid right over the cage that held her beating heart. A promise, a silent vow, that she was the one for me. I knew it plain as day. Hell, I'd somehow known it in the back of that fucking bar and I'd let her go. *Never again...* I didn't know why the fuck I'd been blessed with this second chance, but I wasn't a complete fool. I wasn't wasting it.

She tipped her head forward at the same time I looked up and in perfect sync, we kissed. We kissed and then we came, a lighter, easier thing than what'd happened before; our bodies simply too spent to accomplish anything more.

Bailey just clung to me like some kind of spider monkey while we both took our time catching our breaths, half-dressed on the damn kitchen floor, the ice cream melting in its carton on the countertop above us, the light scent of bourbon perfuming the air under the heavier scent of sex and desperation. A desperation borne of the need to be so close to one another that we damn near went through each other.

"What was that?" Bailey asked between chest heaving breaths.

"I don't know," I lied, "but I liked it." I knew damn well what it was. It was our meteoric plunge into love. For me, it was a plunge so hard, so fast, and so deep, there was no recovery. I think I just found out what it felt like to find your fuckin' soulmate and I wasn't a damn bit sorry for that, no matter what happened next.

"Well whatever it was," she gasped out, "I liked it."

I laughed. "You can have it whenever you want, baby."

She giggled, and I kept right on laughing, and eventually we managed to peel ourselves apart. Nothing short of a shower was going to fix the mess we'd made but first, we had our dinner of ice cream. Pralines and cream with caramel sauce suddenly became my new favorite flavor when licked off of Bailey's body.

14

B ailey...

I winced and Rush cursed a whole hell of a lot sending things crashing off the nightstand as he groped for what I assumed was his phone. He found it and silenced what sounded like the alarm to a nuclear reactor in full meltdown.

"Oh my *God*, was that your alarm?"

"Yeah," he grunted.

"What time is it?" I demanded.

"Two-thirty," he answered sitting on the edge of the bed.

"Oh, hell no. Come back to bed."

"Can't, my boss is kind of a bitch and she'll fire my ass if I'm late."

It took me a full minute for my tired mind to catch up to what he was saying and when it did, I scoffed and said, "Fuck her! Now come here." I pulled him back under the warm blankets and pressed my nude body to his. He came willingly and laid down with me, cuddling me close.

"Is that a request?" he asked, his breath stirring the hair by my ear, causing it to tickle.

"Mm, I wish."

"Sore?"

"Yeah, in all the right ways."

"Sorry about that."

I chuckled. "No, you aren't."

"Yeah I am, if it means I gotta wait to fuck you again."

I laughed and drifted back to sleep surprisingly quickly, wrapped up in his warm embrace.

When I woke again, the sun was streaming through the wooden slats of the blinds casting the room in bars of light. I sat up and stretched and confirmed that, yes, I was alone, and Rush had intentionally let me oversleep. I got out of bed and still took the time to make it the way my nanny had taught me, growing up. I went about pulling clothes out of dressers and armoires, laying them out for use.

I went in and took a hot shower, using the rainfall showerhead feature in my bathroom which, let me say, was *hard* to pull away from in anything under a half an hour, but I managed. I wrapped my hair in one towel and my body in a bath sheet and went back out into my bedroom to get dressed.

I heard the screen door open out in the living area and Rush called out, "Hey, boss lady! You up yet?"

His strange greeting could only mean that he had people with him, so I called back, "Yeah! Give me just a few minutes. Can you get out some refreshments for our guests?"

"Tea or lemonade?" I heard him ask, his boot falls receding against the hardwood as he moved away from the cracked bedroom door toward the kitchen. I heard a woman's voice say, "Lemonade, thank you kindly."

"You bet."

I knew the voice, but I couldn't place it. I chewed my bottom lip and double-timed pulling on my jeans and tucking my camisole into them. I pulled on my boots after I finished sweeping my hair over my shoulder and whipping it into its braid to keep it out of things.

I stood up, grabbed my blouse, a peach plaid pattern, and threw it on over my even lighter peach cami. I didn't bother snapping the buttons closed, my curiosity winning out. Instead I strode out of my room and across the entryway toward the dining room.

Thank God I picked up the kitchen last night, I thought to myself when I saw who was sitting at the table. Marion Cranston, of *the* Kentucky Cranston racehorse dynasty. What in the *hell* was she doing in my kitchen?

"Thank you, Rush. I appreciate it," I said as he set the tray down on the table and poured Mrs. Cranston a tall glass with ice.

"No trouble at all, boss lady," he said with one of his wicked grins and a wink. I tried not to smile and failed.

"Anything I should know before you get back to it?" I asked.

"Moved Starry to the monitoring barn this morning. Stables are all getting a thorough cleaning. Horses have all been fed 'n watered. I'm off to check the mend on that fence in the north pasture and to fill those holes from the old fence posts."

"Okay, grab a radio."

"Yes, ma'am."

He tipped an imaginary hat and went back out the front door. I turned to Mrs. Cranston and smiled brightly. "My apologies for keeping you waiting. I'm not usually so late to rise."

Mrs. Cranston was in her mid-sixties, her blonde hair perfectly styled. She wore tasteful makeup and her green eyes were quick and shrewd as she considered me, tapping a perfectly polished, long nude nail against her perfectly painted rose petal lipstick. She was likewise dressed to kill in a pair of nude pumps that matched the nails, cream slacks, and a lighter cream silk blouse. She practically dripped with gold and pearls. From rings, sometimes stacked two to a finger, to her gold necklace set with a natural pearl. I knew the look, my mother tended to dress the same way when she went somewhere to remind people just who they were dealing with.

Marion Cranston waved one of her hands as if shooing away a fly and said, "It's not like I called ahead. I wanted to talk to you, not your brother and not that pompous windbag Caleb."

I blinked and said, "Me? What about?" I took a sip of lemonade to try and wet my suddenly dry mouth.

"You know those idiot men had the nerve to turn me down when I asked about boarding my baby, Holy Grail, here?"

I promptly choked on my lemonade, spewing some across the table, some of it most definitely coming out of my nose.

"My word! I should have waited until you were done drinking, I do apologize." She pulled one of the napkins from the place settings that were always out on the table and helped me try to mop up, even pounded me on the back as I tried to get some air.

"Why would they say that!? Not only that, but what makes them think they are in any position to make business decisions about this place? This is *my* farm! I'm in charge of the day-to-day operations here."

"I thought it was fishy when they said you were in the midst of closing, which is why I'm here to get it from the horse's mouth!"

I stared at her, horrified.

"Wait, Philip I understand, but Caleb told you the farm was closing?" *That son of a bitch.*

"You need a new trustee, honey child."

I blinked. "My father's will specifically appointed him."

"Doesn't mean you have to keep him, I'd get myself a lawyer if I were you."

I sat there shocked, dismayed, but not at all surprised. It was way past time to face the writing on the wall. Philip was actively trying to tank my dream to further his own greedy agenda. Caleb had been fair and impartial to an extent, but that was clearly right out the window and what was worse? They'd been intercepting clients and turning them away. I mean, how long had that been going on?

"So, I take it you aren't closing?"

"No, no we most certainly are not," I said, and Marion Cranston smiled the most devious smile I had ever seen in my life. *Oh shit, she's a steel magnolia if I ever saw one. An iron southern lady.* I recognized the look, I'd seen it on my mother's face a time or two.

"My mother put you up to this, didn't she?" I asked, everything clicking into place.

Mrs. Cranston winked at me and patted me on the arm, asking in her best southern belle voice, "Why now, whatever do you mean?"

Right.

"You're sure you want to board Holy Grail here at Blue Hills?" I squeaked. We were talking the frontrunner for the next Kentucky Derby here. As in, Holy Grail got his name for being *the* holy grail of race horses. His form, stride, power, *all of it...*

"Why yes, I do, but you seem to have had a bit of a shock now, why don't you come to my home, say this Thursday and we can discuss it at length." She passed me a business card with her address written on the back and I nodded numbly.

"I can do that."

"Excellent! I'm looking forward to it."

She got up, pulling her purse, a Coach bag in creams and golds that perfectly matched her outfit, off the back of my dining room chair. Before I could get up, she patted me on the arm again and stood. "I'll just see myself out," she said and went to the front door. She opened up the screen and called over her shoulder, "And do bring that delicious young man of yours. Mm, he's positively scrumptious."

For the second time that morning, I choked on my lemonade, but honestly didn't have a clue on how to handle this. I needed to call my mom.

15

R ush...

I was filling the holes left just outside the newly repaired fence, left by the old fence posts. They were a hazard, a broken horse leg or human ankle waiting to happen and with laws and shit the way they were now, even if a motherfucker was trespassing, they could sue the property owner and win. I wasn't willing to let that happen so here I was with a truck bed full of fill dirt making it happen.

I was out here probably an hour, maybe more, when Bailey came riding up on Jasper, one of the farm horses. He was a beautiful animal, too. Gorgeous reddish-brown coat with a white star on his forehead and white socks.

Bailey looked solemn and worn out already which sucked considering the day was just beginning for her. I straightened up from my latest shovel full of dirt and asked, "What's up? How'd it go with the iron horse lady?"

She dismounted like a fuckin' pro and walked Jasper the rest of the way, securing him to the fence giving him enough lead to graze if he wanted to. She climbed the fence and took a seat facing me so I could keep going but we could talk. I had no interest in shoveling dirt right that second, though. Not with her sitting there looking like someone'd just kicked her favorite puppy.

"I get two guesses?" I asked.

"You'll only need one."

"What'd your assclown brother do this time?"

She hiccupped on a laugh and said, "Assclown, that's a good one, I've never heard it before."

"You're stalling."

"I'm pissed."

"Most people get pissed off, they fuckin' rage, you mean to tell me you get pissed off and just sit there like a bump on a fence lookin' all pathetic? Come on, now! I've seen your fire, where is it?"

"No, that's me when I'm irritated. Now, I'm pissed."

"I seriously don't fuckin' get you sometimes."

"Rich girl 101, biker boy. If we're legitimately pissed off about something or have a real reason to be angry, it only takes a few times of the men in your life ignoring you, or your mother telling you it's not lady-like to blow up for you to start bottling it up."

"Ah, a conditioned response kind of a thing. Well, we'll just have to break you of that habit, won't we? Any rate, one problem at a time, what's the jerkoff doing now?"

Ooo boy, did she have a whole mess of shit to unload off those slim shoulders, and the more shit she spewed about, the more she got fired up. I don't think the woman had ever had anyone on her side, let alone just listen to her – I mean *really* listen to her.

I was pretty sure I wanted this particular girl in my life for a good long time, so it was the least I could fuckin' do. So, I leaned on my shovel and let her vent, and the more she talked the more pissed off *I* got.

"So let me get this straight, you own two-thirds of this place, you run it, you operate it, and yet your assclown brother and your daddy's golfing buddy are making all the financial decisions runnin' circles around your ass and you've been letting them because…" She stared at me blankly for a full minute and swung around on the fence, dropping to the ground.

"Get over here," she bossed, and I went to the fence. She stood up on the bottom runner and grabbed my face with both hands laying one on me. "Thanks," she breathed, and I raised an eyebrow.

"For?"

"Putting it in perspective."

"What're you going to do about it?" I asked.

"Call my lawyers and see if I can't get through to my mom, she didn't pick up earlier."

"Good luck!" I called as she swung up into Jasper's saddle.

"I won't need it. I'm done with playing by the rules while everyone else runs around getting away with murder."

"That's my girl!" I called after her and she waved over her shoulder, taking Jasper into a trot.

I finished up and threw the tools in the back of the farm truck. I looked out over the place and sure wished that it was worth the problems Bailey was takin' on for it. One of the things that attracted me to the girl was her level of commitment to this place. If she committed half as hard to a relationship? Yeah, I could already tell that she wasn't the cheating type which just made her hotter to me in so many ways. It was just figuring out how to convince her that the world she'd been living in for so long was the wrong one; that she needed to throw some caution to the wind and try mine on for size.

Truth be told, I didn't think I was going to have to convince her very hard. Our vibes meshed really fucking good, now that she's knocked it off with all the pretentious shit.

And her family? Well, her brother, as well as the rest of these rich fucks trying to stifle her? They were doing a great job of driving her right into my arms. Still, I was out of my depth. There was this huge fuckin' rift between us with the way we both came up and I wasn't blind to it.

I jumped into the truck and drove back around to the main garage on the other side of the house, between it and the main stables, and parked it. I put the tools away and felt satisfied with all I'd been able to get done that day. I checked in with Jorge and he was too, sending me off with a hearty handshake and a thanks for everything I'd done for the day. Dude was a natural leader. Bailey had lucked out there. Things were almost running smoother than with Renaldo at the helm and morale? Definitely higher. Still, we were running on the bare minimum of staff, a real skeleton crew, and we couldn't do it forever.

I went up onto the porch to go into the house and stopped when I heard Bailey on the phone.

"I don't care, Caleb. You're blatantly ignoring me. You get those financials to me in the morning, you don't? You're done, period. I've already got my lawyers involved." She paused, listening, and said, "Well, you haven't been listening to me! I don't care what Philip says! He wants this farm to fail. He wants to sell the property to some big development group."

She was calm, her voice barely even raised above a normal talking tone, so her next words pissed me off, "Don't patronize me, Caleb. I am calm. I have every right not to be calm. I have a dead horse, a lead groom and trainer in the hospital, and most of my staff walked off the job all in the span of a week. I own two-thirds of this place, *I* run it, *I* operate it, yet *you* have just about all my assets frozen and won't give me a reason why. Financials, in the morning, or I'm going to have *every* reason to believe you're stealing from me and if you are? You're going to find out just how much my father's daughter I am."

She hung up the line and I pushed through the screen, her head snapped up, those deep brown eyes of hers blazing just like Dragon's or Dray's, just a couple of shades lighter in color. I made an expression as I looked her over that said I was impressed, and I was.

"I want to go for a ride," she said and swallowed hard, as if she were unused to voicing her wants.

I gave her my best slow, panty dropping smile and said, "Well you're going to have to be a mite more specific when it comes to that."

She gave me an answering smile of her own and said, "I know you can go fast, but you can't go *that* fast."

"Well alright, then. Do I got the time to grab a shower and a change of clothes?"

"Absolutely, I have one more call to make." She looked down at her phone, fingertip tracing along the screen before she raised it to her ear.

"Yeah, Mom? I just got off the phone with him. I think I'll be getting what I want by way of the financials tomorrow, but I think you're right that something's not right. I think we're going to need an accountant to go over everything. Someone who's on our side..."

I knew just the person for that job, I also knew just the person to do the digging that needed to be done to find out for sure what was what. Nothing that would stand up in a court, mind you, being that we'd technically be stealing the information, but sometimes when you wanted the truth, that's what had to be done because neither one of these motherfuckers was being honest with her.

I couldn't even imagine not being able to trust one of my brothers. The thought just boggled my mind, I couldn't conceive of it. I wasn't just talking my blood, or the foster brothers I came up with, I meant all of them. My chosen brothers, my club, none of them would even conceive of stabbing you in the back like this. It just wasn't how things were done. When you belonged to something like the club, there was no way any of us would be so dumb as to fuck that up. I mean, sometimes it happened, but the consequences of being out bad? Not worth it.

It was just easier to maintain your integrity than not; I just didn't understand why more people didn't do it. I'm not talking being a law-abiding citizen, don't get it twisted, I'm talking personal integrity as a man. Society had it all fucked up. Integrity wasn't just being a good little law-abiding sheep, especially when so many laws violated common sense so hard.

A man hits you, don't hit him back, boy... No, a man hits you, you protect yourself. You fuckin' stand up for yourself and make sure that same man will *never* make that mistake twice. It's what I'd done, and society reamed my ass a new one over it. I'd already been with the club when that shit went down, but if I hadn't, it surely would have driven me right fuckin' to it. I paid for my 'mistake' by society's fuckin' standards but society didn't believe in second chances as much as they'd have you fuckin' believe.

I showered up quick and dressed even quicker. Bailey was pacing on the front porch, ready to go. She was agitated, but it wasn't out of pocket. If anything, she needed to be, this shit had gone on long enough. I only wished her mamma had reached out before it got so bad.

"Let's go, boss lady."

Bailey shook her head but followed me off the porch. "It's past quittin' time, Rush. I'm not your boss again until tomorrow morning."

I thought about that and asked, "That mean you're willin' to give me a try?"

She stopped and asked, "What do you mean by that?"

I pussed out, I pussed out hard by saying, "Nothing, forget it."

I threw a leg over my bike and started it up the growl drowning out whatever she was going to say. I put a bandana on over my wet hair to keep it down and strapped on my brain bucket. Bailey did the same and we rode out. I'd gotten a text back from Dragon by the time I got out of the shower, and so we headed for Ghost and Shelly's. Data was going to meet us out there and we could round table some of Bailey's problem.

I figured that Shelly could use the money that would come from reviewing Blue Hills' books, while Data could definitely track down if Caleb was doing anything out of pocket. We rolled up to the house and Ghost's tow truck was out front, so was his bike but his regular pickup was missing. Shelly, pregnant with her second, came out the house's front door with her first on her hip.

"Hi!" she called out.

"Hey, Mamma!" I called out by way of greeting. Bailey got off the bike and asked low enough to where I could just hear, "Why did you bring me here?"

"Shelly is the best damn accountant I've ever met. If she can't find anything fucked up in your books, then there ain't anything fucked up to find. Plus, she's not related in any way to either your assclown brother or your father's dick of a best friend."

She stared up at me, her delicate face stony and unreadable before she finally drew in a deep breath and said, "You are *so* hot right now."

I laughed and put an arm around her and led her up to Ghost's front porch. Shelly led us into the kitchen and through the house to the back deck, which was shaded by an awning. She had iced tea waiting and set Harmony into a nearby playpen. The little shit immediately started to throw a fit, so I went over and picked her up, bouncing her.

"Oh, what, what, what?" I demanded and she stared at me, transfixed and held her ragdoll up for me to kiss, so I did. Bailey watched me, transfixed and completely missing what Shelly had said.

"I'm sorry, what?"

Shelly laughed. "Takes some getting used to, doesn't it? These big and burly, badass bikers going all Stay Puft Marshmallow Man around the kids."

"Yeah," Bailey admitted.

Ghost decided that was the time to come out the back door and say, "Babe, I'm back from the store, you want I should fire up the grill now?"

"No, you didn't answer your phone. I want you should go *back* to the store and grab more. Dragon and Data are coming, maybe a couple other of the guys."

Ghost hung his head and I laughed. "Want me to go with you, man?"

"Naw, naw, I got it. You must be Bailey."

"Yes, hi, I am indeed Bailey."

"Ghost." They shook hands and Shelly smiled at her man. I'd wanted for a long time for a woman to look at me the way she looked at him. If anything, it was my deepest desire in life. I still wasn't sure about doing the whole family thing. I could see it, if it were the right woman, maybe.

The table they had out here on the deck was a six-seater, heavy iron and glass with matching chairs. Shelly had set up her laptop at one end and I pulled out one of the chairs, sitting with Harmony on my lap. She was a little fussy, rubbing her eyes and tired. She was coming up on a year already. *Damn time flies.* It definitely reminded me I wasn't getting any younger, not that I was old mind you, just about to turn thirty-seven.

I rocked Harmony and watched as Bailey and Ghost said goodbye for the moment. Finally, she and Shelly returned to the table. Shelly sat down where she'd been working, and Bailey took the seat across from mine.

"So, I'm told that you need an accountant you can trust."

Bailey nodded. "That's the understatement of the year."

"You bring me anything?" she asked.

Bailey shook her head. "It's all online, on my phone. I can print off what *I* have by the way of numbers for the farm but there's no telling what Caleb's numbers look like."

"Gimme what you've got," Shelly said, turning her laptop in Bailey's direction. Bailey took a deep breath and let it out. She looked at me and her gaze clearly read, *I'm trusting you.* I smiled and gave her a careful nod. I trusted Shelly, I trusted Ghost and Dragon, and Dray, and Reaver and all of my club brothers and sisters. Bailey needed to learn who she could trust and clearly, the people she was supposed to trust, had fucked her one too many times for her to do it easy, but she was willing to give it a shot here. That was pretty hot as far as I was concerned.

She pulled up her books and passed the laptop back to Shelly who looked over all of them, her clear blue eyes intent; her head faintly bobbing along the columns of numbers. She looked up at Bailey and nodded.

"It's a start, now I just need something to compare it to."

"I should have those financials for you tomorrow," Bailey said. The timing couldn't have been more perfect, because right then Data slid open the sliding door and stepped out onto the deck.

"Actually," I said, "you'll have 'em tonight and will be able to tell tomorrow morning, once and for all, if Caleb is a friend or an enemy."

"Figured you were going to have me doing something more than slightly illegal when you asked me to bring my laptop," Data said.

"Oh, I don't know about doing anything illegal —" Bailey said and Data beat me to it.

"Pfft, like anyone's actually going to find out or know. Look, I can get you the info, it's just not going to necessarily be admissible in court, not unless I get real fuckin' creative."

"That's my job, anyway," Shelly said. "I have a degree in accounting and a certificate in forensic accounting. I used that time I figured out where Darlene was funneling money out of *Open Road Garage* as my main project. Aced that shit like it was nothing."

"Shelly does all the accounting for all of the club's businesses now," I explained.

"Yep, *Open Road Garage, Open Road Ink, Soul Fuel* and once they open, Evy's *Sacred Grounds* coffee stands. I also do the books for Ghost's towing company and Hayden's interior design company. It only gets hairy around tax time. It's getting to be the point I might need to hire some help."

"Wow, I'm impressed," Bailey said.

Harmony had completely knocked out in my arms, just like my oldest nephew, Noah, had a habit of doing. Hell if I knew why.

"Toddler whisperer strikes again," Dragon said, coming through the slider.

"Yeah."

I let 'Bumpa Dragon' take Harmony from me and he laid her down in her playpen in the shade to let her nap.

He joined us at the table where Data had taken up the seat next to Shelly, displacing Bailey who moved over by me.

"Okay, first things first," he said fingers flying over the keys. "What's the target's name?"

"I'm really not sure about this," Bailey stammered, and I gave her a look like I knew she'd puss out. She frowned at me and said, "Caleb Marsden."

"Cool, give me a minute."

"What're you thinkin?" Dragon asked.

Bailey reiterated her entire discussion with Mrs. Cranston and then subsequently with her mom. "I was really surprised. She was pissed, I mean, I've seen and heard my mom mad before, she's always been sort of stormy, but she was pissed. She didn't even hesitate, she hung up with me and less than ten minutes later her lawyer called me. It's Sunday, the retainer she put down must be huge."

"Wait, your mamma is fronting the money for yer lawyer?" Dragon asked.

"Not like I can, every dime of what I make from the farm has been going right back into it just to keep it going. Caleb barely gives me money enough go to feed the horses and keep the lights on." Bailey sighed and stared off the back porch over the wavering green grass of Ghost and Shelly's yard.

"You're fuckin' kidding me, right?" Shelly blurted and Bailey whipped her head back in her direction.

"I wish I were."

"Oh, now that's some *bullshit*. I'ma kick somebody's ass," she muttered and refocused her attention on her laptop. "Data you better find me something to work with, dude."

"Have I ever let any of you fuckers down before?" he asked and looked at Shelly like she done lost her mind.

Bailey watched them both with utter fascination as Shelly and Data bumped fists. Dragon laughed at them both and fished in his cut for a cigarette.

"Welcome to the family, sweetheart," he said to Bailey and lit up. "This is what you been missin', ain't it?"

"Kind of," she said softly and looked away again, eyes distant. I could tell this called to her and I was glad it did. I could also tell it was tearing her up some inside. I nudged her knee with mine and her dark chocolate eyes flashed to mine. I gave her a reassuring smile and winked at her.

"Relax, baby. We got your back." I turned back to Shelly and asked, "What's for dinner?"

"Steak, if Ghost ever gets his ass back here to grill it."

Cool.

16

B ailey...

It turned into a good old-fashioned family cook-out, or what I imagined one to be. The crystal wine glasses were replaced with red Solo cups, and the china with sturdy paper plates and I wouldn't have it any other way. There was no stiff formality here. There was easy laughter that wasn't at anyone's expense or something so esoteric you laughed so you didn't look like an idiot. It was comfortable, and I was blown away that Ghost, the husband, cooked while his wife worked on my problem.

That *never* would have flown in my father's house. He would have asked my mother to go somewhere else when the business talk began. Made up something that she needed to do in that way when it was time for the men to talk. I loved my father, but he was firmly raised and somehow stuck back in like the 1950s — men did the dealing, women took care of the home. That was the way it was, always. I wasn't allowed to go hunting or fishing, those were activities reserved solely for my brother.

I was amazed when he'd bought me riding lessons, but not for racing, oh no, I was a dressage rider, limited to doing shows and exhibition jumping. I'd been alright with it, mostly because I had been raised in such a bubble as to not realize there were any other things a girl could do, let alone should do.

Boarding school had been both a blessing and a bane. Even being an all-girls school, it had been eye opening for sure. I'd been introduced to things that now made total sense to me, like the concept that *well-behaved women rarely make history.*

I took a drink from the bottle of beer in my hands and stared out over the wavering grass in the vast backyard off the porch. The little one had long since been put to bed, and *that* had been a sight to see. My Uncle José was actually pretty exceptional with kids. Who'd have thought?

Shelly and Data were still playing at their laptops treating their mission with great enthusiasm and zeal. Meanwhile, I stood over here terrified about what they'd find; torn between wanting them to find something to vindicate me, to tell me *yes, you have every right to feel like they're cheating you because they* are and wanting them to find nothing. To know and believe that while my brother may not have the farm's best interests at heart, that he somehow did still value our bond as family enough to not completely fuck me.

My hopes were dashed when Data leaned back in his seat with the scrape and clack of leather and metal fittings against the metal of the patio chair.

"You got it?" Shelly asked.

"Which set of books do you want?" he asked grimly, and Shelly made an 'ah ha' kind of noise.

"Both of them please."

"Bailey," Data called.

"Yes?" I called back.

"I'm going to need you to do something for me when you get those lawyers involved and you're going to want to get them involved fast."

My heart sank and I went back to the table. Before I could sit down in my own chair, Rush pulled me into his lap, his large arms holding me loosely around my waist.

"What's that?" Data passed me a card.

"Get me involved as a securities contractor so I can do this again on the level. Who are your lawyers anyway?"

I gave him the name of my mother's firm and he nodded. "I've done investigative work for them before. I'll get the door open for you to have them hire me on. Shells, your printer up and running?"

"Yeah, fire when ready, Captain Dorkus."

Data chuckled and tapped and clicked through some things. "Well, he fucked up and Shelly's going to be able to find exactly what I'm talking about. He says in his books that he's paying you like three times the amount he's actually paying you. You, obviously, have bank records proving that's a fucking lie but he can't hide that because if he does, it proves that he's not fulfilling his job as trustee, anyway."

"Okay," I said quietly, a numbness setting in.

"So as for where the money is actually going? Looks like it's headed to a 'Giangiulio Development Group', he's using money he's straight up stealing from you to invest in the developer who's trying to take your farm in the first place."

Incendiary rage, hot, fierce, and unlike *anything* I had ever felt before bubbled up inside me. I leveled Data with my gaze and asked, "And you're sure, absolutely sure, you can nail his old ass to the fucking wall?"

"Without a doubt, I've already got it. Even if he goes and erases it, I can fill a bunch of jurors and lawyers' heads with enough technical internet jargon that they'd be willing to do or say anything just to make it stop."

"What if they have their own experts?"

"Problem with that, sweetheart," my Uncle Dragon said.

"What's that?" I asked.

"Ain't none of 'em Data," Ghost said and took a swig of his own beer. Shelly made a pouty face and I realized it was at the beer as she rubbed her swelling stomach.

"Okay," I nodded.

"I'm going to come by and finish rigging the security cameras I started on the rest of your farm tomorrow. Once you blow this wide open and he gets yanked, your brother's gonna be pissed."

I shook my head. "I don't think I can call Philip that. This isn't how family treats each other." Dragon leaned back in his seat and took a drag off his cigarette. I don't think I'd ever seen my uncle look so proud.

"You're gonna be fine," he said, blowing out a plume of smoke. "You got a good head on yah, and real family backing you up now."

Rush gave me a gentle squeeze and a meaningful look. I braved a smile and nodded, when truthfully, I'd never felt so cast adrift in my life. I sighed, closed my eyes and swore in just about every language I knew how to do it in.

Looks were exchanged along with amused looks. "What?" I asked. "I might as well use that fancy education for something, right?" Laughter erupted around the table and I smiled too. I couldn't help myself. Rush's hands were warm and held me firmly and I knew he wouldn't let me fall. Somehow, I knew that extended to more than just me sitting on his lap, too. I wondered about him. I wanted to know more. I wanted to reconcile the man on paper with the man who made me feel so many things, who turned my world upside down and inside out but still somehow managed to make it better.

It was as if we were fated to have met each other, and when we didn't go along with fate's plan, she just came up with another one. I needed to learn to listen to that bitch the first time. We stayed for a while more, Data and Shelly with their heads together oohing and ah-haing over this or that. Copying and printing things, moving things here or there, copying them to an external hard drive Data connected to his laptop.

Finally, it was Uncle Dragon who said, "You two should go on and git. We'll have all this set up the right way. It ain't our first rodeo with the rich folks of this county."

"First one where we were just out to bust them and not –"

"Now, Shelly, that would be club business, and club business you shouldn't be knowing anything about at that."

Shelly shrugged. "Girls talk," she said faintly. "Sorry, Dragon, won't happen again."

"Keep it to your circle of ol' ladies, princess," Ghost said and she nodded, chagrinned.

"Thank you so much for dinner and all that you're doing," I said.

"Hey, got even better news for you. When your lawyers get done with this Caleb guy, we'll all be straight getting paid," Data said.

"He was my dad's best friend," I said quietly. "I still don't think it's quite hit me yet, you know?"

"Yer Aunt Tillie never did like yer daddy."

I shrugged. "My mother never did like *you*," I said. He nodded and sighed heavily. I instantly felt bad.

I opened my mouth to apologize but Dragon beat me to it by saying,

"Well, I can't say she was wrong about that. You two ride safe." I got up and Rush followed suit.

Guilt was churning in my stomach as he said, "Later, brothers," and embraced each man at the table. I hugged Shelly and gushed more about her hospitality and her help because I really couldn't express how much gratitude I was feeling over it.

"Hey, you're family," she said beaming. "It's what we do for each other that defines us as such, not so much when it comes to blood relations anymore."

I smiled wanly and Rush folded my hand into his. I looked up at him and he gave my hand a little shake. "Let's get you back home."

I nodded and we tracked back through the house to the vast gravel drive and his waiting motorcycle. I was quiet, probably more reserved than usual, but Rush didn't push things. Just let me get on behind him and when he was sure I was snug against his back and holding on, he put us in motion.

It was slightly meditative, the ride back to my farm. A little over an hour, the ride was cooler now that the sun had gone down, and I found myself shivering in the last ten minutes or so. When I got off the bike in my driveway, my teeth were chattering and I could tell Rush found it both funny and adorable. I was okay with that, especially okay with it when he tucked me into his side and walked me up the porch steps and into the house.

He walked me straight past the living room and into my bedroom, past the bed; right into the bathroom and then, and only then, did he let me go; and that was only because he wanted to start the shower. He played with the temperature while I watched and then flipped the lever on the showerhead to divert the water to the rain shower head. The sound of gently falling rain against natural stone filled the bathroom and he pulled his tee shirt over his head.

I stood transfixed as he drew me into his arms and looked down at me. No words were spoken, just a meeting of something undefinable between us. He bent carefully, and just before his lips touched mine, I closed my eyes and said, "I don't know anything about you."

"Got all the time in the world to find out, now don't you?" he asked and then he kissed me.

I closed my eyes and let my body do the talking, my arms winding around his neck even as he pulled open the snaps of my blouse, his fingers gently pulling my camisole out of the top of my pants so he could find skin. He touched me, sweeping his hands over my body lightly, an admiring touch, one full of reverence and I couldn't ever remember a time I was touched like that before.

I touched him back and tried to put the same kind of care and admiration in it that he showed me. I trembled finely, still cold from the wind of the ride and too little by way of protection from it. Where I was cold, he was warm, and he crushed me to his body, lifting me. I wrapped my legs around his waist so he could set me on the edge of the marble bathroom countertop, complete with his and her sinks.

His kiss was no less passionate than any other time we'd kissed, however, it held an edge of something different. An almost desperation to it that appealed to me rather than repelled me. He pushed my blouse back off my shoulders and I let him, even though it pulled my arms back, my hands away from his deliciously warm, heated skin.

He didn't waste any time, pulling my camisole over my head and letting it drop wherever it may. I was impatient, rather than letting him go for it, I just unhooked my bra myself. He took his mouth from mine and growled, "I love a woman who knows what she wants."

"Bet you love it even more that I really want you in that shower."

"Yeah, but maybe I'm not up for sex tonight. Maybe I just want to take a hot shower and hold you while we talk."

I froze and drew back a bit searching his face which was so neutral I couldn't read it if I wanted to.

"Are you serious?" I asked.

He nodded. "You've got questions; I've got answers, baby."

That was so… hot. Unexpected and yet totally hot. I swallowed hard and he backed up just a bit, hand behind my knee, sliding along my calf, stopping at the top of my boot as he cupped his other hand around my heel, sliding it off. I watched him with total fascination as he pulled off first one boot then the other, dropping them to my bathroom's travertine tile floor.

He pulled off his boots and socks hurriedly and dropped his jeans so that, for once, he was naked before I was. I slipped off the counter and undid my own pants, a quick shimmy and a shake of my hips and I let them drop, stepping on the cuffs and pulling my legs the rest of the way free. He came back to me, his hands finding my lace-covered ass and squeezing even as he pulled me tightly against his body. He slipped them off, and even if he wanted to keep the evening not about sex, and more about us, his body was clearly having other ideas. The hard length of his erection so tempting, pressed between our bodies.

"Ask me anything," he whispered against my mouth and I smiled.

"Shower first, maybe even a little sex, save the conversation for the bedroom," I suggested.

He grinned crookedly and said, "Get in the shower, on your knees. If you're okay with it, I'd like to fuck that tempting mouth of yours."

I didn't answer him, I just smiled and got into the shower that was easily big enough for three and got on my knees.

He stepped in after me and shut the glass door, his fingers threading through my hair and locking there, holding it back from my face. I wrapped my fingers around his cock and stroked him, looking up the length of his powerful body. He closed his eyes and tipped back his head, letting out a shuddering breath.

"Oh God, baby, yeah. Just like that." He sucked in a longing breath and I slid him into my waiting mouth, carefully, so as not to scrape him with my teeth. He moaned and his hips jerked forward, pressing himself into my throat. He looked down at me, dark desire swirling through his eyes as he gauged whether or not I could take it as roughly with my mouth as I could otherwise.

I let it show in my eyes that I was up for anything and he nodded, fingers tightening in my hair almost but not quite painful. He pulled back, my tongue sliding along the underside of his cock and I took a deep, deep breath before he plunged himself back into my mouth, all the way to the back; the tip of him touching my throat. I swallowed and he moaned again, backing off so I could take a breath.

Again and again, we did the same thing until finally he relinquished control back to me. I sucked him and teased him lightly with my tongue, massaging his balls with one hand while the other I confessed, I slid between my own legs so that I could tease myself. That was mostly for his viewing pleasure though. He shook his head and said, "God, you're such a dirty fucking girl, how did I get so lucky?"

I pulled him from my mouth with a slight little pop and he chuckled, reaching down and wrapping his fingers around my upper arm to help me stand. I turned around and braced my hands against the light, natural stone shower tiles, and put one foot up on the shower's seat, bending forward so he could slide into me.

"Oh, fuck, baby, you know just what I like." He took the invitation and eased into me almost agonizingly slow. Oh God, I totally dug what he did to me. As soon as he was fully seated, he leaned forward over my back, one hand curling against the front of my throat. He pulled me into a standing position, the hand at my neck just holding me, not squeezing, not choking but the potential was just there and lent such an arousing edge to our play I felt my pussy flutter around his dick.

He moved the best he could, but the angle wasn't really made for this, what he was doing, though? Drove me wild. He captured my earlobe gently between his teeth, lightly nipping and kissing down the side of my neck, while the fingertips of his other hand slipped against my sex, looking for that special bundle of nerves.

"Gonna make you come like this, don't care how long it takes. Need you to come a couple of times for what I'm gonna do to you. How's that sound?"

Mm, sounded fantastic, actually.

"Answer me, baby. I want to know you want it."

"Yes, I want it. I want that... make me come, *please*."

17

R ush…

She was languid in my arms, her skin still a bit cool but warming as the water cascaded over us. I needed her pussy good and wet for the satisfaction I wanted to take from her. I held her by the throat lightly, fingertips against her chin as I played against her clit with my other hand.

"Yes, I want it. I want that… make me come, *please*." She was begging now, and I fucking loved that. What really lit my fire was when she sucked my fingertips into her mouth, teasing them with her soft little pink tongue.

I thrust forward to make sure I was as deep as I could go and teased her clit. She probably wasn't even aware of it, but she was writhing against me, her pussy slipping up and down my cock, not by much, but enough to drive me nuts, that was for sure. I loved that Bailey was all-in when it came to sex. She didn't just lay there and take it like a dead fish. She writhed, she moved with me and against me causing the most delicious friction.

It really hadn't been my intention to fuck her tonight, but who the fuck was I to say no? Plus, she wasn't wrong, I probably would be a little more relaxed and willing to answer her questions after a good round of fucking.

She tightened around my shaft and I held her harder, pressing her back to my chest and swirling a fingertip around her clit. She was getting close, fast, and I couldn't say that was a bad thing. Still... I had a better idea.

I pulled my cock out of her and turned her around dropping to my knees. She made a yip of surprise and stumbled a bit, catching herself against the shower wall with her shoulders and arms, bowing her head so she didn't smack it on the tile. I lifted her, knees over my shoulders, letting the shower wall hold her the rest of the way and pressed my tongue against her pussy, licking her from slit to clit, sucking on that little kernel of flesh.

Bailey's eyes, which were fixed to mine, squeezed shut and she tipped her head all the way back with a short cry. Her breaths came heavy and uneven, more ragged gasps than breaths as I played her body with my tongue, returning the favor. She cried out again, the pitch a little higher and I willed her to come, silently urging her with every fiber of my being to do it, to come on my face so I could turn her around, shove myself back in, and make her come all over again.

She was beautiful; her lithe, fit body shuddering above me, an honest body honed by working her craft as a rider. She made eye contact with me one more time just as I happened to flick my tongue over her clit right at that magic point in time. It was a beautiful thing watching the explosion of her pleasure go off in those brown eyes of hers before it hit the rest of her body.

I tortured that oversensitive nub until she collapsed against the tile panting and spent, then I returned her to her original position and did just what I said I was gonna do. I put my cock in her as far as I could get it and I pulled her back flush against my chest. I murmured in her ear, "That was one, now we're gonna do it again. You ready?"

"Oh, God, yes, bring it, biker boy," she said and I had to bite the inside of my cheek to keep from laughing and ruining the illusion of control I'd spent so much time putting into place. I brought it, and when that first flutter, that first expansion of her body started around my cock, threatening to squeeze down and milk me, I bowed my head, putting my forehead between her shoulder blades.

She jerked in my grasp, a long thin wail slipping from between her lips as she came for the second time. I couldn't keep the satisfied grin off my face if I wanted to. I rode her orgasm out until near the very end of it and growled in her ear, "Put those hands against that wall and brace yourself."

She did what she was told automatically, and I gripped her hips firmly. I pressed into her hard and deep and tipped my head back, letting my body do the rest of the talking for me. It was a punishing set of strokes and she had me so fucking worked up, it didn't take me long. My balls had already tightened up on me, that tingling sensation had already started before I even bent her over.

It probably only took me a dozen strokes or so before my body crashed into hers a final time and I spilled inside of her. She arched, standing up a little straighter and I held her body against mine as we both panted and settled back down to earth. I pulled from her body and gasped, groaning that I might have done it a little too soon. I was still sensitive myself.

"I fucking love that you can take me like that," I whispered, laying a kiss behind her ear.

"You fit fucking perfect," she murmured. "Any bigger it would hurt, any smaller and you wouldn't satisfy."

Nice.

"Guess we were made for each other, huh?"

She turned in my arms and wrapped hers around my neck, staring deep into my eyes before she said, "It depends, can I trust you?"

"One, have I ever given you any reason not to?" I asked. She shook her head and I nodded carefully. "And two, ask me anything. No bullshit. No lies."

"You mean that," she said startled.

"I mean that. Anything, anything at all."

She looked thoughtful but didn't say anything right away. I could see the wheels turning and I could be patient. To fill the time, I picked up her bath poof thing and lathered it up, running it across her skin. She closed her eyes and sighed and whatever stress or worry that'd caused her to stiffen up melted away. I liked that I could do that for her. Liked even more just how relaxed I felt.

I took my time with her and chose not to worry about what she would ask me, deciding I liked where things were headed and that I liked even more that with every corner and every curve we took, things just seemed to get *more* comfortable, not less. Nothing had ever been so easy or comfortable for me. Nothing until her. I was beginning to think I'd do just about anything to hold on to that. Anything except compromise myself as a man. That I couldn't do. It just wasn't me.

18

B ailey...

We lay cuddled in bed. I'd washed and taken the time to blow my hair dry. I didn't waste the time drying it because I'd wanted to, but because if I slept on it wet it would have turned into a mess of tangles and waves that I wouldn't have been able to deal with. We'd washed one another, and had kissed, but I could tell he was waiting me out. He hadn't spoken a word in all that time, and I just had so many things I wanted to ask that I just couldn't settle on any *one* thing to start with.

"Logan," he muttered against my hair, finally.

I looked up at him sharply and he pressed me into his side a little more firmly. I dragged my leg over his and snuggled closer asking, "Is that your name? I mean, your real name?"

"Logan Fisher," he said nodding.

"Funny," I said, "I never in a million years would have guessed you were a Logan. A Kevin or a Donnie maybe but Logan never even crossed my mind." I searched his face and had to smile. "It suits you."

"Glad you like it."

I licked my lips, a sudden thought sobering me as I said, "Tell me why you went to prison?"

He swallowed hard and said, "I was still pretty new to the club. Patches on my cut hadn't even had a chance to get dirty yet, you know?"

I nodded and he sighed. "I was at the local grocery store and this little guy was lookin' up at me all wide-eyed and curious and I asked him, "'You like motorcycles?' Kid couldn't have been more than five or six, you know?"

He paused and I could see whatever it was still hurt his feelings, even today. "Anyway, his mamma starts yelling at me, makin' this big ol' fuckin' scene about not talking to her kids, throwin' around phrases like 'people like you' and shit. Then she drops the thermonuclear bomb of insults. She accuses me of being a fuckin' child molester. I'd been putting up with it up until that point but fuck that shit, you know? There's disrespect and then there's *disrespect*."

He gave a big sigh, his hands smoothing aimlessly against my skin as if he were subconsciously afraid that by the end of the story, I would never want him to touch me again, and so he was trying to commit the feeling of my body to memory before it was gone from his grasp forever.

"Go on," I urged quietly, twining my fingers through his, then looking at our hands. I knew in my heart of hearts that I couldn't promise anything. If what came out of his mouth next was that he hurt that woman in front of her son? I just didn't know if that was something I would ever be able to forget or let go of.

"I popped off at her, started yelling back about fuck her and her bull-shit preconceived notions and this guy comes in and starts yelling at me and getting in my face. We're yelling back and forth exchanging choice words and then he goes and does it... he hits me."

He fell silent and I was confused, *I mean, if he was the one who was hit, then why did he go to jail? Why didn't the other guy?*

"I swore after Duncan and Norma-Rae, I would never let another man lay hands on me again. He just flipped my switch and it was like I blanked out. I fuckin' raged. I beat him into a three-day coma. I don't even remember doing it. It didn't matter that the guy threw the first punch. I went away for aggravated battery. Didn't even try to take it to trial. Prosecution had the store surveillance tape and any jury would have locked my ass up in a heartbeat for the maximum. I was looking at a ten to fifteen-year sentence. I plead it down to eight, and thanks to overcrowding and good behavior, I was out after three."

I swallowed hard and squeezed his hand. I don't think I could blame him for his reaction. I had a feeling I knew, but I had to ask any way just to be clear, "Who are Duncan and Norma-Rae? Your foster parents?"

"Yeah," he said unhappily, and I felt my heart squeeze down into about the size of a quarter in my chest. I ached for him. For the lost little boy that he'd been and the damaged young man he'd become as a result. Still, for as awful as his childhood had been and as hard a mistake he had made in the beginning, I still couldn't help but be impressed at the man who held me close and occupied my bed with me.

"Why did you come here to help me? I mean, you didn't even know it was me, and when you found out, you *still* stayed, despite my being a bitch."

"Dray said his family was in trouble, he's my club brother, a bond we treat as almost thicker than even blood. One of us asks for help, we all answer. There is no other option there. You don't answer, you're a liar. We all took an oath when we put those colors on our backs to be there for each other and to do right by one another. We take that shit seriously."

I laid my head on his shoulder and bit my bottom lip. I wanted to ask, *and now?* I really did, but I was scared about the answer. Still, if they could be brave and strong and do these things for me, then I could face the truth no matter what it was.

"And now?" I said it out loud and steeled myself for the answer.

"Now, even if Dragon ordered me to pull out and leave the situation alone, I couldn't even if I wanted to."

"Why?"

"Because that would mean leaving you high and dry and I couldn't do that."

"Why?"

Silence. Too long of a silence. I pulled myself up and propped myself onto one arm so I could look down at him. He had an expression as if a very real war were going on inside and I straddled his hips and stared down at him, waiting him out, scared for the answer myself. My heart thundered in my chest so hard I felt my pulse point leaping out of the side of my throat.

"Because, Bailey... isn't it obvious?" He swallowed hard and I think he was freaking out on the inside as hard as I was.

"I think I want to hear you say it," I said.

Again with the nervous swallow, his gaze trapped, staring at my face as he reached up and traced some of the fall of my hair behind my ear.

"Fuck, you're really going to make me say it, aren't you?"

"Would it help if I said it first?" His smile said that yes, yes it would, but more than that, it said he was overjoyed that I might feel the same way.

"How about on the count of three?"

"One," I murmured.

"Two," he muttered.

"I think I love you," we said together. There was a mutually stunned pause and both of us started to laugh at the same time.

"Come here, you," he said and pulled me down, pressing our mouths together. I let my eyes close and kissed him back, but still worried that love couldn't or wouldn't be enough. I mean, our worlds were so different and to ignore that?

Well, I could ignore it for now if he could.

19

R ush...

I worked my ass off around that fucking farm while Bailey dealt with not only her lawyers and meeting up with that Cranston woman, but soothing a never-ending stream of prissy ass fuckin' rich snob assholes. All of them were demanding shit way out of pocket to ensure that their precious horsemeat was safe. We had guys on rotation, Jorge's idea, sleepin' in the fuckin' stables at night, waking up every hour on a stagger to check things out.

What's more, and what no one knew, we had a couple of our guys from the club around keepin' an eye on things. It was quiet for a while. Almost too quiet, to be honest, which typically meant one thing and one thing only; they were gearing up to cause more trouble. I didn't like it, but honestly it was nice getting a bit of a reprieve.

I'd been missing my shop and needing some fresh clothes. Bailey had said she would be fine and to get some 'me' time in. I appreciated it. Loved it even more that I may have found a woman who got my need for some time to myself, just me and whatever chunk of wood I happened to have in front of me.

I'd been doing okay, hand carving some little pieces in the evenings and spare moments, but I'd really been missing my shop the last couple of days. The current piece I'd been working on was seriously calling my name and I got so absorbed in what I was doing I completely lost track of time. I also completely missed the fact my two brothers ended up on the stools I had set up in the corner of the shop. They sat at a bar height table, several brews between 'em and a couple dead soldiers back in the six-pack they'd come from.

"Hey, guys… what's up?"

Nox laughed and Archer being his typical deadpan self said, "We were wondering when you were planning on coming up for air and stop hittin' that rich pussy to go back to hittin' your shop."

"Man, if I could I'd hit that rich pussy *in* my shop." I was surprised that our typical foolin' over a girl was suddenly sitting wrong with me. I felt like, I don't know, like I was somehow betraying Bailey by talking about her like that. That'd never happened to me before — that kind of reaction.

Nox picked up on it first, he always did. He searched my face and said, "Well, Arch, I do believe we get to welcome Rush here to the fold."

"What the fuck you talking about, boy?"

Nox twisted the top off a fresh cold one and held it out to me. I went over and took it and clinked bottles with him and held it out for Arch to do the same. He did, and we drank and Nox said, "I do believe my twin here has finally found love."

"The fuck, you say?" Arch leaned back on his stool and frowned. "How the fuck do you guys tell this shit about each other with one look?"

"It's a twin thing," I told him, knocking back some more beer. "You wouldn't understand."

Nox laughed while Archer made a face and gave me the finger. I smiled and laughed a little too and asked, "To what do I owe this pleasure of having both my brothers in one place at the same time?"

"Noah and Chandler are wondering where their Unca Rush is, and so is their mamma."

"Club business," I said and Archer scowled at me.

"I fuckin' know that, asshole. I'm a part of this club, too, or did you forget?" I shook my head and smiled.

"You already missed a couple of Sunday dinners now, you best not miss this one."

"Might need to set an extra place setting," Nox said and Archer nodded.

"Done deal, bring the rich girl with you."

"Jesus, Arch, she has a name," Nox said shaking his head.

"Ain't none of you fuckers said it yet," he admonished and drained the rest of his beer in two pulls, cracking another one and drinking half of it in one go.

"Bailey, her name is Bailey," I said laughing. Mel had rubbed off on Archer in a lot of ways over the last year, but in a lot of ways, Archer remained stubbornly the same.

"Right, well bring *Bailey* to dinner on Sunday or Mel an' the boys are gonna have my balls."

"Right, and we wouldn't want that."

"Fuck no, we don't want that!"

Nox was laughing so hard he was gonna fall off his stool, but Archer, he was smiling. I kind of liked the softer side of my hard-ass older brother.

"So, you two love birds trading 'I love yous' yet?" he asked and I knew he meant to yank my chain but my silence must have tipped him off. I mean, I didn't know what to say about that one. I wasn't about to lie, not even a white lie, to either of my brothers. We weren't like that, ever.

Nox scoffed in disbelief and said, "You're fuckin' serious?"

"Dude, it's just... fuck, I don't know, it's just *right*, me and her. Hell, both of you know."

Archer looked thoughtful. All of a sudden, he was taking great interest in peeling the label off his bottle of beer. He sighed finally and it was heavy.

"And the pendulum swings," he muttered darkly.

"And just what the fuck is that supposed to mean?" I demanded.

Nox hung his head and raked a hand back through his black hair. "If I had to guess, it means she sure as fuck won't be into you for money but dude... How many bitches back in Arizona get with us because of the bad boy image, and how well did that end for any of us?" he asked.

"I don't think it's like that," I said. "Bailey's different."

"Yeah, we've heard that song and dance outta you before," Arch said skeptically. He wasn't wrong, but this time I could feel it, down to my fuckin' bones.

I looked my twin in the eye and told him the fuckin' truth, "I'm pretty sure I feel the way I do about Bailey the way you do about Maren. Fate's cruel joke, man. If I recall we *just* threw down over that shit not long ago."

"Yeah, yeah we did..."

"I'd really fuckin' hate to repeat that experience, bro. It was so not one of my favorite things."

"Jesus," Arch said, his eyebrows shooting up into his hairline. "You're fuckin' balls deep into this chick and then some, ain't yah."

"Not ready to make her my ol' lady or anything yet, but yeah, bro; I dig her. I dig her the way I've never dug another chick in my life."

Nox and Arch exchanged a worried look, and Arch nodded, finally. "Just be careful, Rush. We all know you like to leap before you really look, and it's burned you but good in the past."

He had me there. I nodded and sighed, saying, "I promise you, I got both eyes wide open this time and it seriously feels like the stakes have never been higher."

"Do you at least got a good feeling about this?" Nox asked, grimacing. I looked my brother in the eye.

"When we're together, I ain't got a fuckin' doubt in my mind that if it weren't for all the extra bullshit, she and I would be totally cool."

"But?" Arch said.

"I don't think it would be money that fuckin tore us apart. If anything, it'll be her rich mamma or the club that'll do it and that scares me. It really does."

Archer squinted at me. "Are you seriously sayin' what I think you're sayin'?" he demanded, and I jerked back and asked, "What the fuck you think I'm sayin'?"

Nox blew out his cheeks and said, "It seriously sounds like you're saying you'd leave the club over this girl if it came down to a choice between them."

"No, man. I would *never* leave the club over pussy. I'd stay, but what I am sayin' is it would hurt way worse than a case of road rash. The scars would be the same kind of forever, too."

"You sure she feels the same way?" Archer asked me.

I nodded. I'd seen it in her eyes that night, the words, cheesy as they were, echoing faintly through my brain... *One... two... I think I love you.*

"Yeah, man, I really do."

"Then you'll figure it out," Nox said. "If you guys are meant to be, the club will rally, man. They did with Maren."

"And either her family will get on board or they'll lose her."

"You haven't even met her, what makes you so sure?" I demanded.

"I've met Dray, and she comes from his mamma's stock, don't she?"

"She's his cousin, yeah."

"'Nuff said, that kind of ornery don't skip a generation. It's solid in the bloodline."

"God, we are *so* fucked when it comes to Noah and Chandler," Nox said, rolling his eyes and the look on Archer's face had us both busting up laughing.

"Yeah, don't I know it?" he asked, and killed his beer.

There wasn't enough beer in the world.

20

B ailey…

I laughed and leaned against the kitchen counter and said, "That'd be great, thank you, Dray."

"No problem," he said into my ear and stuttered for a second, stumbling over his words as if he were trying to decide if he wanted to speak. He, of course, did… he was his mother's son after all. "Hey, Bales, you got a thing for our boy, Rush?"

I pressed my lips together and thought to myself, *way more than a thing,* but still, I was *my* mother's daughter in some ways and needed to decide just how much to share. I decided on honesty with Dray, thinking that surely he wouldn't use it against me later.

"Yeah, yeah I do… I uh, I'm not sure what to do with that, you know?"

I heard my cousin let out an explosive breath on the other end of the line before he said, "Well whatever you do, don't tell your mom until you're absolutely sure about things." I could hear the unease in his voice and tearing a page out of Rush's manual, I waited him out.

"Just, go easy on him if this is just a fling for you, Bailey. Dude's been hurt a lot."

"I don't know what this is, Dray. It's not like anything I've ever experienced before, but it's not my intention to hurt anyone. I'm just trying to save my farm and what's left of my family here."

"Not sure a relationship with one of us is going to help your cause on that last part," he said, and I know he was just being honest, but the truth hurts, doesn't it?

"I wonder if this was how Aunt Tillie felt," I said chewing my bottom lip. A long heartbeat of silence and Dray cleared his throat.

"Only one person you can ask about that, Bales, and that's my pops."

"Yeah, I guess so."

"It was a little before either of our time. Do you want to talk to him?" he asked.

I shook my head realized he couldn't see it, and said, "Not right now, I honestly just want to cook some dinner and get some sleep. It's been a long day."

"Right, I'll go find Rush and send him in your direction."

"Thanks, I kind of figured he'd lose track of time."

"It's nice you want to cook for him, thanks for treating us like human beings."

"You guys are human beings, and you're helping me. Why wouldn't I treat you as such?"

"I really ain't got much to say to that, Bales."

"Right, my mom, I should have known the answer to that one. I'm sorry, I'm just really, really, tired. All of this is just so mentally and emotionally draining."

"I know when the shit gets heavy, being with my Em makes everything better," he confided.

"That's sort of what it's like when Rush is around, it's just easier somehow."

"That's a keeper, Bales. That's a keeper. I'ma go get him for you."

"Thanks."

"No problem."

He ended the call and I set my phone on the dining room table. I sighed and went into the kitchen. Rush had told me it took forty-five minutes to an hour to get here from the club where his woodshop was, so that meant I had about that time to do my prep work and start cooking. I liked to cook, I just didn't have much occasion to do it. It was no fun cooking for one and a lot of the farmhand's wives had them bring me food all the time.

Renaldo said it was a sign of respect and gratitude, to turn them down would hurt feelings, so I had way more than enough to feed myself and the guys if need be. I shared where I could and before my dad had died would do a quarterly picnic and barbecue potluck. I hadn't precisely stopped the tradition, but I may have missed it with everything going on and no one had seen fit to remind me.

I reminded myself staunchly to schedule one and get the preparations in order sometime this week. That I couldn't let morale slip any further. Renaldo was out of his medically induced coma but it would be weeks if not months of rehab before he could return to work. *If* he could ever return. It was still too early to tell and that was depressing. I'd gone to visit him, and he'd been upset. He didn't know why this had happened to him and swore up and down that he'd just placed that bet and had lost, that the money wasn't even due, and that he would have been able to cover it easily.

I'd told him not to worry and that there would be a job waiting for him, regardless. That even if he couldn't come back full time, or do things the way he'd used to, that there would always be work somewhere in some way at Blue Hills for him.

The whole thing was just so damn depressing, so I fought to look on the bright side. To do something nice for myself and for Rush. A quiet evening in. I think we both needed it. I'd even bought ice cream.

I set about the kitchen, pulling out ingredients and utensils, setting up pans that I would need and setting out the steaks to rest. I was busy chopping up the vegetables I was planning to roast for the recipe when I froze. The front door opened, and I looked up from what I was doing. I'd locked it. I know I'd locked it, and there were very few people who had a key. Philip, my mother, Caleb, and Renaldo... Rush didn't, in fact, the person who came through the door shouldn't, but then again Ken was my brother's best friend, so it wasn't like I needed more than one guess as to where he got the brass colored key he used to let himself in.

"What do you think you're doing?" I demanded by way of greeting.

"You're locking your doors now, Bailey? Since when?"

"Since a bunch of men beat the shit out of my lead groom and someone poisoned my horse; that's when, and when were you going to answer my question?"

I set down my knife on the cutting board and leaned on my hands. If I had to guess, I'd say it'd been a half hour or so since I'd gotten off the phone with Dray. That meant I only had to hold out as long as it took Rush to get here. I most definitely didn't trust Ken, but we'd known each other since we were all kids, so while I didn't trust his motives, I didn't think he would do anything to physically hurt me.

He sighed and his shoulders dropped, he turned the chair at the head of my table out so he could face me and dropped into it.

"Wow, this whole thing about the farm has really done a number on you guys."

"No, really? I hadn't noticed."

He held up his hands palm out, the offending keys to my house dangling from his thumb. "Whoa, girl. I'm not the enemy here."

"No, you're just my brother's best friend which doesn't exactly put us on the same side here, Ken."

He covered his heart with his hands and said, "Ouch, Bales, that really hurts."

I tried to see if he was being genuine, but you never could tell. Not with the jet set. Fortunes were built and equally destroyed by thinking the wrong person was your friend. You had to be shrewd, you had to be cutthroat to really belong to the upper crust. Qualities that I may possess but didn't really have the heart to act on.

I sighed and came around the kitchen island and leaned against it, crossing my arms. The least I could do is listen to Ken's pitch, even though I was pretty sure I wasn't going to like it.

"Fine, why don't you just tell me whatever it is that Philip sent you here to tell me." I said it tiredly because I *was* tired. Tired of the whole damn thing.

Ken looked me over and sighed. "I really hate seeing you guys go through this, and Philip didn't send me over here to do anything. This is all me. That being said, I do have to ask, why won't you consider the offer on the table? You stand to benefit from it the most, being the majority owner of the place. They're offering *a lot* of money Bailey. Enough you could buy yourself another horse farm."

"I don't want another horse farm, Ken. I want my dad's farm. Blue Hills is way more than just another Kentucky thoroughbred racehorse farm. It's one of my dad's legacies, and my granddad's before him. I can't imagine that he would leave it to the three of us and want us to immediately sell it."

Ken snorted and leaned back, kicking one leg out; his pressed jeans fitting him well. He had the rich playboy look. Handsome, like he belonged as a poster boy for J. Crew. He was too perfect, and it didn't appeal anymore. Granted, I'd crushed hard on him when we were teenagers, but we weren't teenagers anymore and I was disillusioned. I wanted something real. I wanted a man like Rush. Honest, what you saw was what you got with him. It wasn't always pretty, but I was realizing honesty won out over pretty any day of the week.

"We talking about the same ol' man?" Ken asked, and I heard my brother's disdain for our father echoed in his voice. I hung my head and shook it.

"He may have been a shark in the boardroom, but he had some sentimentality when it came to a few things."

"Like what?"

"Like this place, like our mother, like us..." I wanted to believe it, but sometimes I had a hard time believing. My dad had been multifaceted, that's for sure. Strict and not always fair, but I sometimes wondered how much of that was him and how much of it was the way he'd been raised.

"Is that why he shipped you off to boarding school then?" Ken asked.

I knew why I'd been shipped off to Connecticut. The problem was, no one else did. My mother and father did it to protect me from the reporters surrounding the rape allegations against my brother. What they didn't realize was that they couldn't protect me from the scandal itself, not even so far away. I could read and use the internet, not that I really needed to. Not when my classmates were following it so closely and never gave up the opportunity to fill the rapist's sister in on what was going on. They grilled me about Philip every chance they got until the faculty caught on and held an assembly telling the school to leave it and me alone.

It did more harm than good, I was pretty much shunned except for a close circle of friends. I was okay with that, though, keeping my circle small. You sort of had to in this lifestyle. God forbid your friend's parents meet because of you and started brokering deals. I'd seen it destroy more than one friendship, burning everything to ash. This life was just pretty on the surface, believe me.

"You don't know everything, Ken, stop pretending that you do."

He sighed and got up, coming to me and putting his hands on my shoulders, giving me a little shake. "Bales, it's me, seriously, there's no need to get hostile. I'm just trying to figure out where your head is at on this, that's all. You seem to be going through a lot of stuff and it's like you're not thinking clearly. I'm worried about you."

I stared up into his hazel eyes, warning bells going off inside my brain. One of those moments where if you tried to explain precisely what it was that was freaking you out about a situation, people would look at you like you were crazy. I mean, Ken was a friend to my family, not just my brother. Hell, he'd been my first kiss as embarrassing as that was to recall right now.

I'd been seventeen and – hey, don't judge, all-girl's boarding school, remember? Anyway, he was twenty and I was home for spring break. There was an abandoned quarry in the county that had filled with water and made a fantastic swimming hole. Much safer than a lot of the lakes and rivers in the area. River drownings were especially common because of unexpected currents, so we used the quarry.

I'd been the one to kiss him, and he'd let me down pretty easy, considering. We'd been horsing around in the water and it just sort of happened. He'd set me back and had told me thanks but no thanks and said I was his best friend's little sister, and how weird would that be? It'd hurt and been embarrassing, but as far as I knew, he'd kept it to himself. Still, it was embarrassing for me, even to this day which is why his proximity made me blush so hard right then.

He tipped my chin with the side of his finger so I'd look up at him and said, "Man, I should have gone for it back then, I actually really regret it now."

I pushed past him into the free space between my kitchen's island and my dining room table and said, "Yeah, but you didn't and it's too late now."

He grabbed my wrist, and I'm pretty sure it was supposed to be some compelling romantic gesture, but all it was, quite frankly, was terrifying. I whirled and jerked it back, but he didn't let it go, his grip tightening.

"Yeah, but it doesn't have to be, right?" he said. "Seriously, Bailey, you should take the money, offload this place and move on. Buy out one of your competitor's, renovate; make the place yours. You'd still have plenty left over and I could help you invest and grow your money. What do you say?"

He was close now, way too far into my personal space for my liking. I shook my head and said, "You haven't heard me at all, Ken. I don't *want* to sell Blue Hills. I love it here, it's my home and I'd like you to leave." I stumbled back and he just kept coming. I tried to pull my wrist free and said, "Let me *go!*"

"Bailey, come off it! You need to listen to me and stop this foolishness!" He had me back up against the table, the chair digging into me but I wouldn't sit down. No way. Instead I leaned back and almost climbed the damn thing to get away from him. It was awkward but I couldn't focus on that right now, I needed to focus on him and figuring out a way to get myself out of this situation.

Shit.

"I'm done listening to Philip and I'm done listening to you. I mean it, Ken. Get out of my house!"

He backhanded me with his other hand and I yelped, stars exploding across my vision. He batted the chair out of his way and before I could register what was happening, he had me up and I was flying, weight-less for a moment; but what goes up must come down and this was no exception. I slammed down onto the hard wood of my dining room table top and Ken loomed over me, pinning my body with his, situating his hips between my legs and pinning me down.

Fear spiked in the center of my chest and dread unfurled in the pit of my stomach. Ken shook his head, his hazel eyes cold and his face a mask of irritation below which cold fury roiled, looking for any excuse to escape. It was one of the most terrifying things I'd ever seen but I had to stay strong, I had to stay calm.

"Let me go, or I'm going to scream."

"No dice, princess. You know, I told him you wouldn't go for it. I said I'd try to talk you into it, but I knew it would probably come to this. I don't want to hurt you, Bailey, but your obstinacy is about to cost Philip and me, a lot of money. We can't have that, so you need to sign on the dotted line."

"It'll be a cold day in hell before I do that," I said and he shook his head.

"I thought you'd say that," he said and went for his belt. "I'm going to enjoy this a lot more than you are, Bales."

My eyes went wide and I opened my mouth to draw breath to scream, kicking out, trying to fight, but before I got the chance, my front door crashed inward on its hinges and a blur of muscle and hate barreled past me and pulled Ken off.

I pushed myself up, eyes wide as Rush knocked Ken onto his ass, kneeling over him. Rush wrapped one fist into the front of Ken's shirt and pulled his other back. Before I could shout or do anything else, the fist he'd cocked back barreled forward into Ken's face with a sickening crunch. Ken shouted and went limp, but Rush didn't let up, he was going to kill him.

"Rush! Stop! Oh my God, stop! You're going to kill him!" I wrapped my arms around his one and pulled back and he miraculously stood up.

"He deserves to die, touching you like that." He spit on Ken's prone form and turned to me and all I could do was stare openmouthed.

21

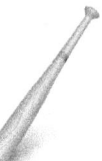

R ush...

I almost turned around and went back down the porch steps when I saw them through the fucking window. It hit me in the center of the chest like a blow from a hammer. My first instinct was *fuck she's been playing you all along* but then I saw her hands, pressed against the wood, palms down as she tried to push away from him. He put one hand in the center of her chest, between her breasts and went for his belt as she tried to get away and I'd seen enough.

I tried the front door but it was locked, like that was going to keep me from getting to her. I hauled back and kicked that fucker clean off its hinges, the doorframe exploding into slivers and shards of wood. I moved in and I brought the fires of hell with me. Dude put up his hands to fend me off. *Aw yeah, it was a lot fuckin' different when you weren't the biggest dog in the fuckin' yard anymore, wasn't it?*

I let fly and put my fist right into the bastard's face. Then I did it again, and I was going to keep doing it, if Bailey hadn't stopped me. I stood up, chest heaving and spit on his unconscious fuckin' ass before I turned to my girl. She stared at me, skin ashen, brown eyes way too wide and her sweet mouth slightly agape.

"You alright?" I demanded.

"Are you?" she demanded back.

"Yeah." I pulled my piece out of the back of my pants and pointed it at him.

"Say the word and I'll pull the trigger, baby."

She stared at me, the wheels and gears clicking and whirring. She shook her head and I put up my gun and pulled out my burner phone instead.

"Who are you calling, the police?" she asked.

I snorted. "Fuck no, I'm calling the cavalry," I said. Dragon picked up on the first ring and without preamble I said, "Dragon, its Rush, we got a situation. Bring the crash truck."

"Dead body?" he asked and didn't sound the least bit grim, more like he was asking the status of the weather out here.

"Not yet, gonna be though."

"Bailey alright?"

I looked her over and said, "Shocky, but yeah, she's a tough cookie."

"On our way."

"Thanks, man."

I hung up the old school flip phone and shoved it back in my pocket. Bailey was pouring a bourbon, her hand shaking so bad she slopped half of it on the counter. She lifted the glass and downed what she managed to get in it in one shot.

She was staring at the douchebag's unconscious body and I stepped over it. I went to her and pulled her into my arms, tucking her head under my chin. I pressed her into my chest and her arms went around my waist. She trembled against me and I sighed.

"It's okay, baby. You ain't got to be strong over this one. You do what you need to do. I'm here, let me be the strong one this time."

It was like she needed permission or something and once granted, she sagged against my chest and just lost her shit. As far as girls losing their shit went, I would take Bailey over just any broad any day. It started with a broken sob at first as she turned her face away from the mess I made on her dining room floor. She buried it into the front of my tee shirt and clung to me.

She cried, sure, but they were these tiny, heart-wrenching, hiccupping sobs, not the great bawling mess I was accustomed to out of most women. No screaming, no theatrics, she just clung to me and wept as quietly as she could. It felt as if her heart had been shattered in a million fuckin' pieces and I couldn't be sure it hadn't. I didn't know who the guy was, I didn't care. He really was a dead man. You didn't put hands on Sacred Hearts' property like that and live, and make no mistake; Bailey was *mine*. I think this shit just clinched it.

By the time Dray stepped through the ruin of the front door the storm had passed and Bailey just stared mutely, dispassionately at the groaning pretty boy on her floor who wasn't so fuckin' pretty anymore. She wouldn't let me go, and I was okay with that, her arms tight around my waist, her smaller figure pressed tight into the protection of my larger frame.

"Who is this guy and what the fuck happened?" Dray demanded.

"Ken Sias, my brother's best friend; I thought one of my friends..." She shut her mouth and bit her lips together, taking in a deep breath through her nose and letting it out slowly.

Dragon who'd come in after Dray stared down at the dude, face neutral and asked, "What'd he do to deserve this treatment?"

Bailey didn't answer so I did for her, "Put his hands on her." Dragon's mouth turned down and he surveyed the damage, finally giving a little nod.

"Good work," he said dryly.

"What do you want to do with him?" Dray asked.

"Kill him," I said matter-of-factly. Bailey inhaled sharply and I rubbed her back.

"Relax, baby. The man asked me what I wanted to do with him, he didn't tell me what we were gonna do," I murmured.

"Right, think he'll be missed?" Dragon wanted to know.

"Yes," Bailey said, then swallowed and asked, "Shouldn't we call an ambulance for him?"

"Nope," Dray said and put his hands under the dude's armpits. Dragon took his ankles.

"Where are you taking him?" Bailey asked.

"Hospital, have Doc patch him up and then when he wakes up, we're gonna have a conversation," Dragon said.

"I'll fix the door in the morning."

"Right, see you two later and thanks for all the fish," Dragon said then he looked at his son and said, "One, two, three, lift!"

Bailey's mouth fell open as they carried the injured man out and put him in the back of Dragon's old pickup. Bailey and I had kind of naturally just followed them and we stood in the ruin of her open doorway.

She hugged to me tightly and shuddered and I sighed. "Well, that's it then," I murmured. "You've seen the worst of me."

"Would you have really killed him?" she asked quietly. "If I'd said so, would you have shot him?"

"Without hesitation."

She closed her mouth and had a faraway look on her face for what seemed like a long time. She let her arms slip from around my body and took a step back and my heart sank.

"I think I need another drink," she said, and her tone was brittle and empty… soulless.

"We can do that, then I'll clean up this mess."

She nodded and we went back into the kitchen, our boots crunching over broken glass, the dinner she'd been preparing left forgotten where its components lay. I looked it over and she uncorked her bourbon bottle and took a drink directly from it, her dark eyes never leaving mine. She coughed a little and passed me the bottle saying, "Man up, we're drinking dinner tonight."

I couldn't help but smile at the brass pair she was sporting, my hope rising a bit that I hadn't just killed it completely, but I could see she had questions. I took a swig out of the bottle and waited for her to ask them.

22

B ailey...

I laid in the dark, wide awake and losing yet more sleep over my asshole brother, but it wasn't the main thing keeping sleep at bay. I couldn't stop seeing Rush's powerful fist plowing into Ken's face over and over again. His model perfect looks would never be the same again. I knew that in my heart of hearts, but what scared me about the thought wasn't the thought itself, it was the fact that I felt *nothing* about it. Well, that wasn't precisely true, what I felt about it was satisfaction. Did that make me a terrible person?

Rush jostled me slightly and I jumped, his voice softly penetrating the dark of the room and the miasma of my thoughts to ask, "Hey, you okay?"

"I don't know," I said honestly.

"What's eating you? What I did to that guy's face?"

"That's part of it," I confessed.

Rush grunted. "You ask me? That was some karma right there. No girl'll ever be suckered in by his pretty boy face again. He tried it on you, Bales, there's not tellin' how many he's succeeded on."

I blinked and my heart sank, not for me but for the fact that Rush was right. I suddenly didn't feel like such a monster for not feeling bad for the cockroach. Still, if it ever got out what happened to his face, it would be my fault, just by virtue of being a woman. Never mind associating with a criminal element capable of such barbarism. I sighed, and Rush pulled me a little closer in the dark.

"Scared the shit out of me, seeing you like that. I just wanted to kill him. Make sure he could never touch you like that again. I still should have broken his damn hands. Maybe Dragon and Dray did it for me."

"You mean that," I said.

"Damn right I do."

"I'm not used to this," I said looking up at him. I couldn't see him in the dark, the light through the blinds illuminating my face but leaving his shadowed.

"I know. Things are a lot simpler where I come from. More basic. You touch a man's property, his woman, his bike, you best be prepared to have your face smashed in."

"Is that what I am to you?"

"What?"

"Your woman, your property?"

"Well, yeah, Bailey. At least I'd like you to be." I swallowed hard and pushed away from him, getting out of my bed.

"Get out," I said, and it nearly broke my heart to say it but it needed to be said.

"Call someone else to come sit with me, I don't care but get out." I was shaking now, and he sat up completely, clicking on the bedside lamp and leaning back against the headboard.

"Talk to me," he said, and I could tell by his tone I'd hurt him.

I shook my head and said, "Just please, get dressed and leave."

"Not until you tell me why."

I sniffed and stared at the ceiling, willing the tears to remain where they were and not spill but no such luck. It was like the tap was loose or something and wouldn't quite shut off.

"Don't you understand?" I demanded. "My whole life I've been told to shush. I've been shuffled off to the side in favor of the Berling golden boy. Told what I'm going to do, when I am going to do it; paraded in front of people to make my parents, my father, look good to his cronies and to impress clients or whatever. I'm not a show piece, damn it! I'm a woman, a person and no one's fucking property!"

He started laughing then, hanging his head and shaking it a little just like every patronizing male in my life ever had as a way to discount the girl, *oh don't mind her, must be that time of the month,* sort of thing. I hated it, I hated it so much and all of that venom, the poison I'd been ingesting since I first drew a damn breath just boiled to the surface and I just completely blew a gasket.

"Get out!" I screamed at him and stomped into the bathroom and slammed the door, locking it.

He tapped on the other side of it a moment later while I paced over my travertine floor and seethed.

"Bailey, open the door."

"I mean it, Rush, either you leave now or I'm calling the police."

Silence met that proclamation and he said, "Come out here and talk to me."

I ripped open the door and demanded, "And say what?"

"What the hell's gotten into you would be a good start," his expression was stormy, and he was getting angry too.

"Men! Men's what's gotten into me. Men thinking they know what's best for me, men thinking they can do whatever they want to me and blowing me off every time I have a problem with their shitty attitude or way of treating me like I'm nothing more than a cute little pet!" I went to slam the door in his face, but it was stopped by his broad palm.

"And I'm one of those men, huh?"

"Yes! I'm not your fucking property. I might have been your girlfriend, but good luck with that now, biker boy!"

That tipped him over the edge. He got right into my face, nose to nose and said, "You rich bitches are all the same. Judgmental little cunts in it to ride some bad boy cock for a few nights then can't handle it when shit gets real even for a minute. Then what do you do when we clean up your fucking mess for you? Trash us like we ain't shit. News flash for you, rich bitch, I'm a person, a man, and I've got feelings; I'm not fucking disposable, not that you'd know anything about that." I recoiled from his low vehement tone and the horror of what I'd just done had only begun to sink in.

My mind raced, repeating over, and over, and over again, *you broke it. You broke this, you broke this; you broke this...* even as my mouth betrayed me further by saying dully, "Just get out, leave."

He yanked on his clothes while I watched from the bathroom doorway and when he finished swinging on his leather vest, he came to me with his gun in his hand.

"You know how to shoot this?" he demanded.

"No."

He clicked a little lever on the side and said to me, "Safety is off, it's a point and click application, aim for center mass; that's the chest. It's not hard. I know your spoiled ass is used to having everything done for you, but I think you can handle it. Just do me a fuckin' favor and don't shoot me in the back, already hurts from your knife."

With that, he turned and walked away, ducking out the bedroom door. I heard his truck engine start up outside and the tires slide in the gravel as he romped on the gas and left. Just like I'd asked him, no... *demanded,* he do.

I stared at the big black gun in my hand and knew fear. Not for what might happen to me, more for what wouldn't now... I really loved him. I knew it by the breaking of my heart, but at the same time, I couldn't blame anyone but myself.

What have I done?

I slid down the door frame to my bedroom floor and wept. What else could I do? You know the trouble with crying, though? It didn't really fix anything. Sure, it made you feel a little better for the moment, but when you were done? Nothing was different. Nothing was changed.

I got dressed and went to my kitchen. I had to pass the ruin of my front door, but I couldn't bring myself to care. I looked around my house and shook my head. All of it was just stuff. I'd had the potential to really have something with Rush, something more real than anything I had ever had with anyone before and I'd just taken a keg of dynamite to it. White washed any future I might have had with the same prejudiced brush of my past.

What is wrong with you? I asked myself, but I didn't have an answer. I honestly didn't have an answer at all. I made coffee and curled up in one of the chairs on my front porch. I set the gun next to the coffee cup and stared at it for a long, long, time wondering why he'd left it.

It was around seven in the morning when Dray pulled up on his bike, the sun had risen, the birds were chirping, and my cousin looked pissed. He stormed up onto the porch and made a disgusted sound.

"What the hell did you do, Bales?" he demanded, and I looked up at him with a tear-streaked face.

"I fucked up," I said, and he shook his head, gripping the back of his neck and swore.

"No, shit. What did you say to him?"

He dropped into a seat across from mine and I stared at him. "What does it matter? He left, I drove him away and he probably hates me."

Dray rolled his eyes and said, "Oh, for fuck's sakes, talk. *What did you say?*"

I told him everything and he bowed his head, nodding. "You're right," he said, "you fucked up. You didn't let him get a single word in edge wise, did you?" I stared at him blankly and shook my head. "Didn't think so. If you had, you'd know that to be considered property of one of us is just about the highest honorific a brother could give you."

"I don't understand that!" I said. "How does that make sense to any normal person?"

"It's not *supposed* to. Not for a citizen like you," he shot back, and it wounded me. Dray had always been patient with me before, teasing, but now? Now, he was harsh and unforgiving, and I wasn't used to it even if I did deserve it.

"Listen," he said finally, "I'm only going to explain this once..." and he did, and I would be lying if I said it didn't boggle my mind. I sat there and absorbed it all and finally came to the conclusion that there wasn't really anything to understand about it. It wasn't something, like he said, that fit into any neat little box constructed by the average person to explain it. It just was for them. As natural to them as the air they breathed.

"How did you know to come here? That I would be alone?"

"He left a fuckin' voicemail. Shit, Bales, get your fuckin' ass up and let's go."

"To do what?"

"So you can fuckin' apologize."

I nodded. As much as I didn't want to do it because, *God*, so many reasons… embarrassment being chief among them. I nodded and said, "Let me grab a pair of boots and tell my lead that I'll be gone for a bit so that he can keep an eye on the house."

"Make it quick, I ain't got all fuckin' day. I'd like to get back to the club and my girl." He picked up Rush's gun and put the safety on, swearing. "You're lucky you didn't shoot your fuckin' self."

I tipped my head and said, "I'm not completely stupid, Dray-Dray."

"No, just naïve as fuck."

I nodded, I couldn't argue that when it came to his world. I went and did the aforementioned errands as quickly as I could. When I came back, Dray was already astride his bike which was running. He shoved his helmet at me, and I put it on and got on the back of his motorcycle. It was a little weird riding with my cousin, not knowing where to hold on and such. I mean, he was my cousin… I don't know. I guess I was just being dumb.

It was both the longest and shortest ride of my life. I spent the entire thing trying to get my exhausted, stressed out mind to work. Trying to come up with an apology big enough to suit the situation.

I'd never been to my uncle or cousin's motorcycle club, and I craned my neck as we pulled up into the lot, trying to get a good look. Dray stopped and I got off, taking his helmet off as I looked over the low-slung cinderblock building. He backed his motorcycle into the line of them out front and shut it off, leaning it onto its kickstand. He took the helmet from my hands and led the way to the door.

He opened it for me, and I went through. A girl straightening up from the front of the bar, gave me a flat, unfriendly look.

"Who the fuck are *you*?" she asked, but her thick Irish accent made it come out more like 'Who th' feck are ye?'

"Excuse me?" I asked.

"Aye," she said addressing Dray, "club business, ye say? Who the fuck is she, Dray? Huh?"

"Jesus, chill out, Em."

"Oh? Gettin' up this early an' leavin' without so much as a kiss? Ye come ridin' up at a half past eight in th' mornin' with this lassie on yer bike and I'm supposed t' stay calm? Club business my arse!"

Fire sparked out of her steely blue eyes and I just kept my mouth shut. I didn't know what was worse, that she was accusing my cousin of sleeping with me or the fact she was doing it in front of an audience, a mostly grinning audience.

Dray went to her and grabbed her by the upper arm. "It *is* club business, Em, now get over here," he said and started dragging her toward the darkened back of the club.

She raised her voice and dug in her heels and said, "Not until ye tell me who she is!" She turned her attention back to me and said, "Ay, ay! Who are ye? Can't ye talk?"

I blinked and remained silent, just watching the mess start to unfold, Dray hauled on her a little harder and said, "Em, Em, EM! Get over here, alright?"

"*No!* It's not alright! Who the feck is she, Dray?"

It blew up into a full-scale quarrel at that point. I looked over and saw my Uncle Dragon, Ghost and a few other men and women sitting around scattered tables laughing and watching the show Dray, and his girl, Em, were putting on. They were shouting at each other and I watched him thrust her through an empty doorway into a room beyond.

He followed her in and bellowed, "Jesus Christ, Em! What is your fuckin' problem?"

"Ye want to know what my problem is, I'll tell you what my problem is!" she shouted, then raised her voice even louder and screamed, "I'm pregnant!" right before the door slammed shut on a ringing silence. My jaw dropped and several of the men were laughing beside me. I looked and my uncle Dragon was beaming.

"Congratulations, *Grandpa!*" a man crowed. He had bright, twinkling blue eyes and his hair was smoothed down to a point between his eyes, an almost Mohawk without actually being one. Dragon laughed for real then, a lot of them did, laughing almost until they cried. The first thing that was evident was that Rush was not among them. I pinched the bridge of my nose and let out a pent-up breath... *I so don't get these people...*

"How you doin', Bailey?" Ghost asked and I dropped my shaking hand, my nerves shot from the stress and gave him a weak smile.

"Seen Rush?" I asked softly, dodging the question.

"Out in his woodshop, sweetheart. Straight ahead, zag left at the media room and go down the hall next to it and out the back door. Big fuckin' building on the left, last bay. You can't miss it," my uncle said, dark eyes roving over me. Silent disapproval radiating from them, but I couldn't say I hadn't earned it.

I pressed my lips together and nodded, my chest tight with fear and anxiety. I put my hands in my back pockets and followed my uncle's directions. I heard the first man that'd spoken, congratulating Dragon on him impending grandparenthood ask, "He do that to her face?"

"Nope, that's been handled already."

"And you didn't tag me in? Awww!"

"Don't you worry about it, your turn's a comin'," Dragon said, and he didn't sound happy about it. The other guy, on the other hand, was all too pleased. I heard him give an excited, "Yay!" and the rest of their conversation was lost to me as I made my way deeper into the clubhouse, dread ticking fingers down my spine. They were so casual about violence and I found that so frightening.

Still, I was distracted by the man's first question. I wondered what they were talking about when it came to my face, and I realized I had no idea, that I hadn't looked in a mirror yet. I went to the back door and there on my left was a small bathroom. I ducked into it and looked into the cracked mirror above the sink.

A bruise stained my face, the color of old coffee, on my chin by my mouth. I bowed my head and shook my head. It hadn't been Rush, he hadn't laid a hand on me despite how pissed off he'd been before he'd left. *Before you kicked his ass out,* I corrected myself.

Rush hadn't hit anybody first, I thought to myself. Ken had... Rush had just come in and finished what Ken had started. I shook my head and scrubbed my face with my hands, tiredness making everything a small irritation.

I went back out into the dimly lit hall, switching out the light to the bathroom and squared my shoulders at the back door. I took a deep breath in through my nose and let it out through my mouth and opened the portal into the too bright summer sun. Rush had been right, he had cleaned up the mess made last night regardless of if it being my mess or not, and I couldn't even give him the benefit of hearing him out. I'd been too busy clutching my damn pearls. Ugh...

It took me a minute to let my eyes adjust, not that I needed them. I could hear the sound of tools off to my left and ahead of me; I probably could have found him by sound alone. I followed the asphalt track around to that side and up a gentle incline until I was even with the shop. The first and second bay doors were firmly shut but the third was flung wide open to the air. I could hear what sounded like a hammer and chisel at work and I could almost picture him bent over whatever piece he was working on.

I wanted to see that, for real, not just in my imagination, but I was afraid. More afraid of rounding that corner and having him reject me before I could even say I was sorry. He had every right to... I hadn't listened to him. I hadn't even given him the chance to say a thing. It'd serve me right if he told me to fuck right off.

Tears collected on my lashes before I could even round the corner and I didn't bother to try and dash them away. All it ever accomplished was making them worse, the oils from my skin liked to get into my eyes and started burning which just made them water even more. It wasn't worth the trouble, so I just stepped around the corner and there he was, just like magic, leaning over a slab of wood, a mallet in one hand and a chisel in the other. He leaned up and lowered the tools to his sides, staring at me through a pair of clear safety glasses.

"Hi," I murmured, and his gaze flicked over me from head to toe.

"Hey." One word, cautious, suspicious, my heart broke a little more.

Tears welled up hot and fierce and my voice broke when I said, "I'm so sorry."

Tools clattered to the piece of wood he was working on and he came around it making a beeline for me. He pulled me tight against his chest and kissed the top of my head.

"I'm sorry, too," he said roughly, and my tears turned to ones of relief.

"I didn't understand, I still don't, but I want to... Dray showed up this morning and explained some things, but this is all my fault. I should have let you talk. I should have just *listened*."

"Shh," he soothed, and held me close. "I hate it when you hurt," he said with a sigh and I laughed a little brokenly.

"I hate that *I hurt you*."

"Water under the bridge, baby. I'm a big boy, I can take it. What's killin' me is the shit I said to you. I lost my temper, called you names, and that shit just wasn't right."

"I don't understand something," I said, and I could hear the slight smile in his voice when he said, "What's that?"

"Why'd you leave me your gun?"

He chuckled faintly and said, "I love you, babe, and loving someone means tellin' 'em to go to Hell and worrying the whole time they're travelin' on if they're gonna get there safely."

I laughed then, I couldn't help it. It was one of the most ridiculous things I'd ever heard that made perfect sense. I'd been awake all night doing the same thing, worrying on if he made it back here safely. Wondering if it could be fixed, wondering if he hated me.

"It's the same reason I been out here since I got back, building you a new front door."

I looked up at him and told him the truth, "I don't know how any of this is supposed to work. I don't want to screw up again."

"Me either," he said, "but it's gonna happen. We're human, baby, and this is part of it."

I held to him tightly and muttered the first thing that came to mind, "Well then, I don't want to be a human anymore. I want to be a horse."

He laughed for real then, a deep rolling laugh that made me smile. It smoothed some of the jagged edges just to hear it, but I was far from healed. I was afraid I'd done too much damage for that, and the world in which I lived, the kind of damage that was inflicted by feeling like you slighted someone at a golf game would follow you for years. Keeping you looking over your shoulder waiting for the consequences to appear. What I'd done was unforgivable where I came from, that he was just willing to forgive me, just like that? It was unheard of and usually came with strings attached at some point. I was afraid, and so I told him so, stumbling over my words, trying to make him see.

He leaned back and smoothed some of my tangled hair out of my face, his gaze drifting to the corner of my mouth and hardening for a moment.

"That may be how your rich world works, but that ain't my world, baby."

"I don't feel like I belong anywhere," I whispered, and he tightened his hold on me, giving me a reassuring squeeze.

"Sure you do, you belong with me."

I looked up at him and he was ready for it, his lips gently finding mine before I could say anything. The kiss so light and so careful, it took my breath away.

23

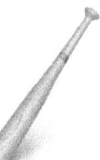

R ush...

"Hey, you guys okay?" my twin's voice startled us and I looked over.

"Yeah. Yeah, man, I think we are. Babe, I'd like you to meet my twin, Nox."

"Oh!" Bailey sounded startled but she smiled and it transformed her whole face, despite her damp lashes. "Hi, I'm Bailey," she said and held out her hand. Nox gave it a shake and smiled back.

"You two look like shit; no offense. Seriously, you should get a nap. Dragon's orders, actually. He wants everyone rested for your big family meeting." Nox made a face and Bailey laughed a bit nervously.

"Um..."

"Shit, man. I gotta finish this door and –"

"Later; Reave and Trig already headed out to Bailey's farm, Data too. You guys go in, get some sleep, fuck, do whatever you're gonna do, but no one wants to see your asses until some kind of rest happens."

When we didn't move right away Nox rolled his eyes and said, "Seriously, bro. Your girl looks like hell. Get some sleep, honey. You need it."

"Close up the shop for me?" I asked and Nox nodded. "Thanks, bro."

I held Bailey close and guided her to the outbuilding that housed my room asking her, "Ready to see how the other half lives?"

She smiled a bit wanly, and said to me, "I'm ready to see how *my* other half lives."

Chills. Motherfucking *chills*. I tightened my arm around her shoulder and leaned over kissing the side of her head. I wanted her in my bed, between my sheets, her body twined around mine. I wanted to kiss her, I wanted to hold her, and I wanted to move inside her slowly and savor that shit. I knew when I'd left her place last night that it wasn't the end; that I would see her again, but I didn't know what form or shape that meeting would take. I hadn't expected tears. I hadn't expected she would come to me or so soon.

It was everything I ever wanted, a strong, beautiful, funny, and committed woman who wanted *me*, flaws and all. That was intense. The fact that I was definitely in love with her back was just mind-blowing. I seriously never thought in a million years it would happen to me but here we were.

I opened the door to the outbuilding for her, the outside walls made from cinderblock like the main clubhouse, the roof sheeted with tin. It was long and held doors down both sides. A lot fewer than what'd been here before, which had been cells for the old juvie facility. We'd completely gutted the place when we'd first got here and built it out the way we wanted it. First thing we'd done was put a roof on the building, then completely knocked out the interior walls and re-studded, partitioning out the new rooms.

I was telling Bailey about it as I led her to my room. "We tore out all of the existing plumbing and electrical, put a bathroom at either end of the hall." I opened the bathroom door at this end and told her, "The other bathroom is on the opposite end opposite side of the hall from this one."

"Reminds me a little bit of a locker room's kind of vibe."

"Yeah, we went for efficiency over style, that's for sure." Each bathroom in the outbuilding had three showerheads in a very gym-like setup with drains set into the tile floor. On the other side of them, there were three bathroom stalls and against the back wall as you walked in, two urinals. To the right, just through the door, was a pair of sinks with a mirror over it. I grinned wryly and said, "Have to admit, I like your bathroom better."

"It's nice in here for what it was meant to be." She hugged me tight around the waist and I smiled pulling the door shut.

"Come on, my room's up here." I opened the door for her and let her go through and she just stopped about half a step inside. It made me smile knowing what it was that stopped her. I had a king-sized bed taking up the majority of the room, but what stopped her was the rustic head and footboard. I'd used a light, honey colored mesquite to do it and it'd turned out pretty fantastic. The headboard carved in a desert scene of saguaro cactus over a rock landscape, surrounded by a different, but prettier cactus flower than the saguaro produced.

The flowers I'd modeled? The ones I'd carved into the headboard and footboard of this piece, had come from a much smaller and much spinier cactus I'd found growing in a pot outside Mel's old place. They'd had wide centers and the layered petals, white toward the center and a light, dusky pink toward the outer, delicately curved to a point, the petals had captured my attention like no other. I just knew I had to do something with them and so I'd created this piece. Probably one of the most labor-intensive I'd ever done. Hundreds of hours had gone into this bed, and I didn't regret a single minute of it.

Bailey went to it, her gait slow, and touched the footboard, running fingertips along the top of the satiny wood, her eyes wandering the landscape in front of her.

"It's so beautiful," she murmured.

"Eh, it was the only way to bring home with me... I miss Arizona sometimes. It's a different kind of beautiful out there."

"I can see that," she murmured.

I pulled back the corner of the native blankets piled on the bed revealing the black sheets under them and said, "Sit."

She did and I kneeled in front of her, cupping one heel of her boot with my hand and the other behind her knee to steady her lower leg. I pulled off her boots and set about getting her naked. I was serious about everything I'd listed earlier, and it all started with getting us both naked.

"There's something about taking a woman to your bed when you're a man," I murmured.

"Yeah?" she asked, a little breathy as I carefully pulled off her clothing a piece at a time.

"Since I built it, I've never had a woman in this bed," I confessed. "Fucked plenty, sure, but never in this bed. We've got general purpose rooms around this place for that."

She smiled a bit wryly and said, "How romantic."

"I'm not trying to be romantic, baby. I'm trying to make you under-stand something."

She fell silent and tipped her head gently, searching my face. Finally, she said, "I'm listening."

"You're the first woman I have brought to this bed, and I never intended on bringing any woman to it that I didn't feel like she would be the last."

"Oh."

"Stand up," I ordered and she did. I hooked my fingers in the waist-band of her jeans and she gave that little shimmy of her hips to help me ease them and her panties down in one go. It drove me crazy, absolutely wild, to see it.

I stood up and pulled my shirt over my head in a single easy move-ment. Bailey put her hands to my waist, head bowed; the fingertips of her one hand gently grazing the one percent diamond I had tattooed on my ribs.

"What you thinking?"

"Is it always like this?" She circled the dark ink under my skin with a fingertip.

"Only when people fuck with what's ours. Our family, our lives… We won't stand for this shit." I tipped her face up to mine and gently touched the stain under her skin where the bastard had hit her.

She closed her eyes and nodded, and I tucked her into my bed while I finished stripping out of my clothes, letting them lay where they fell. I didn't care about being neat right now, I cared about holding her close, about getting some sleep, and yeah, I'd be lying by omission if I didn't say I was thinkin' about getting in that pussy.

First, though, we needed some sleep, the both of us. I had her turn on her side, back to my front, the little spoon to my big, and pulled her into the curve of my body. Kissing the back of her shoulder, I let the peace of having her near, our emotional wounds on the mend, lull me into a restful sleep.

I think she was out before I was.

The next thing we knew, the door to my room was swinging open. We'd shifted in our sleep, Bailey might have gotten up at least once to pee or something, because while she'd started out with me between her and the door, she was tucked into the front of my body on that side, now. My shirt a puddle by the bed that said she'd worn and discarded it. I liked that.

"What the fuck, over?" I demanded, scowling at Dray while Bailey hid her face in my chest. The blankets had slipped while we'd slept, and her back was bared to the cooler air of the room. I didn't move, adjusting her coverage meant I'd probably expose more of her rather than just the relatively safe zone that was already showing.

"See, I told you she was fine," he said and Bailey's mom stepped halfway into the room. Bailey twisted around and looked over her shoulder.

"What the hell, Dray?" she demanded and hid closer to the front of my body. I scowled at my club brother and let him know with my look alone that there would be some kind of reckoning for this down the line.

His smirk told me that his aunt had been a special kind of pain in his ass and that whatever was comin' was gonna be worth it just to take her down a peg or two. To her credit, Bailey's mom didn't flip out. If anything, she went total ice queen and said quietly in a voice and tone that was completely crisp and even, "Get dressed, I'll be waiting with your uncle José. We have things to discuss." And with that, she turned and strode from the room and back down the hall outside, the heels on her fashionable and likely expensive pumps muffled by the office style carpet out there.

"You're a real dick, you know that?" I shot at my VP.

"Can't be sorry, was totally worth it," he said. Bailey turned and glared at him.

"Worth it for you and your point zero two seconds of revenge, nice to know you totally give a fuck about how it's going to affect *me*. Thanks, so much, Dray."

His expression darkened and he went out, shutting the door behind him. Bailey let out a breath and bowed her head. I palmed the back of her head and drew her forehead to my lips.

"It'll be alright," I told her.

"Easy for you to say, you don't know my mother," she groused and pushed away so she could get up and get dressed.

"Glad I'm not the only one gettin' tired of mitigating family drama and emotional damage."

"I swear to Christ I'm getting ready to inflict some," she muttered darkly, and I gave her a crooked grin as I pulled on my jeans.

"That's what I like to hear, now you're gettin' it."

She gave me a slight smile that screamed she was callin' me a smartass and I couldn't disagree with her. I pulled my cut off the hook behind the door and put it on. Bailey took my hand and I grabbed the knob, giving it a twist and dragging the door open. Whatever shitshow was about to go down, I needed her to know I was with her.

We went to the barroom where we held church and found Dragon, Dray, and Trudy sitting around a couple of tables that'd been pulled together. Trudy had her legs primly crossed at the knee, her arms crossed over her chest and was sitting there in an isolating cold silence. Dray was leaned back casually in his seat, a slight smile on his face while Dragon? Dragon just looked *tired*.

Trudy's dark, gleaming eyes went to rake angrily over her daughter but the second they fixed on the bruise staining her face, they hardened, and I could tell her anger had redirected. I didn't know what to make of Bailey who was half a step behind me but still clung to my hand. It was as if she were back to being a small child or something, waiting for the wrath of her mother to come down. I suddenly had images of Joan Crawford screaming *'no more wire hangers ever!'* in my head. It'd been a favorite movie of Norma-Rae's. She watched it every time it

194

came on the damn TV and I swear to fuck, I hated that goddamn film. Especially after the first time she picked up a wire coat hanger against *me.*

Trudy's eyes trailed from her daughter's face to mine and she asked so calmly it was scary, "Did you kill the man who did this to my daughter?"

"No, ma'am. Not for a lack of trying. Bailey just wouldn't let me. Your daughter's a good woman."

"Did you at least break his hands?" she asked and Bailey's mouth fell open.

"Mother!" she cried and Trudy lifted her hand, palm out to stop her daughter's objections.

"No ma'am, I broke his face. Bailey didn't let me get to his hands."

"No worries, Trudy. I broke his hands for you," Dragon said and Trudy turned to look at him.

"Thank you, José."

"No problem."

I pulled out a chair for Bailey and she dropped into it saying, "It's like I'm in some kind of alternate dimension!"

"Think they call it the *Twilight Zone*, baby."

"Think for our generation it's an episode of *Black Mirror*," Dray said.

I shrugged and told him, "Haven't seen that one, dude."

"It's on Netflix, you should check it out."

"Enough," Trudy snapped and looked disgusted. Bailey's hands were over her mouth, her elbows propped on the edge of the table, I dropped into an empty seat near hers and put a hand on her knee under the table, propping my elbows on my own.

"Great, so now what?" Bailey asked.

"Now, you listen to your mother," Dragon said, clearing his throat. He leaned back in his seat and Trudy leaned forward.

Bailey looked like a deer caught in the headlights.

24

B‌ailey…

Not how I wanted my mother to find out about Rush. I didn't know how I wanted her to find out, but this certainly wasn't it. I sat with my hands over my mouth half because I couldn't believe what was coming out of hers and half to keep from screeching at Dray. I was so pissed. I was well aware my mother could be an unyielding pain in the ass but that was no reason to sell mine down the river.

The fact that she was asking the men around the table if they'd *killed* a man and was genuinely disappointed when the answer was 'no' just left me reeling. The only thing steadying me at that point was Rush's hand massaging my knee under the table.

I stared at her and said nothing, ever the obedient child, I'd never gone against her wishes, not once. Though she'd never specifically said who I could and could not be with, I knew damn well her views on Uncle José and his men. *Miscreants, dirty, thieves, murderers, rabble, a bad element,* all words she'd used to describe them at one time or another. She missed a few descriptors from what I could see though, *passionate, committed, honest* and *honorable* were on my list, though I understood that while they were all of the things I listed, it wasn't necessarily by regular societies' standards. Of course, my family *was* regular society, and look how we turned out…

"I've made several mistakes in my life," my mother said quietly. "I never imagined your brother would be chief among them."

"Mom!" I cried, horrified. She put up a hand and shook her head.

"I don't want to hear it, Bailey. What he is doing to you and the people who work for not just you but *him*… I can't…" She pursed her lips.

"Yer brother put his buddy up to what happened last night, didn't even have t' break his hands to get it out of him." Uncle Dragon looked sad to have to say it but not one bit surprised.

"There's spoiled, and then there is what your brother has turned out to be." My mother's eyes welled up and she looked at the ceiling trying to get it together which just made me want to cry. It was a worldwide main event when my mother cried, the kind of thing to rock you to your core if you knew her at all. She'd always been the strong one, a real iron lady, so to see her careful façade crumbling really distressed me in a way I couldn't even begin to convey.

"Mamma, don't cry," I said, and she looked at me so full of sorrow and disappointment my heart seized in my chest automatically, even though I knew the look wasn't meant for me.

"I am so proud of you, Bailey."

Her words caught me off guard and I said, "I don't understand."

"For turning out the way you did. For turning out better than your brother despite what a failure I am, and that your father was, as a parent."

"Mom!" I cried. *So not how I wanted their approval… so not. Damnit!*

"No, Bailey. No arguments. My own son sent a man to my daughter's home *with a key* with express instructions to hurt her badly enough; to scare her into submitting to his will… and for what? *Money.* We *have* money! We have enough money for your brother, you, *and* me to live comfortably and never work a day in our lives! If that isn't a monumental failing at parenting my child, I don't know what is."

It sounded like something Philip would do, as much as you never want to think of any kind of family that way, and he wasn't wrong. Girls like me were raised to think if it happened to you, it was your fault. Leave it to Philip to go there, if Ken had succeeded, my brother would have swept right in while I was shattered and shaking with the paperwork to sign. Probably with some song and dance about how if I'd only signed in the first place, it never would have happened to me; that my own stubborn willfulness had been the cause.

He missed the part where I'd been sent to an all-girl's boarding school. One that actually educated its girls that it was *never* our fault. It just went to show, rape really wasn't about sex, it was about power. Well, newsflash, I wasn't giving mine up under *any* circumstances. I stared across the table at my mother's tear-stained face and not for the first time had to wonder about her and why she would allow half of the things she had under her roof. Of course, the short answer was, *because of my father.*

Scary.

"Begging your pardon, ma'am… but your son is what, two, three years older than Bales here?" My mother's attention went right to Rush who had spoken. His voice, likewise, snapping me out of the deep well of thought I'd fallen into.

"Yes."

"That makes him what? Thirty, thirty-one?"

"Yes, I don't understand what that has to do with anything, though."

"Well ma'am, if your boy is thirty to thirty-one years of age and don't know what he's doing is wrong, I don't think there's a parenting tactic in the world that's been invented to handle that kind of wrong. He's old enough to know better, he just don't care."

"There's a word for that, Trudy," Dragon said and my mother turned her tear-stained face to him.

"Sociopath," Dray supplied when it was clear she wasn't getting it.

"I don't know if there's any help for 'im if that's the case," Dragon said. "But we can sure try."

"How do you propose we do that?" she asked, squaring her shoulders.

"Fire with fire?" Rush asked looking grim.

"Not quite ready to turn Reave or Cell loose on 'im just yet," Dragon said leaning back in his chair.

"There *is* one more possibility," Dray said.

"What?" I asked.

"Could just have a really bad fuckin' case of that affluenza goin' around the country."

I made a face. "Spoiled little asshole is way more my brother's speed. I'm pretty shocked he would go so far, I mean, are you *sure* Ken wasn't saying just anything to get away from you?"

"That could be, too."

"Because it's family, let's err on the side of desperation. What would make Philip so fuckin' desperate he would stoop so damn low?" Rush put out there gently and my mother looked positively grateful for him casting the line of hope out there that maybe, just maybe, she wasn't completely to blame.

"Only one man's gonna have the answer to that question," Dragon said.

"Data," Rush and Dray said in unison.

"Where's he at?" Rush asked.

"I told you, he was finishing up rigging security gear at Blue Hills. I imagine he's still there with Trig and Reave. I know the farm hands fixed up a new door frame for Bailey's front door.

Rush grimaced. "Gonna have to buy one to put in it for now. I ain't finished with the one I'm makin'."

"That's fine," I said with a smile. It was sweet he had tried to make me a new front door rather than just going down to the local home improvement depot and picking up a new one.

"Only one thing for it, let's take a ride," Dragon said pushing to his feet.

"I'll grab my spare helmet and be right back," Rush said and leaned in and kissed me quickly on the lips before I could say or do anything. My gaze immediately went to my mother's whose dark eyes I'd inherited remained shuttered.

"Let's take a walk, Son." Dragon got up from the table and Dray echoed the movement. I swallowed hard and they left out the front door.

"Dray's girlfriend is pregnant," I said, and immediately followed up with, "I don't know why I just said that." Actually, I did. I was so nervous about the ass chewing that was likely to come from my mother's mouth that I would say just about anything that could and would draw fire. Unfortunately for me, it put her on the wrong track when it came to her train of thought.

"Are *you* pregnant?" she asked and I blinked wide-eyed.

"No!" I said startled, which wasn't precisely true. I was on one of the birth control shots, but Rush and I had been having *a lot* of unprotected sex. Still, my damn period was ridiculously fickle before the shot. After, it was really hit or miss. I hadn't had one yet, but that wasn't too surprising with all the stress… still, I was reminded, I needed to get checked up or take a test, just to be sure.

My mother searched my face, decided I wasn't lying, and sighed. She turned her face to look anywhere but at me and said, "I was always so jealous of my sister. Hated her, in fact, for a long time."

"What?" The change of subject was so abrupt I almost couldn't follow.

"She had the courage to follow her dreams, to do what made her happy. While me? I always tried to do what was *right*." She raised her hands and put the word 'right' into air quotes.

She laughed, a short, self-deprecating sort of sound and said, "I used to tell her how my children would grow up to be healthy, happy, productive members of society. That I was giving them a better life than she was providing for herself and Dray. I used to tell her I worried about how Dray would turn out, living around such a criminal element. I'm ashamed of that now, but I wholeheartedly believed that I was doing the right thing."

I swallowed hard. "And now?"

"Now, I feel the fool, but at least I am an honest one with the best of intentions."

Silence stretched between us for a span of heartbeats while I tried to decipher what my mother was trying to tell me. Finally, I ventured out hesitantly with, "So you're not mad about Rush and me?"

"I'm not happy, but I'm not angry, no."

Why? Why is the fact you aren't happy with me so absolutely soul crushing? I wanted to demand to know, but instead I just sat there, still, silent, and trying not to let my eyes mist too hard.

"Oh, don't look at me like that, Bailey! What am I supposed to think? My sister's involvement with this club is what eventually ended her life! I don't want that for my only daughter."

"No, I get it…" I said quietly the first tear sliding free.

"I'm not angry, Bailey. I'm scared. Scared that in my desperation, I've put you on a path that you can never come back from."

"Mom, you need to stop. It's not all on you! God, Rush was right – Philip and I both are old enough to know better and right now, I know that Rush, Uncle Dragon, and Dray have my best interests at heart, just like you. I have to make my own decisions now. That's part of being an adult."

"I understand that, Bailey Lynn Berling!" my mother snapped, and I felt about five inches tall when she used all three of my names like that. "What you need to understand is no matter how old you are or how big you get, you will *always* be my little girl."

Okay, well, point well taken.

"Right," I said and hugged myself a little.

"I love you," she said and she sniffed, her own tears spilling over. I blinked, taken aback. My mom rarely, if *ever*, uttered those three words. It always took me by surprise when she did, and worse? I always had this little internal voice crop up that said, Y*eah, right*, because I knew in the front of my head, even if the back of my head didn't get the message, that you didn't treat people you really loved like cast-off objects. I'd always been an afterthought to my family unless they needed me for a photo op, or to make them look good... and I always, *always*, did stellar at it because I craved their approval over everything else... their love... and of course, never felt like I had it or got it.

"I love you, too, Mom," I said and I meant it – even if it did feel wooden coming out of my mouth.

It was a picture-perfect family moment after that. We got up and hugged each other and that was how Rush found us. Hugging and crying, just generally being a couple of girls, but it felt so incredibly *fake* now. Especially considering I was sure I'd finally experienced the real thing and he was standing right there, waiting us out. When we broke apart, he cleared his throat to let us know he was there in the gentlest way possible. I knew, but my mother startled. She hadn't known, and it was then that it hit me, she meant everything she was saying… there wasn't anything fake about it and with all the baggage of my childhood and growing up the way I had? I nearly missed it.

Thank God for Rush… if he only knew.

"Come on, let's go see what we can find out," he said holding out his hand to me. I frowned and took it, wondering where his spare helmet was.

My mother stared at our hands for several moments but said nothing. We went outside to where my mother's car and driver waited, Dragon and Dray leaning against their bikes, smoking and talking to him.

The driver snapped to and scurried to open my mother's door for her. Rush got on his bike and tied a red bandana onto his head. Dray did likewise, tying a black bandana over his raven locks. He handed me his spare helmet out of his storage container on the side of his bike and winked at me and I felt my shoulders drop. I tilted my head to the side with a silent '*really?*' and he chuckled quietly. I mean, I could see it but couldn't hear it over the bikes.

I got on behind Rush, buckling the helmet on, my mother's silver Jag pulling smoothly past us, her face worried as she stared at me through the glass.

I wished she wouldn't, knew she would, and held onto Rush tightly as he started the bike, hating the clash of confusing emotions, my heart squaring off against my head once more. The wind was a soothing thing, the fierce wildness of it stripping off some of the insecurities, infusing me with a bit more confidence. I was beginning to realize things were all much more clear-cut when I was with Rush, my uncle, and my cousin. They didn't say one thing and then do another like my mother, brother, and father did.

Everything was much clearer, and there was something to be said for having the ability to take things at face value. Something you could *never* do in the circles I had been raised in. I was quickly starting to prefer and enjoy who I was and how things were with Rush, over who I was and the constant checking over my shoulder that I needed to do with my family and anyone I had been raised around. I knew in the front of my head, this wasn't supposed to be how things worked. It was how I was certainly raised, too... but it wasn't at the same time. There were the rules on the surface, then there were the rules underneath, and they rarely, if ever, were the same rules. I was really enjoying the fact that my cousin and his people lived by one set of rules, even if those rules were simply just theirs, and that they adhered to them so strongly.

There were three Sacred Hearts on my front porch when we arrived. Data with his laptop out at my table, a cord running through my window which had been lifted a crack to allow it to run to a power source inside. Then there was the man with the bright blue eyes who had congratulated my uncle on becoming a grandfather. Finally, there was a huge mountain of a man with a blond ponytail. I didn't know him, either.

The man with the blue eyes was helping some of my men finish up installing a new front door and he looked like he knew what he was doing. We pulled up, and I got down, Rush, Dragon, and Dray backing their bikes into line with the other three already present in front of one of my porch railings.

"Was wondering when y'all were gonna get here," the big blond guy said. "Data's already got something."

"Seriously?" Rush asked.

"Fuck, like you're surprised!" The blue-eyed man said.

My mother and I were given the right of way to mount the steps and Uncle Dragon gave the introductions.

"Bailey, Trudy, these here are my men, Trigger and Reaver. You've already met Data."

"Hello," I murmured, my mother simply giving an elegant nod.

"Hey, darlin', nice to meet you," Trigger said to me.

"Man, you gonna tag me in? I really wish you'd tag me in," Reaver said to Dragon, bouncing on the balls of his feet.

Dragon eyed him and said, "After the shit that went down with you, Cell, an' that little fuckwit? I'd be lyin' if I said I wasn't more 'n a little reluctant."

The man *pouted*. Like actually stuck out his lower lip and made a sad faced pout like a little kid before he whipped around and started working on my door again saying, "That was all Cell, man. We aren't even the same type of crazy."

Trigger, Rush, and Dray laughed, and I could tell Uncle Dragon was trying really hard not to. He shook his head and I sighed. "There's more room inside at the dining room table. Are we good to go through that door?" I asked.

"Yeah," the man, Reaver, said and his tone was dejected. He opened the door and ushered us all through. I immediately went to my kitchen to raid the fridge for cold drinks while everyone settled around the table. That done, I settled in to hear what Data had to say.

"Sorry to be the bearer of bad news, but it looks like your nephew is in deep with this development group on a few projects. This one being only one of them."

"What?" my mother asked and tried to peek at Data's laptop screen. He turned it so that she could see, and her expression became grim.

"I don't follow," Dragon said. "Real estate ain't never been my thing."

Cue a bunch of long explanations about loans, flipping properties, budget overages, and a bunch of contractor mumbo jumbo that *I* could barely follow. It seemed that my brother owed this development group *a lot* of money and in exchange for some forgiveness on some of those loans, they wanted his help in acquiring Blue Hills for their development plans for the area. My mother looked crushed, meanwhile, I was just mad. I shook my head and scrubbed my face with my hands.

"There's more, and I'm not sure what y'all are going to want to do with this…" Data trailed off and looked like he really regretted what he was about to say.

"Out with it, dude," Rush told him, tone encouraging rather than impatient.

"I managed to hack into some emails that went back and forth between your brother and the lead developer. They already know his attempts to sway you into their corner didn't work. They sent back a one-line email that's concerning. It reads: 'Fine, I'll handle it.'"

"Shit," Dray swore and my mother looked at me pointedly.

"Your meeting with Marion Cranston, how did that go?" she asked.

I swallowed and said, "I went to her home just yesterday… or was it the day before?" It was the reason why Rush had had the time to play in his woodshop. I'd completely forgotten about the results of that meeting given everything that'd happened since. I also had completely lost all track of time.

"And?" my mother pressed.

"And I think that I need to call her and that I definitely need to do what she suggested."

"Which was?" Dray demanded, arching a brow.

I shook my head and looked pointedly around the room. Data looked startled and said, "Oh, yeah!" He reached into his pocket and tossed a handful of small circuit boards and bits of wire onto the table.

"What are those?" my mother demanded.

"Bugs," Dragon told her.

"What?"

"Listening devices, Mom."

"I know what a bug is, Bailey... I just never thought –"

"That's why Marion Cranston wanted me to go to her place to discuss business," I said.

I told them what she'd told me. One, that she was sick of the way the south treated its women in regards to business and horses, and two, that her informational sources had told her that things weren't going well at Blue Hills and that she'd like to help – up to and including housing the horses kept here in case of an emergency. I was sure this qualified at this point.

"You and Rush can do it on yer own?" Dragon asked.

"Yes, shouldn't be too hard."

"Need to do it by cover of night and you need to start tonight; there's no tellin' when these fellas are going to show."

"How do we know they aren't watching?" Rush asked.

"We don't," Trig said.

"Right, tag Reave in. Go find 'em and do what you do," Dragon said.

"On it, P." Trigger got up from the table and opened the front door, he said to Reaver outside, "Nice work, you've been tagged in. Let's go."

"Woo hoo!" Reaver responded and the door shut on the rest of their conversation.

"You okay, Bailey?" I startled and looked at Rush who was looking at me, concern written all over his face.

"I, uh, yeah?"

"What's wrong, sweetheart?" Dragon asked.

I shook my head and said, "This stuff just doesn't happen in the real world... this is the kind of thing that happens in movies and on TV. This isn't *life*."

The men around the table shared a laugh and I frowned, perplexed. Data leaned forward and said, "Where do you think they get the idea to put this shit in movies and on TV?"

I thought about that, and the answer came from Dray, "It's art imitating life more often than not, Bales."

I sat there and spent the rest of the conversation quiet, not knowing what to say after that. Not realizing how naïve I'd really been until the veil had been unceremoniously snatched off my eyes. I guess I now really understood the phrase *ignorance is bliss*. It really was. I mean, I didn't know what to do with myself now that I could really see.

Rush reached over and took my hand under the table and threaded his fingers through mine, giving it a reassuring squeeze. I looked to him and sighed, and he gave me a warm smile that said, *We've got this.*

Yeah. It was overwhelming, sure, but I'm sure he was right... we had this.

25

R ush...

We got the call about three hours later that Trig and Reave had located the dude watching the farm and had taken him to Point Nowhere. It was a bummer finding out it was an inside man – an even bigger bummer to find out it was Jorge.

I should have seen that one, honestly. The dude was a little too eager to step up when Renaldo had gone down for the count. Reave and Trig were gonna sit on him. See what they could do to get Jorge on board with our way of thinkin' and flip him. Either way, Jorge was going to help us by feeding the fuckwits what we wanted while we moved shit around.

There wasn't any telling if any of the other guys were on the douche's payroll, so we had to wait until everyone had gone home to do anything. I'd taken on the responsibility of sleeping in the stables that night, so no one had a reason to be around. It was a responsibility everyone had been keen on skipping out on in favor of a good night's sleep, so that worked out well.

It was both a blessing and a surprise when Marion Cranston's crew showed up at around eleven o'clock at night to help get things moved out. We worked all night, too. Right up 'til dawn, and had no trouble at all, even when it came to Starry Eyed Dreamer, the super pregnant mare. It was a hell of a thing, moving all that horseflesh in one night. An even bigger thing that even as we were moving the thoroughbreds out, we had lesser bred but similar in appearance horse stock coming in to replace the five or so client horses we were boarding. We were fortunate that it was the time of year that it was and that anything that was racing was either on the circuit or with their owners. It wasn't the right time of year for active breeding, which was a bonus.

Trig and Reave were calling in with regular updates on their progress on the burner. Jorge was swearing up and down that there wasn't anyone else at the farm that was feeding information to the Giangiulio Development Group, the GDG for short, but we weren't going to take any chances on this end.

Add to that, for once, we were actually working *with* the cops. Well, Bailey's mom was. She went in with a pile of paperwork to the local sheriff's department and demanded to speak with detectives. She brought a thumb drive with everything her 'private investigator' had uncovered to boot. She and Data had signed and backdated a bunch of contracts and paperwork so everything on that front was legit and above board. He had his PI's license even though he didn't much use it and the backing of some big security firm that he worked for as a day job. Mostly as a 'consultant' read – hacker. Again, not all of what Data had dug up would stand up in court, but Bailey and her mom's lawyers had it all and it was the lawyer's job to make shit stick, not anyone else's.

It'd been a long, long, day after that. Bailey and I couldn't afford to sleep during the day and tip any of the guys coming in that we'd been up to anything. We'd managed to get through the day with Bailey runnin' the show and the excuse that Jorge was out sick with some kind of summer cold. It hadn't been pretty, but we powered through on coffee and I think even a prayer or two.

Finally, fuckin' finally, the last of 'em left. Now it was just us and the quiet of an empty house.

"I'm ordering a pizza," Bailey said and I nodded, kicking back in a chair at the dining room table. She stared at me for a long minute and it took me forever to fuckin' realize it wasn't me she was staring at with that vacant look, but rather the place I was sitting at.

"Call for the pizza, baby," I told her and she snapped out of whatever waking nightmare she'd been in.

"Then what?" she asked, suspicious.

"Then I'm going to lay you on this tabletop and lick that sweet pussy. I wanna see if I can make you come in thirty minutes or less."

She scoffed and laughed, her amused and incredulous expression melting away to total disbelief. "You're serious," she said finally, and I nodded. "Why?"

"Replace the bad with the good." I gave a shrug. "At least I'd like to try, anyway."

She came over to me then and straddled my lap, lowering herself into it. She pressed her mouth to mine and the kiss was everything and nothing I'd ever experienced before. I wrapped my arms around her and held her to me, tongues mingling, bodies pressed tight. She broke the kiss and I smiled, amused and said, "Call for that pizza then get your fuckin' pants off."

"Sausage and pepperoni okay?" she asked breathlessly.

"Don't fuckin' care," I whispered.

She stood up and tucked the phone between her chin and shoulder pulling off her boots while it rang. She fuckin' strip teased the entire time she was ordering, all the while her voice innocent and her wide brown eyes full of mischief. As soon as she hung up the damn phone, I snatched her off her feet. She squealed, laughing, and I set her on the edge of the table, nudging the dining room chair out of the way. I kneeled between her legs, shoulders bracing her knees apart. Her chest rose and fell with heated breaths as I licked her, one long slow stroke of the flat of my tongue.

"Oh, God!" Her voice deep with desire, she arched and I teased her opening with my fingertips. Oh yeah, she was wet, ready, this was going to be a snap. I wondered if I could make her come twice before the pizza guy got here and thrust two fingers inside her. She groaned, her hands sliding over her body, smoothing over the fabric encasing her torso provocatively.

I teased around inside of her, looking for that secret spot that if you were a dude and had half a fuckin' brain when it came to sex, wasn't a secret at all. She moaned, her hips arching when I found it and I couldn't help but smile. I worked her up, stroking over that slightly more textured patch of skin just inside and on her roof. She sighed and gripped the front of her blouse, knotting her fingers in the cotton.

I teased gently at her clit with my tongue and she let out a rush of breath and a soft, "Holy shit," which meant I was doin' something right, so I kept at it. Her breathing steadily ramping up and becoming more labored, her pussy tensing down around my fingers, a sure sign I was definitely going to beat the delivery time and I was definitely going for doing it twice.

She arched and cried out sharply, her body going as taut as one of Archer's bowstrings and I smiled, backing off so she didn't clamp her legs around my head and suffocate me. Don't laugh, it's happened, usually with alcohol involved. Bailey finally went limp, spent and panting on the table.

"Oh, my God!" she gasped and I chuckled.

"Ride ain't over yet, baby."

"What?"

I didn't answer, I just went back to work.

Her body arched, and she let out a long, low cry of passion just as the doorbell rang. *I win*, I thought to myself as I got up, wiping the back of my hand across my mouth. I opened the door to a wide-eyed pizza delivery kid, took the box and handed him a fifty out of my wallet. All the while he tried to peek around the door that kept my woman hidden. I smiled and said, "Thanks kid," and shut the door on his curious face.

Bailey lay breathing hard, sprawled on the table, eyes slightly unfocused and glazed, staring at the ceiling. I smiled and dropped the box at the head of the table and went around to the side, leaning over her.

"How you doing, baby?" I asked softly.

"Good," she moaned, head lolling languidly on her neck to look at me.

"Yeah?"

"Yeah, just give me a minute."

"Oh no, no, you take your time." She was floatin' and I smiled, putting my hand under her shirt to caress her ribs. She closed her eyes and shivered at the little touch. I waited patiently until she went to sit up, then I helped her.

"That was hot," she said and I laughed.

"What can I say? I like my dessert first."

"Mm..." She gestured and I bent down to kiss her. She kissed me back and it was beautiful.

"I love you," she whispered uncertainly against my mouth and it was music to my ears.

"I love you, too, babe."

I considered her, sitting there, sex-tousled, her eyes dilated with afterglow and lips swollen from my kiss, and pulled off my tee. I helped her out of her blouse, little tank top thing, and bra and slid my shirt over her head.

"Sit right there, I'll get plates."

She nodded, swinging her feet a little and I brought over plates and the little bleach disinfecting wipes from under the sink to clean up. It was a good way to spend our evening. I had no complaints.

A long shower together to relax us both the rest of the way, and for once I was too tired to even try to get mine. We fell into bed and were both out like a traffic light inside two seconds. I think that's why it took so long for me to come to, to realize something was even wrong. Bailey was shaking me, and the room was illuminated by the orange glow of fire.

I sat up, just as the next bottle crashed against the front of the house, and just like in the fuckin' movies, it went up with a 'fwoosh' sound that was just fucking unbelievable. I leapt out of bed, Bailey already up and pulling on my discarded shirt, grabbing up her phone. I pulled on my pants and grabbed my gun off the nightstand. I looked around for a half a second, still a bit disoriented from sleep, and grabbed my cut off the wingback chair, swinging it on over my bare chest.

"Come on, let's go!"

I grabbed her hand and we bolted out of the room for the front door. Flames were already licking on the other side of the glass window set high into it, so we turned tail and bolted for the back door, just as what looked like a flaming mason jar crashed through the fucking back window. It shattered on the hardwood and the flames lit up the inside of the house, effectively blocking our escape, the fire leaping up, the heat and adrenaline already having me break out in a sweat.

"The barn!" Bailey choked out between coughs and we ran for the door that adjoined the house to the smaller barn. I put my cut between my hand and the knob and gave it a twist, not knowing what to expect and hoping like hell it wasn't on fucking fire out here too. My eyes watered and stung from the smoke pouring through the house. A mix of camp-fire and burning plastic assaulting my nose, overwhelming in its intensity.

I pulled open the door and nothing, smoke poured into the barn from the open door behind us, but it wasn't on fire in here… yet.

"Get in the truck," I ordered, and Bailey went for the driver's seat, already on her phone, talking fast, almost too fast, having to stop and repeat herself to the emergency operator on the other side. We'd parked one of the farm trucks in here, backing it in in case of emergency. I think this more than qualified.

"Yes, I already said that, we're trapped inside!" Bailey cried into the phone and I went to the barn doors and unbolted them, just as the sound of breaking glass hit the other side – again, with that sound of flame catching on an accelerant. I shook my head and went back to the truck and got in on the passenger side.

"Punch it, go through it; don't stop, Bailey."

She cried, aghast. "What!?"

"It's on fire, now go through it!"

She pulled down on the shifter, putting the automatic in drive and popped the emergency brake.

"God, I hope this works!" she cried and romped on the gas. I hoped so too, the barn doors opened out, so it was a fair chance we'd make it out just fine but not so much if these assholes started shooting at us.

We hit the doors and they crashed outward, the truck lumbering through and out into the night. A pop and a ping, and fuck me swing-ing, they *were* shooting at us.

"Just keep going, baby! Don't stop!"

Bailey ducked low over the steering wheel and cried out when there was a loud explosion, the truck swerved in the gravel and she fought the wheel. They'd hit a tire, fuck…

"Ride it on the rim!" I cried, "Don't stop!" The back window shattered, and I turned around in my seat, knocking it out. The house and barn were in flames, and I mean roaring total-loss flames. I finished knocking out a bigger hole in the back window's safety glass and couldn't see anything to shoot at but returned fire anyway, popping off two rounds, hoping the motherfuckers would dive for cover.

Bailey kept going, in the initial chaos, while we could still breathe, she'd called fire and rescue. Who the fuck knew if they would get here in time to mitigate any damage to the house and honestly, who the fuck cared? I was more concerned with keeping *us* alive long enough for the cavalry to arrive, be it fire and rescue or my brothers.

Another pop, and the driver's side window, Bailey's window, shattered, a bullet hole punching through the windshield. She screamed, overcorrected and we went into a skid on the gravel drive. I flung out an arm to pin her back against the seat as the truck careened into the ditch off the side of the driveway and went right into the goddamn split-log fence of the second paddock. I pulled Bailey across the bench seat, toward me, the truck was leaning pretty heavy to my side and at an angle, providing some decent cover if we could get out and use it to our advantage. I needed to get Bailey to cover before something happened to her.

She slid out of the truck and into my arms and I ducked down, looking for our assailants. They were good, pros if I had to guess. Sirens were wailing in the distance and I peeked over the bed of the truck. Lights were flashing out on the highway, still a good distance from the mouth of the driveway. A shot rang out and I ducked. It pinged off the side of the truck and Bailey screamed, huddling in a tight ball against the back tire. I popped up and returned fire, but I still couldn't see what the fuck I was supposed to be shooting at.

I pulled Bailey into my arms and held her as the sirens drew nearer and the hidden threat melted back further into the dark. I pressed the gun into Bailey's hands and said, "My brother, Nox, lent this to you because of the threats. You got it?"

She nodded dumbly and I pressed her close, holding onto her tight as gravel pinged the other side of the truck, the fire truck lumbering past to set up and start working on the blaze. We were saved, after a fashion, but the motherfuckers that'd done this? They best be afraid. I was coming for them, and I was bringing hell with me.

26

B ailey...

The sheriff's deputy and a paramedic found us crouched behind the truck and once again they tried to put Rush in handcuffs, simply judging him by his vest. I started screaming at them to leave him alone and clung to him and that seemed to settle things down. My house, along with the attached smaller barn were burning in the near distance and I was helpless, forced to watch as my life, livelihood, and sense of safety burned to cinders with it.

I was sitting on the back step of an ambulance, Rush curled around me, wrapped in one of those Mylar blankets and shivering despite the warmth of the evening. Rush tightened his hold around me as Uncle Dragon, Dray, and a few of the other men of the Sacred Hearts pulled up. Nox was the first to reach us, crushing both me and Rush into a hug.

"You okay, man?" he demanded and looked so relieved I thought there might be tears.

"Yeah, fine."

"Do you mind?" the paramedic asked. Nox backed off and she went back to work, dabbing at a cut in my hairline from flying glass from the truck.

"She alright?" Dragon called and the paramedic turned with a scowl.

"He's my uncle," I said by way of explanation and she looked perplexed for a second.

"You don't look Mexican," she said, and I didn't even have it in me to feel outraged.

I rolled my eyes and added, "By marriage."

"Oh." She was turning bright pink under the glare of the lights from the back of the truck and the incendiary look she was getting from my uncle and cousin. We ignored her pretty much completely after that.

"I'm fine, Uncle Dragon, just really shook up. Can someone check on the horses we have here?"

Archer grunted, "I'm on it," and Rush unfurled from where he'd wrapped himself around me.

"I'll go with him if you're good."

"I'm good, I'm good, just go check on them, please." They may not have been the thoroughbreds worth hundreds of thousands of dollars, but they were real, living creatures and were probably terrified by the smoke. Guilt swamped me that I was using them the way I was.

Dray sat down next to me and grabbed my hand, squeezing. "You okay?" he asked low and controlled and I shook my head, staring past the paramedic tending my small cuts at my burning house.

"No, Dray-dray. I'm really not okay," I confessed, if only to get them to stop asking.

"It's just a house, sweetheart. We'll rebuild it, it ain't nothing compared to you or Rush. Our people, we can't replace."

"What am I going to do?" I whispered and my cousin put his arm around my shoulders. I leaned my head on his and took the comfort for what it was, remembering when we were kids, before my mother's true colors had the chance to affect us and start the divide.

"You ain't gotta do nothing except hold firm. We've got this now." The look on my uncle's face was terrifying. I don't think I had ever seen it before. What was more terrifying was the look on my cousin's face, one that mirrored his father's near exactly. Both of them had the flames of the house reflected in their glittering black eyes and for a moment, I could believe it wasn't a reflection so much as the hell of wrath projected from within themselves. I shuddered and Reaver came up.

"I got Hayden bringing a cage to take you back to the club," he said. I shook my head.

"I have my truck."

"Honey, your truck is sitting in the ditch over there, the front end pushed in by the fence." It was a redheaded man who'd spoken. He raised a Bic lighter to the cigarette dangling from his lips and cupping the flame, lit the end taking a strong pull off of it.

"That's the farm truck. My truck is in the garage," I told him.

"Well excuse the fuck out of me," he said.

"Cell." Dragon's tone held a note of warning and the guy turned neutral brown eyes on him but didn't comment any further.

"Impressive," I muttered to my uncle, and the man said, "Ain't got nothin' to do with obedience. Don't get it twisted. I just really want to be tagged in on this."

I wanted to ask why but the paramedic was still here, and Dragon barked, "Duracell!" The man smirked and walked a ways away, the coal on the end of his cigarette glowing in counterpoint to the embers that my house was becoming.

"Told you it wasn't me," Reaver muttered and Dragon shot him a withering look. Reaver held up his hands in surrender, a mischievous sparkle in his blue eyes but it was Trigger who started talking.

"Let Reave's ol' lady drive you back to the club, honey. You been through a shock. You just ain't fit to do it."

I nodded and just kind of gave up, a wave of exhaustion and emotion just sort of swamping me.

Rush and Archer returned with the news that the horses were spooked, but by all appearances, doing just fine. The firefighters had the blaze under control and the house and smaller barn attached seemed to be the only losses so far. The police took a statement from me and then Rush while I sat there and shivered in nothing but Rush's tee and the stupid emergency blanket. All my clothes, all my belongings continued to burn throughout the rest of the night.

Finally, as dawn began to light the eastern horizon, we were told we were free to go. I stood up from where I had been relocated to the back of Hayden's SUV. She was incredibly kind and vivacious, taking the evening's events in stride like they happened every day, which worried me to tell you the truth. Rush had retrieved his bike from the garage and leaned on it nearby. His warm, cognac eyes roaming over me, fixed on me, all while his older brother, Archer, and his twin, Nox, talked to him in low even tones.

The set of his broad shoulders told me just how furious he was about the whole thing. I, on the other hand, was too emotionally drained to really feel anything one way or the other about anything except for my desire for a hot shower, a real bed, and some real clothes. Hayden sat down on the tailgate of her Lexus with me and said, "My dad boards his horses here sometimes."

I blinked and turned toward her. "Who's your dad?" She gave me a one-thousand-watt smile and said "Jacob Michaels."

Well, now *that* was a name I recognized. I blinked stupidly and just barely managed to keep my mouth shut on the burning question, *How the hell did Jacob Michael's daughter end up marrying a biker?*

Hayden laughed and winked at me leaning in to say in a conspiratorial whisper, "I can see it all over your face, and it's a long story. I promise to tell you when the boys put us all in lockdown to go take care of business."

I frowned and she smiled, and it wasn't entirely happy. I didn't quite know what it was, but it was something I was likely going to find out and soon. Rush came over and the guys started moving around like we were making ready to leave.

"I can't leave the horses," I blurted and Rush came over to me.

"You aren't, baby; look." He pointed at the driveway and the line of three pickups coming down it. I frowned and then realized, "Oh, God. No one called the men to tell them not to come to work today."

"It's okay, I'll handle it." He kissed my forehead and said to Hayden, "Take her home for me, make sure she gets a hot shower and tucked into my room safe."

"No problem, Rush." Hayden said, and Rush led me to the passenger side of Hayden's SUV.

"I love you, baby. Go try to get some rest, I'll be right behind you."

I nodded and kissed him back, his lips warm and comforting against mine. I didn't want to let him go, but I supposed that was the price you paid for growing into your own and shouldering the mantle of 'adult.'

The car ride was silent for the most part until Hayden broke it with, "They can be heavy-handed sometimes, you know? Not telling us everything. It can be infuriating, but it's for our own good... God, as much as I *hate* having to say that."

I turned from the window and looked at her, frowning. "I don't understand."

"No, I suppose I need to explain a little better, don't I?"

"It'd be nice."

"Okay, I've been around the club for a few years now. In all that time, I've never seen any of the guys get violent for the sake of being violent. I've never seen one of the boys do something to start shit, but I've seen them finish plenty."

I blinked. "Why are you telling me this?"

"Because word is, your mom has filled your head since practically birth that these guys are all violent rabble rousers who go out and cause a bunch of mayhem at every opportunity." I blinked again, long and slow and tipped my head thinking about it.

"Yeah, okay, I can't say you're wrong there, but that's kind of how things were, I mean, before –"

"Before your aunt died?"

"Yeah."

She sucked in a deep breath and let out a gusty sigh. "I know, and that must be a really hard one for you to wrap your mind around, but I'm telling you, I've *never* not *once* seen these guys do anything to anyone that didn't do something to them first."

"Okay, again, why are you telling me this?"

"Because I can see this is tearing you up something awful and that you *really* like Rush."

"I do," I said softly.

"Okay, I'm going to give you the super short version on what happens next."

"Okay."

"The guys are pretty much going to call all the ol' ladies and their families into the club. Unfortunately, as the women and children, we get to do a lot of hurry up and wait while the boys go out and take care of business."

"And just what is *that* supposed to mean?" I asked. "What does '*taking care of business*' look like?"

"Aggravating as hell, but we don't get to know what that looks like. It's for our own safety."

I shifted uneasily and Hayden sighed. "I'm not doing a very good job of explaining this, am I?"

"Not really, no."

"Look, you're tired, you've been through a lot; can we table this talk until after you've had some food, a shower, and some rest?"

"Sure," I said. I didn't want to sound bitchy here, but I honestly wasn't in the mood for this conversation. I didn't want to meet new people, I didn't want to be fawned over; I just wanted to be left alone.

We pulled up into the club's parking lot and when Hayden went to park, I asked her, "Can we just go around back, closer to Rush's room?"

"Sure, not feelin' like dealing with other people right now?"

"I hope that doesn't make me a complete bitch."

"Not at all, honey." She laughed a little and pulled around onto the asphalt track, taking the long way around so that the passenger side of the car would be closer to the door.

"Thanks," I said softly.

"No problem, I'll go find Disney. He's the keeper of the keys around here. He'll have the spare to get into Rush's room. In the meantime, take a hot shower. I'll scare up some towels while you're in there."

"Sounds good," I said, adding, "Thanks."

"No problem."

I unfastened my seat belt and slid from the car into the cooler morning air. It was still pretty warm and promising to get hotter as the day went on, so I was grateful to slip into the cinderblock building and out of the punishing rays of the sun.

I went into the bathroom at this end of the hall and stopped in front of the mirror. There wasn't anything amiss about my appearance, really. Hair tousled, skin a bit too pale from my ordeal, my summer tan almost floating on top and looking wrong, somehow. I had a bit of a scab just at the edge of my hairline to the left side of my forehead from where the flying safety glass had nicked me. I closed my eyes on the sudden well of fear that opened up and swallowed me whole. Watching that windshield spider web, that hole opening up, the passenger side window disintegrating… God, a few inches to whoever fired that shot's right and I wouldn't be here right now.

I leaned heavily on the white porcelain sink basin and finished taking stock of my reflection. White tee hanging on me several sizes too big, spotted with my blood, streaked with black soot. I shuddered, and turned away, not wanting to see anymore. I pulled the offending covering off my body and dropped it into the wastebasket, stepping into the nearest shower and turning it on. I waited for it to heat up to a tolerable level and took a deep breath, thrusting my face into the spray.

It felt good, even though the tiny cuts to my scalp and even some to my feet stung like a mother. It felt even better to be washing the nightmare of the past several hours away, though the thought, *if only it were really that easy*, did come to mind.

The door opened and I looked back over my shoulder and yelped. A tall, skinny, and heavily tattooed biker with long brown hair held up one hand, a set of keys dangling from them and cried, "I'm the gay one! It's cool, it's cool. I just came to bring you towels and the key to Rush's place. You remember which room it is?"

"Yeah, yeah! I do, just get out!" I tried to cover myself with no success and he at least kept his eyes averted.

"Right, sorry, I thought you knew!" he said lamely and bolted. He ducked out the door and I stood there, chest heaving and started to laugh. Once I started, I couldn't stop, until finally the laughter was drowned by my tears. I ended up on my knees under the punishing hot spray and cried until I didn't have anything left in me to cry out. It was a super shitty way to end my night, I finally decided. Alone, afraid, in tears, on a strange bathroom floor with no home left, no clothes, no car – my keys including the spare having gone up with the house, and just the unanswered question of *Why didn't I just sign the fucking paperwork*, making slow, lazy circles in my head.

I used the large pump action bottles of body wash, shampoo, and conditioner sitting in the metal bracket bolted to the wall between this shower and the next and cleaned up to the point that if I kept scrubbing, I was going to take skin. Finally, I realized the kind of dirt and grit I was after to wash away wasn't a physical thing, at least not anymore. So, I gave up and shut off the water. I went out to the bench where the tattooed biker had left everything and found a regular-sized bath towel on top of a larger bath sheet towel with a key ring sitting neatly in the middle of it all. I set the key aside and listened to it slip and fall to the floor as I wrapped my hair in the first towel and dried off with the second. Finally, I wrapped the larger bath sheet around me from armpit to knees and sighed. I plucked the keyring off the floor from where it had fallen and went in search of Rush's room.

It was the second door I tried, and I stepped into it, grateful that it locked but missing Rush keenly. I swallowed hard and went to the dresser that was carved to match the beautiful bed. I opened drawers until I found what I was looking for. I don't think Rush had ever worn the boxer shorts, but that was okay. I kind of liked the easier access without. I pulled them on, then pulled one of his classic white tee shirts on over my head, knocking the towel loose.

I pulled it out of the neckline and off my hair and used it to rub my hair as dry as I could get it, staring at myself in the mirror above the dresser and wishing he were here. Afraid for what he might be doing. I knew they were operating outside the confines of the law now. I understood why, but I had so much to be afraid for… that he would get hurt, that he would go to prison for whatever he did, or the very worst thing of all… that I would never, ever, see him again because he was killed.

I sat heavily on the edge of the bed, and stared sightlessly at my reflection, turning all of this over in my mind. God, the implications were awful, and my state of mind was such that it couldn't and wouldn't go anywhere good no matter how hard I tried to make it.

A light rapping fell at the door rousing me a bit. I stood up and went to it, unlocking it and opening it a crack to a small woman with long black hair and her deep blue eyes peered up at me through a fringe of bangs.

"Bailey?"

"Uh, yeah…"

"I'm Dani, Red-Thirteen's ol' lady."

"Oh, hi…" I didn't want to be rude, but I didn't want to just let her in to Rush's room, either.

She smiled and helped me out by saying, "I don't want to come in; I just thought you might be interested in some of my party favors." She held out her hand with a tiny little pill on it and I recognized it immediately. It was hard to grow up rich and *not* know what Xanax was.

"I really want that," I said and hung my head.

"Hey, no shame in that. I know how it goes, believe me." I held out my hand and she dumped the tiny pill into it and brought her other hand into view, a glass of water in it.

"Try and get some sleep. I was supposed to get your sizes so we could get some clothes for you, but if you want to wait, that's cool too."

"Oh, um… I wear a size eight jeans and a large shirt."

"Great, we'll see about rounding something up for you so we can take you shopping."

I groaned, "Oh, God, my purse, my wallet, *everything* went up with the house!"

"It's okay, we'll figure it out. Just take that and try not to worry about it for now."

I took the damn pill and downed the water handing the glass back. "Thanks Dani," I murmured and she smiled.

"No problem, we'll see you later."

I closed the door, mind racing while I waited for the little pill to kick in and even me out. I didn't even know what had happened to my cellphone. The last time I remember having it, I was panicking and talking too quickly to the emergency operator, telling her we were trapped in my burning house.

I pressed the heels of my hands into my eye sockets and took a bunch of deep breaths trying to keep from bursting into another fit of useless crying. I was anxiety-riddled, pacing Rush's room like a caged thing and for a half second, I almost panicked, wondering what would happen if I got stuck like this and the pill didn't work.

I tried to make myself useful, but Rush was so damn neat I didn't have anything to do. I picked up my towels and hung them on the hooks set into the back of the door, having no place else to put them that wouldn't ruin furniture or cause the carpet to go musty.

After that, I turned to Rush's beautiful but too-large bed. I pulled back the blankets and got in, pulling the pillow Rush used most against my chest, hugging it tightly, breathing in his smell. I don't remember anything after that. Like nothing. Maybe the pill hadn't been Xanax after all, maybe it had been something more potent. In any case, whatever it was? I think I liked it.

27

R ush...

Ringing came from the cab of the truck. *Shit, Bailey's phone.* She hadn't been gone ten minutes, my brothers and I still standing around surveying the damage in the new light of day. Bailey and I had been asleep in that house which was now burned halfway down to the foundation. I shook my head and went down the small embankment, ripping open the bullet-riddled truck's driver's side door. I scooped up the phone and swore.

"What is it?" Dragon called.

"Bailey's mom," I called back and swiped a finger across the screen. "Hello?" I answered. Silence on the other end of the line for a span of one seized up heartbeat.

"Where is my daughter?" Bailey's mother demanded.

"Safe, on her way to the club," I answered. "This is Rush."

"It's all over the news," she said and I looked up.

"Well, that *does* explain the helicopter," I said.

"What happened?"

"I'd better give you to Dragon."

"I'm asking *you*," she said. "You were there, with my girl, what happened?"

"Alright, damn!" I told her in as few words as possible.

"But she's alright?" she asked incredulously.

"Shook up, a few cuts from flying glass, but yeah. She's gonna be fine."

"My poor Bailey," she whimpered. A mother's love, I guess. I wouldn't know myself, but I'd heard about it often enough to believe it existed.

"It's going to be okay, ma'am. I'm going to take care of it."

"You do that and don't you worry about a thing. I have the best legal defense team."

I snorted, I didn't plan on getting arrested, but if it happened? I didn't think for one minute, Bailey's mom would follow through. With the way her son turned out, I fully expected her to leave my ass to rot ensuring her daughter was safe not only from the big bad developer, but the big bad biker, too. It was how these rich bastards were. They operated above the law, while us? We just operated outside it.

I just handed the phone to Dragon at that point and went over to my bike which Archer and I had pushed out here. I was lucky I kept my keys in my cut and I'd grabbed it, otherwise I'd be sitting here fucked without a way out of here other than sittin' bitch 'til I could grab my spare.

"Where the fuck you think you're going, brother?" Archer demanded.

I dug through my saddlebags and cursed. No spare boots. Fucking damn it. I must have taken 'em in the house.

"What size, dude?" Duracell called and I looked back over my shoulder at him.

"Twelves."

"Woo hoo! I can hook you up," Reaver said and flipped open one of his bags. He came up with a pair of paint stained work boots.

"Nice," I muttered and pulled them on without socks.

"They're eleven-and-a-half's but they might work."

"A bit snug, but fuck it, I ain't got better."

"Here, put this on under your cut. You look like a –"

"Cell!" Dray barked and Cell corrected at the last second from what he'd been about to say to "Tool."

He tossed me a spare black wife-beater. I shook my head, knowing full well what he'd been about to say. We were all trying to get him to fuckin' fix it on a kind of Disney and Aaron. The last thing we wanted was Disney to get in a beef with Duracell over something he'd picked up and used so often in prison that he kept on with it on the outside. He didn't think about it, he just said it. Bad habits being a pain in the ass to break and all of that.

My twin held my cut while I pulled the shirt on over my head. Dragon was still on Bailey's cell, talking to her mom, nodding every so often and saying things like 'right' and 'I hear yah.'

I held out my hand for my cut and Nox handed it to me; he gave me a meaningful look and I shook my head. I couldn't promise him what he wanted, that I wouldn't do something stupid or wind up in jail. His shoulders dropped and he tilted his head, his expression screaming *Really, dude?*

I had one word for him, "Maren."

That shut him up. He sighed and hung his head. He'd pulled some stupid shit for his girl only around six months ago or so. Stupid shit

232

that could have and would have ended his career and ruined his clean record. He wasn't one to fuckin' talk. Only luck and some strong-armed tactics by cover of night kept his ass straight and the cops out of it.

"I don't plan on killin' nobody," I said softly so only he could hear. "But I *am* about to fuck some shit up."

"Just be careful," he muttered.

"Careful as a virgin on her wedding night," Archer said sucking his teeth.

"Man, fuck you dude. You have Mel and the boys to worry about now," I told him.

"I get locked up, the club'll take care of things 'til I get out."

"Jesus, Archer, there's more than just finances and shit to take care of now. Those boys don't need an absentee father," Nox hissed.

"It's a moot fuckin' point. Nox, Arch, take your asses back to the club-house and post up. Watch your brother's girl. Rush, Reave, Cell, Dray, you're with me," Dragon ordered.

"Trig, Blue, Data, head on back to the club with Nox and Archer and wait for our phone call. Data, listen to the scanners and have bail money ready should it come to that."

"Yeah, you got it."

"Em is gonna fuckin' kill me if I get locked up," Dray griped.

"It's fuckin' family," Dragon said. "You're in this to win this because you got a boy on the way."

"We don't know it's a boy, yet," Dray protested.

"It's a boy," Dragon said and grinned.

"Girl pops out, I'm going to laugh at your ass," I said.

"Girl pops out, I'ma be like, 'you better put that back,'" Dray said.

Laughter went around and we mounted up. I'd added one thing to my bike for the trip we were agreed on and about to make. It was time for a public display of what happened when you fucked with a Sacred Hearts' man's family – let alone the president's. I patted the end of the bat sticking out of one of my bags and hit the ignition on my bike, starting her up. I fell into formation and when we reached the highway went right toward the freeway that'd take us to the city, while the rest of the boys peeled off left to go back to the club.

I was amped, I was ready, and I was gonna hurt a motherfucker. I was gonna hurt him bad. We rode out toward the GDG and hell rode with us. When we got there, we stopped about two blocks away and put on shades, covering the lower half of our faces bandito style with bandanas and pulling on baseball hats, generic black – nothing with a logo or traceable. Last thing we did was take duct tape to our rear plates to cover them up from any eyes in the sky. We were as prepared as we were going to get. I straddled my bike and pulled on a pair of gloves, everyone else doing the same. Wouldn't do to leave finger-prints behind.

We rode right into the lot of the office complex that housed their offices, gliding right up to the front of the place, parking the bikes haphazardly and pretty much taking up all their parking. I pulled the bat out of my bag and went to the front door, locked and on a buzzer. Well fuck that shit.

"Batter up!" Duracell crowed and I adjusted my grip, tested my swing, and took out the front door. The glass shattered on the second or third hit, crumbling in a sparkling fall. Safety glass, like the shit that had cut up my Bailey last night when the hired goons this motherfucker had sent shot out her fuckin' truck windows.

"You can't come in here, I'm calling the police!" his secretary was screaming, and Cell pointed his gun in her face.

"You ain't doin' shit but sitting down and shutting the fuck up while we have a chat with your boss!" he snarled.

"Which way?" Dray demanded. She stood with her hands up and pointed down a hall. Dragon led the way with me right on his heels and Reaver right on mine. Dray stayed back with Cell to keep him on a leash.

Dragon stopped in front of the big man's office, reared back, and kicked that fucker in with one blow. The door flew back and hit the wall, swinging forward violently. The man behind the desk, olive skinned and dark haired wasn't no slouch. He was a bigger dude, the cut of his suit screaming 'tailored to fit' but it looked like he knew how to throw down.

I walked right up to his desk as he set his phone gently back in its cradle saying, "I've called the police."

"Bully for you," I breathed and he leaned back.

"Get up," Dragon ordered.

The man stood up slowly, cautiously and came around the desk. I backed off and gave him some room. Dragon who was a head and shoulders shorter than the guy looked up at him.

"You know what happens when you fuck with our family, *culo*?" It was everything in me not to laugh. Dragon was pouring on his stereotypical, Mexican gangbanger, hood rat persona; which he only did when working on problems like this. It fucked with the cops when they came knocking looking for the Mexican dude expecting him to sound a certain way, only to have D. come out sounding like a down-home country hick. He'd adapted entirely too well to his environment, comin' up around these parts, and despite his appearance sounded like a white ass, country bumpkin, motherfucker when he talked.

"I'm sure I have no idea what you're talking about," Giangiulio said and was pretty much sneering at our president.

"You *really* don't want to find out, dude," Reaver said smiling.

"Oh?"

You know, I really hated these rich ass fuckwits who thought their money could get them out of any problem that came along.

"We're going to ruin your life," I said and Dragon and Reaver froze at my tone. "Pull down everything you've built brick by fucking brick. You try to touch anyone in any way that doesn't have to do with a boardroom, or whatever legal way you have to fuckin' deal with 'em, and I'm gonna find you and I'm gonna fuckin' kill you."

He laughed, or started to, but I gut checked him with the bat. He doubled over and I brought it down across his back and wasn't too gentle about it. He sprawled face first on his nice office carpet.

"You've graduated to the major leagues, motherfucker. Don't think for a minute we ain't serious. We're watching you," Reaver said and his gaze was as cold as a winter's sky. Dude coughed and tried to get up, so I served his ass more of a beatdown.

"That's for Renaldo Hernandez," I said. "You don't even want to know what the retribution for Bailey Berling is gonna look like. You've got two days to wrap the shit up surrounding Blue Hills. Two days to drop whatever pipe dream of a project you got surrounding that place. You don't, I'm comin' back and hell's comin' with me. I meant it, mother-fucker... brick by goddamn brick."

We needed to leave if he had called the cops, so we did. When we went back out the lobby, Dray and Cell went first, Dragon next, then me, then Reaver bringing up the rear. We got on our bikes and rode out, taking the opposite end of the office complex that the sirens were coming in from. We got out, by the skin of our teeth, now it was on to phase two of our little plan. We were pretty much expecting a raid on the club as well as some of us having our asses thrown in jail, at least for questioning that night, but there wasn't going to be much the cops could do with all of us giving each other alibis.

The cops could and would hassle us for a few hours, but that was all they'd be able to do. We knew how the game was played and we were all-in. It was just a question of if we were gonna get away with it.

Right now, we couldn't worry about it. We got about five miles from the place and put our cuts in our saddlebags. The cops were going to be looking for Sacred Hearts' guys, not single riders. Next, we pulled the tape from our plates and availed ourselves of our baseball hats and bandanas, throwing them in a random dumpster. We split up from there, taking a joy ride in any direction for about ten, fifteen minutes before turning and heading back toward the club.

I didn't get stopped, and I didn't see any of the other guys stopped and getting hooked up for a ride back to the pokey. Looked like we were in the clear until the police came knocking. It'd take them a while though.

I parked my bike back at the club. Dragon was already here and Reaver, but Dray and Cell were still in the wind. I gave a nod to Dragon when I came through the door and he came up to me. No women were in sight, it was just us guys out here. Good deal.

"Dray made it home just fine. He's got a damn fine queen in that woman, she'll cover his ass. She gets it."

"And Cell?"

"Stopped at the diner to eat and see that waitress of his and Blue's."

"Them fuckers ever gonna pull the trigger on that?" I wondered out loud.

"Don't know, not my business. I guess Dani gave Bailey one of her anxiety pills and it knocked Bailey on her ass. She's been asleep in your room. I think now would be a good time for you to get cleaned up and look in on her."

I nodded. "Might be a minute before I get to see her again if we missed something."

"Even careful criminals fuck up eventually," Dragon agreed.

"What's next?"

"Data's been monitoring their shit, you fucked up Giangiulio pretty good, broke a couple ribs. They transported him to the hospital out there in the big city."

"Too bad they didn't take him to Mercy General."

"Right?" Dragon chuckled an evil little sound.

"I'm gonna grab a shower and see about Bailey. I suppose we'll know if and when the cops get here."

"Might be a few days, but yeah. Yeah, we will. Take care of that bat," he ordered.

"Already on it."

I took it out back and to my woodshop, sliced it into kindling and dumped it in the firepit out back. A little lighter fluid, a match, and presto, one piece of evidence that wouldn't be of any use. Especially since I dumped a bunch of cookies from other projects and similar woods in with them.

"Little early for a fire, isn't it?" Dani asked from her shop and I smiled.

"Figured barbecue for lunch," I called back.

"Ah," she said all-knowingly. I laid the cooking grate over the fire and gave her a nod.

"She's out cold," she called after me. "Probably will be for a while yet."

"Thanks for looking after her," I called back.

"Of course."

I went to my room and unlocked the door. Something fell on the other side of it at as I pushed it open, making it tough to get the door open. It was slow going, I didn't want to break anything, not knowing what it was, but I got it open far enough that I could slip through. Turns out it was towels that'd fallen off the back of the door. Probably where Bailey had hung them after using them. I picked them up and the big one was mostly dry, the smaller one still quite a bit damp.

She was fast asleep in my bed, her hands tucked beneath her cheek like some sort of angel. I watched her for a lot longer than I had a right to before I grabbed my toiletry kit out of my dresser drawer and went back out and down the hall to the bathroom.

I showered and scrubbed up, took my time to shave off the five o'clock shadow that had just plain gotten away from me into a full-on scruff. Reaver poked his head in and I said, "Cops here?"

"No, man. I was just coming after my work boots."

"Oh, they're right there," I said and pointed. I was still shaving, face half full of cream so I kept at it.

"Hayden's pissed again," he said a bit glumly and I turned.

"What that you might get arrested?"

"Yeah, but she gets it."

"Go fuck the ornery out of her," I suggested.

"I think I might need a new trick," he said wrinkling his nose.

"Tried flowers or chocolate yet?" I asked.

"Oo! Hey, good idea. I'm going to have to try that."

"Hey, Reave?" I said as he was halfway out the door with his boots in hand.

"Yeah?"

"Thanks, man. I don't want to see your marriage take a hit because of this, so if you gotta stand down…"

"I will if I need to, the whole Florida and thinking I was dead thing? It wasn't maybe such a good plan. There's still a lot of shit there from that."

"She thought she lost you forever, man. I can't really imagine what that's like."

"I love her," he said and it sounded like a confession which was weird. Usually Reaver wasn't this fuckin' sappy, at least not with me.

"I know, man."

"You love Bailey, you know what it's like now," he said, glacial eyes boring into mine with an intensity that creeped me the fuck out. "Welcome to the club inside the club, brother," he said, and with that, he bounced; ducking back outside the door and taking off back up the hall.

"Fuckin' weirdo," I muttered, but I'd be lying if his words hadn't meant something to me. They'd actually touched pretty deep.

I finished up with no more interruptions and went back to my room, slipping in quietly. I shut and locked it behind me and put my shit away. I opened up the closet and ditched the wet towels in the hamper I had in there and rolled the door back shut. Bailey didn't even stir. Not even when I got into bed and pulled her into the spoon of my body, laughing to myself when my hand caressed the curve of her ass to discover one of the three pairs of boxers I owned.

The laughter died when I thought about how she literally had no clothes now – not even a pair of shoes for her damn feet. I pulled her close and she whimpered in her sleep from me holding her a touch too tight, but damn... I don't even want to think about how close last night and early this morning had been. The bullet hole through the farm truck's windshield, if the trajectory had been just a few inches different I wouldn't be holding her. I'd be sitting somewhere covered in her blood trying to figure out how to watch the whole fucking world burn.

"Rush," she murmured and I looked down into sleepy brown eyes.

"Sleep, baby. I'm right here." She twined around me, throwing her leg over both of mine and cuddling into my side, her head on my chest, arm across my ribs, and it was perfect. I kissed the top of her head and closed my own eyes. Sleep came quickly, her warm, toned body pressed safe into mine.

28

B ailey…

I stirred sometime after dark. I knew it was after dark, because when I opened my eyes, I could barely make out the glow of light from the high window over Rush's bed. I pushed off of him and made a frightened sound when I realized the shifting light was firelight. *God, had they followed us here? Was the club burning?*

"Easy, babe. It's just the firepit going outside."

More masculine laughter erupted, and I swallowed hard, realizing what it was that'd woken me up. Rush pulled me back against his nude body and ran his hands over my skin, under his shirt.

"Sorry, I think I'm going to be jumpy for a while."

"Can't say I blame you."

"When did you get back?" I asked.

"You don't remember?"

I shook my head. "Mm-mm."

"You were *out*, then. You said my name and everything."

"I don't remember."

"It's cool, don't sweat it. The shit Dani gave you was *good shit*. I'm kind of surprised you're awake at all."

"Me too, to be honest."

"Still groggy?"

"Yeah, it's like I'm hung over from whatever she gave me."

"Yeah, that can happen. You hungry?"

She frowned a little. "Starving, actually."

"K, let me get dressed, we can go raid the kitchen in the main house."

"Um, I'm not sure I should go out there like this."

"Your ass is covered, it's fine, baby." He climbed over me and got out of bed, pulling on a pair of black lounge pants. He pulled on a black wifebeater over his head and I sighed, watching the black material slide over his golden skin, obscuring the tattoo and musculature of his back.

He pulled me to my feet and shrugged his into a pair of rubber soled sheepskin house slippers. Looking over his shoulder he asked, "Ready?" I nodded and took his hand and followed him down the hall to the door to the outside. He opened it up, but before I could step outside in bare feet, he picked me up. I yipped and put my arms around his neck, and he carried me smoothly to the back door of the club's main building.

"Hey, Bailey!" one of the guys called from over by the fire and I blushed furiously, glad for the cover of darkness and called back, "Um, hi!"

Rush set me down inside the back door and called, "Back in a minute guys, gotta forage for food."

The big blond, Trigger, called out, "My Sunshine's in there, you won't have to search hard."

We found a small woman in the kitchen with long auburn hair, along with Reaver's wife, Hayden.

"Hi," she said softly with a megawatt smile, "I'm Ashton." She came over wiping her hands on her apron and shook my hand.

"Bailey, nice to meet you."

"We were just talking about you," Hayden said and I blinked.

"You're about Evy's size, um, Dray calls her Em. She's going to bring some clothes tomorrow and we were going to see about picking you out some clothes," Ashton said.

"I think a girl's shopping trip is probably just about something you need right now."

I put my hands on the counter and leaned on them, thinking furiously. "I'll have to go by the bank in person and pull some cash," I said and Ashton smiled, nodding. "Except I don't have ID anymore. Everything went up with the house."

"No passport?" Ashton asked meekly.

"In the safe, in my house."

"Might have survived," Rush said.

"Wasn't a fireproof safe, just more anti-theft," I said grimacing.

"Well, to be fair, you weren't expecting the place to burn down because a greedy developer threw Molotov cocktails at it."

"I don't think *anyone* expects that shit," Hayden said laughing.

"Your old man is rubbing off on your language choices," Rush teased.

"Damn right he is," Hayden said grinning.

"Trigger's my old man," Ashton said to me and her smile turned seven different kinds of amazing. I looked at Rush and sort of had the inkling that I was beginning to know the feeling.

"Listen, Sunshine," he ventured, and she put up a hand. "I know she's good for it, she's a Berling. Don't worry about it, Bailey. We'll get you something decent to wear and take you to the DMV to have your license replaced tomorrow. You can pay me back."

"Oh, I can't ask that…"

"You didn't," Hayden said with a wink. "We offered and it's gonna happen. It's really nothing."

"Thank you," I murmured, surprised at how much of a weight was lifted off my shoulders.

"We take care of each other, it's what we do," Hayden said with a wink and took a drink from her beer.

"I'll get you two some dinner if you want to get settled somewhere."

"What do you think? Taproom, media room, or out by the fire?"

"Anywhere but near a fire," I said meekly.

"I'd avoid the news stations if I were you," Hayden said taking another swig from her beer.

"Can I get one of those?" I asked.

"Yeah, sure. Come on out here." Rush took my hand and led me out into the taproom and to an empty table.

"Food will be right out," Ashton called after us. "I'm just going to heat it up."

"Thanks, Sunshine!"

I took the chair that Rush pulled out for me and he went behind me, back around the bar. The hiss and plink of bottle caps being removed and he was back, handing me a beer, two to a hand, and setting down a glass with a bit of bourbon in it.

I smiled. "Trying to get me drunk?" I asked downing the bourbon first.

"Trying to get lucky," he said with a wink.

"Pretty sure that's in the cards," I said and he pulled an arm back and said, "Ungh! Yes!"

I laughed at him and a moment later two plates were set in front of us and silverware was handed out. I smiled and thanked Ashton, already more at ease, relaxing bit by bit with every kind gesture and every little comfort. The food was barbecue ribs, potato salad, and corn on the cob and all of it was fantastic when paired with the crisp hoppy-ness that was the beer.

"Feel better?" he asked when we were done eating.

"Much."

"Good."

I eyed him carefully. "What happened between the time I left the farm and you came back here?" I asked him evenly.

"Can't tell you that, baby. That's club business."

"Will you get arrested?"

"Maybe... probably... but your mamma *did* offer to pay my legal defense." I stared at him and blinked.

"She did not!" I burst out and leaned back in my chair laughing. His expression wiped the look clean off my face. "She totally did, didn't she?"

"Yep."

"Wow."

"Think she meant it?" he asked tipping his bottle to his lips.

"I... I don't know."

"Some fucked up food for thought, isn't it?"

"Yeah. I mean..." I didn't finish the thought, I mean what was there to say? I pressed fingertips into my eyes and rubbed, sitting up and leaning forward some.

"This is all so bizarre, you know?"

"Not for me, babes. This is just *life*. Nothing out of the ordinary about it for me. People, *citizens*, are shitty human beings to each other, which is why when you find yourself a tribe of good people, you do everything to protect that."

"I'm a citizen though, aren't I?"

"Eh." He gave a one-shouldered shrug. "We're working on that."

He winked at me and I leaned back in my seat laughing, saying "Oh, fuck you!"

He waggled his eyebrows at me and said, "Every intention just as soon as we've had some time to digest."

"What do we do in the meantime?" I asked.

"When was the last time you watched a movie?" he asked. I shrugged and shook my head.

"Let's go see what they got going on in the media room then. Bring your beer, or are you almost out?"

"Almost out."

"Want another one?"

"Um..." I thought about it a second and finally shook my head. "No, I'm okay, thanks."

He held out a hand and I took it, letting him lead me back to a room with couches, some recliners and a large screen TV. It was empty and he led me to the couch.

"Sit," he ordered and I dropped onto it. It was so cushy, it nearly swallowed me whole, the black leather cool against my skin. He rifled through the DVD's on the shelf and picked one.

"Gotta go with a classic," he said and I frowned.

"What is it?"

"*Big Trouble in Little China,*" he answered and I made a face.

"Never heard of it."

"The 80s," he said. "You had to be there."

I laughed and he put it in and came over to the couch dropping onto it and stretching out. He patted his chest like I was a cat or something, but I didn't complain, stretching out and laying on top of him. The movie was weird, silly, and dumb but awesome at the same time, with these god-awful effects and neon lights meant to make things look all mystical. It was hysterical, and Kurt Russell and Kim Cattrall looked so *young.*

When the monster popped up on the back of the bobtail tractor trailer at the end, I threw back my head and laughed asking, "Are you kidding me!?"

"No, it's like the best thing ever, isn't it?"

"Oh my God, it was sooo bad! Is there more?"

"What? No, that's the end!"

"Are you serious? There's not a sequel?"

"Nope."

"Oh man! There needs to be a sequel."

"Well, there isn't."

"Ahhhh!" I hugged him tight and Rush chuckled.

"Come here," he said, and I crawled the few inches up his body to put my lips against his. His hands drifted down my back and cupped my lower back, just above my ass. I flicked my tongue against his bottom lip, and he moaned appreciatively and let me in.

We kissed like we weren't two grown adults, but rather like we were a pair of teenagers, discovering one another for the first time. There was something different about this time rather than any other time we'd kissed. Something deeper, more appreciative, more… fragile.

We parted naturally, breathing slowed, his caresses, heavier, more languid. I found my hands tangled in the front of his shirt, holding on for dear life. He smiled and looked at me, tracing some of my hair out of my face, tucking it gently behind my ear.

"I think I'd like to go back to your room, now."

"I think I'd like that, too, babe."

I got up and he turned off the TV. We went out and around to the back door, and once again he swept me up into his arms.

"Oh, well, looks like they're going to fuck," I heard someone say, followed by a burst of laughter as I gave them the finger behind Rush's back as we passed.

"She's related to Tilly alright," I heard a grizzled, older voice, say. Some more laughter, fonder and almost reminiscent. I knew how they felt. I missed my aunt too, even though it'd been years before she'd died, since I'd last saw her. She'd been one special lady.

Rush didn't set me down inside the door this time. Instead, he carried me up the hallway, all the way to his bedroom. I bit my lip as he stooped and managed to get the unlocked door open without dropping me. He pushed it open and kicked it shut behind us, flinging me onto the bed. I squealed and landed in the softness of it laughing, bouncing twice.

Rush wasn't laughing. He was stripping his tank over his head, stepping out of his slippers. He pushed the lounge pants off his hips and to the floor and snatched me by the ankle, turning me on my stomach and peeling the shorts off my legs. I gasped, and pulled his tee off from over my head, struggling a bit where it was trapped under my body.

He licked a wet line, dragging his tongue from my heel all the way up the back of one leg, nipping my left butt cheek with a little playful growl. I yipped and arched low and his hand crashed into the right, leaving a deliciously stinging handprint.

I fisted the covers and writhed a little from it and he groaned. I looked over my shoulder and clearly saw just how much he appreciated the view. His cock standing straight up and at attention, his gaze leaving a tingle of warmth where it traveled over my skin. He wrapped his hand around himself and pumped his erection through his fist. I gasped again, a sharp little exhale of breath, and my pussy gave a delighted little anticipatory throb.

I wanted that. I wanted him inside me, and I wanted it *hard*. I wanted him to fuck me so hard it left a permanent impression of my body in his mattress and I wasn't afraid to beg for it. I whined and raised my ass up off the bed, an offering. An offering which he gladly took, straddling my thighs and working for the right angle. *There!* He pressed into me and I cried out, thrusting my hips back onto him.

Too slow, he was moving too slow, too careful. I *wanted it* and so I said, "That all you got, biker boy? I thought you were gonna fuck me."

"Oh, is that how you like it?" he asked, voice tinged with amusement.

"Yeah," I gasped. Still too slow, still too careful, his hands on my shoulders, pressing me into the mattress, hard, pinning me so I couldn't do anything about it.

"Beg me, rich little bitch," he said. "I want you to beg for that cock."

"Please," I whined, "give it to me, Rush. I *need* it."

"Oh, you need it, huh? You gonna die without it?" he asked and he was being such a teasing prick.

"Yes!" I gasped as he surged forward a little harder.

"You want it hard?"

"Yes!"

"What like this?" he gave it to me a little bit harder, but it wasn't enough.

"Harder," I demanded.

"What like this?" He pulled back and surged forward again, this time our bodies meeting with a slap.

"No, *harder!*" I cried.

He gave it to me for real, then. Drawing back and slamming into my body so hard I moved several inches across the bed. It felt so good. Pleasure and pain rolled into one until I didn't know where one left off and the other began.

"Yes!" I cried. "Like that, just like that! Oh, God, *fuck me!*"

Oh, God, he did. He totally gave me exactly what I asked for and then some. I was right on that edge, so maddeningly close and he held me there. It was like he just needed to go in that quarter to a half an inch more to touch that spot, to scratch that itch, and then he did something no man had ever done before. He grabbed me by my upper arms and hauled back on them like they were reins and I completely understood why the French called it 'The Little Death' because I *died* a little inside, it was so fantastic.

He shoved into me so tight, so hard, with the added pull, it was the most exquisite kind of torture. I screamed in the best way possible as my body exploded into light, and fire raced along every filament and nerve.

He thrust into me one last time with a shout of his own as I, swear to God, flopped like a landed fish underneath the weight of his body with the intensity of my own orgasm. I felt him twitching inside my pussy and I tried three or four times to regain enough control of my motor function to tighten myself down around him.

He gasped and cried out again when I did it too, as we lay there a panting mess, skin sheened with cooling sweat.

"I don't know what that was," I said, pausing to draw breath, "but I liked it."

"Oh yeah, me too. You gotta tell me any time you're in the mood for that, baby. I don't ever want to miss out," he said between panting breaths.

I laughed and he laughed, and it was *so* good.

29

R ush...

"You ready?" I looked Bailey over, the new clothes she'd bought fit her well and looked nice. I'd had to go do some shopping myself; replace my helmet, motorcycle boots and shitkickers. I could afford it with what she was paying me, even if it now felt weird taking money off her.

"As I'll ever be," she said and I smiled. I'd bought her a little something too, and I had to say, her motorcycle boots looked good with her country look. I pulled her into my arms and kissed her, loving how her body responded, relaxing and melting into me.

"This is going to suck," she said and I nodded.

"But then we can come back here, where it *sucks* but we *like it*." She slapped me on my cut and pulled away, turning so that I got a fantastic view of her ass as she sashayed it out the door. I locked up my room behind us and walked out into the Kentucky summer sunshine; I missed the drier heat of the Arizona desert but the green out here couldn't be compared. I'd take the green of lush growing things over the brown of the desert any day of the week.

I caught up to my woman and wrapped my arms around her waist, lifting her off her feet and spinning her. She squealed, a happy sound full of laughter and I loved that. I set her on her feet, and she took my hand and we walked through the club and out front to my bike. I tied a spare black bandana over my hair and put my helmet on. Bailey put hers on and smiled at me while I started up the bike. Sunglasses went on my face, and she got on behind me with her own mirrored lenses firmly in place. She'd gone with a pair that was an old throwback style that the cops used to wear back in the day. God, what the hell had they called them? Aviators! That's right. They looked good on her. Fit her face and her style.

I pulled us down the drive, and she hugged tightly to my back, cuddling up to me. I didn't like that I was headed to the farm without a gun, but the cops were supposed to be there; along with Bailey's mother, the insurance guy, Caleb, and her asshole brother. It wasn't going to be pretty, that was for sure.

The ride was a good one, weather perfect, sun not too hot, wind warm as it washed over us. We pulled into the long gravel driveway of Bailey's farm and I had to watch it. It was always tricky riding on uneven, shifting surfaces and this was no exception. I pulled us up in among the semi-circle of vehicles facing Bailey's burned-out house and I felt pretty grim.

I didn't want to go to jail today but depending on what came out of Junior's mouth, I might be. This… this was bad.

The house was soot streaked and blackened from about halfway down. The top half? Spindly and black where any of the structure remained, like a burned-out matchstick. To think… we'd been asleep in there. Fuck, man.

I tapped Bailey's knee to get off and she did, her movements stiff and mechanic as she surveyed the scene in front of us, too. She took off her helmet and wordlessly handed it to me as I leaned the bike onto its kickstand. I took it and hung it from one of the handlebars before I started working mine off.

"What is he doing here?" a dude that could only be her brother demanded, looking at my cut with disdain. I tensed. I should fuckin' let fly into his pretty boy mouth just for that disrespect alone.

"Rush is my boyfriend, not that you have anything to say about it, you creep."

Her brother looked at her like she'd gone insane, Caleb echoing the look, but Bailey's mom just went over to her daughter and hugged Bailey's arm. Both of them sort of entranced by the house.

The insurance guy was already up closer, snapping photos and writing things on his clipboard. Caleb opened his mouth next, "I would advise not telling the insurance company anything about the Giangiulio Group or your brother's involvement with them. You do, and the claim will be dismissed as he *is* a partial owner of this farm."

"He won't be when Bailey's lawyers get through with him, just as you will no longer be trustee." Bailey's mom's tone was absolute as she turned her head to glare at Caleb.

"Bailey, I had no idea that…"

"Shut it, Philip. You had *every* idea, you just didn't care. All you care about is money, your name, and your reputation." Bailey wasn't having any of it either. I was proud of her.

"Mom," he tried to appeal to Trudy, which was a bad idea. She turned her head slowly and the look she gave him was sub-zero ice queen at its finest.

"You are your father's son, Philip. I certainly didn't raise you to be this way."

Philip sneered then. "You didn't raise me *at all*. You had the nanny for that, remember?"

"Be that as it may, as far as I am concerned, Bailey is an only child at this point."

"I wouldn't say anything else, if I were you Philip." Caleb's voice was brittle with barely suppressed anger.

"Neither one of you should say shit anyway," I said, casually leaning against my bike. "You do, and I'm liable to take you both apart. Take a good hard look at that house, boys. Bailey and I were both inside, asleep when that started. They made sure to hit all the entrances and exits to the place. If we hadn't parked that truck," I turned up the drive and thrust my chin at it, "in the side barn? We'd be a couple of crispy fuckin' critters. At some point, y'all might have to answer for that." They blinked at me, and just finally started looking nervous as the implications sank in.

"You might want to rephrase that a little, baby," Bailey said and I raised an eyebrow. She smiled and it wasn't nice. "At some point they *will* be answering for that."

I nodded and Philip looked like he was about to burst a blood vessel somewhere. "Are you threatening me?" he demanded.

"Why that would be illegal!" I cried.

"Consider it a promise wrapped with all the love I have left for you," Bailey shot back, and her mother patted her hand. A classic gesture of 'that's enough for now.' She was right. She hadn't even turned around, but the crunching gravel could only be one person.

A sheriff's cruiser was coming along the driveway, the last piece we needed to finish this sorry song and dance. It appeared it was the man himself by all the bars and trappings on his uniform and it'd be very telling who he went to first. I watched him get out of his car and walk up to Bailey's mother and shake her hand exchanging some words. He got to me last, but we didn't even bother shaking hands, just exchanging a nod instead.

"My God," he said, turning and letting his gaze roam the burned-out husk that'd been Bailey's home. "Fire Marshall's preliminary report says it's arson, which is consistent with your accounts of what happened. Tell me more about this mess with the Giangiulio Development Group."

"I will let my son tell you," Trudy said and her eyes sparked fire. We all stood around while Philip spun some sort of fuckin' fairy tale about how he had no idea what Giangiulio was planning and how he was totally innocent or some shit. One of the lawyers that Trudy brought with her opened up an expensive looking folio and walked forward, wordlessly handing the sheriff a single sheet of paper.

"The findings by our private investigator disagrees with Mr. Berling's account of the events leading up to this tragic loss of Ms. Berling's home," he said, and the sheriff looked up from the paper and raised an eyebrow at the lawyer.

"You can save that kind of talk for the courtroom, mister. This is enough for me and enough to make an arrest. Mr. Berling, turn around."

The insurance adjuster was furiously scratching notes on his clipboard and almost none of us had even noticed when he'd drifted up.

"Mother, are you seriously going to let him arrest me!?" Philip cried, incredulously.

"It is a lesson you should have learned when you were sixteen," she said coldly. "Your father isn't here to protect you from the consequences of your actions anymore, Philip. I, for one, am not willing to sacrifice one of my children over the other. You nearly got your own sister *killed* and for what? A piece of property that wasn't even yours to begin with —"

"I own one-third of this place!" he screamed, lunging at his mother and that's when Bailey snapped. She rounded and kicked up, hoofing her brother right between the legs. Poor fucker was already handcuffed so he couldn't even defend himself. He dropped like a fuckin' stone and the sheriff had the good sense to let him drop.

Bailey looked the law man right in the eye and said, "Arrest me if you have to." Meanwhile Philip's civil attorney was screaming about suing her; I stood up off the bike and turned in the suit's direction and he shut his mouth.

The sheriff nodded and looked back at the house and I could see what he was thinkin'. He shook his head and said, "I think you earned that one free and clear, miss."

Jaws dropped and Bailey nodded, the sheriff looked at me and said, "Say, you wouldn't happen to know anything about what happened one county over yesterday, would you?"

"Wouldn't know, sir. I left here and went straight back to my club with my girl. We were both mighty shook up. What happened?" I feigned innocence and Bailey came over and wrapped her arms around one of mine, hugging it.

"Seems some biker types went and roughed up the very same Giangiulio wrapped up in this. Hurt him pretty bad and put him in the hospital with some broken ribs."

"That's a shame," Bailey said without much feeling. "But it's like he says, he was with me in his room at the club yesterday. We stayed in all day. He was trying to help me cope with…" she turned her attention back to her house and the sheriff gave a nod.

"Any rate, it's out of my jurisdiction, I figure that the sheriff's department or the big city cops will come a knockin' at some point."

Well I'll be a son of a bitch, I do believe we were just warned that the boys in blue most definitely would be coming by. I gave a nod and said, "They've gotta do their jobs and we ain't got nothin' to hide. We're a law-abiding club after all."

"Uh-huh, firmly in the 99 then I take it?"

I grinned. "You can count on it."

"Come on, boy. Let's go." The sheriff hauled Philip to his feet and walked him to his cruiser. Philip didn't have much to say, which was probably a good thing. Bailey shot me a worried look, but this wasn't over yet. Still, it was up to the lawyers and insurance company for the remainder of the visit. We just had to stand around and listen while they fought it out.

By the end, we were mind weary and, of course, nothing was really resolved. The insurance adjuster left, Trudy had some choice words for Caleb and then he and his attorneys left, and Philip's attorney took one look at the whole goddamned mess and shook his head.

"I will advise my client to retain other council, you can expect to hear from them," he said, then he left until it was just me, Bailey, and her mom.

"Well, *that* was thrilling," Bailey said and rubbed her forehead.

Trudy sighed and took her daughter's hands and it looked like she was about to tell Bailey someone had died. Aw, fuck... I took a deep breath and held it and waited her mother out.

It was pretty much as bad as I thought it was going to be. Bailey had enough money in her accounts to be set for finding a modest place to buy or rent, but the shit with the insurance company could drag out for a couple of years and what Bailey and her mom *didn't* have was enough to rebuild this place in the meantime.

The farm might survive, all of its actual facilities intact, however, while the garbage went on with Caleb, all of the farm's assets were in trust and pretty much frozen there. So, there was money to rebuild but none that could be touched while the investigation happened into whether or not Caleb was fit to remain trustee.

Bailey looked crushed as she looked back over her farm and realized the writing was on the wall. She hadn't lost, and Giangiulio hadn't won, but what was clear was neither fuckin' one of them was going to get out on top. She'd pretty much lost this place. It could continue to run with a government trustee, but no one was going to want to board their animals here with what had just gone down. Not with any kind of threat coming anywhere near their precious investments.

Bailey's shoulders dropped and she hung her head. She shook it finally and looked up with tears streaming down her face.

"I think I'd like to go for a ride," she said.

"I think I can help you with that. Come on." We left and took a long ride. I took her back to the meadow by the river where we could just be for a minute and talk. Maybe come up with some new dreams or find a will to fight.

God, I hoped it was the latter, and Giangiulio? If Bailey wasn't coming out of this with her dream intact, neither was he. I had plans for that guy.

30

B ailey...

I lay by Rush's side, deeply depressed and discouraged. My
mother was right. Blue Hills, whether I liked it or not, wasn't going to
survive if there were no client thoroughbreds to board or breed. I was
better off letting the clients I had out of their contracts and selling the
land. I wouldn't be selling to the GDG though. They could go fuck
themselves.

"Baby," Rush said softly, and I turned my head to look at him.

"Not the way any of us wanted this to go down, but I'd like to think
you still scored in some ways, I mean, right?"

I couldn't help but smile then and pulled myself up to kiss him. He was
right. There was more to life than money, property, and status. Plus, if I
were being honest with myself, there was so much more I could be
doing than living my father's legacy through Blue Hills. Like I could
be focusing on my own, I just didn't know how...

"Tell me something good," I murmured and he smiled.

"I love you," he said and I smiled, too.

"And?"

"Oh, you need more than that?" I gave him a look and he chuckled. "You got some of your family back," he pointed out and that was a double-edged sword.

"I lost my brother, though."

"No, your brother lost *you.*"

"Splitting hairs," I said and huffed out a breath.

"True enough," he admitted, then with a smile said, "But it doesn't make it any less true."

"Nice play on words." I let out a sigh while he trailed fingertips along my cheek.

"What do you want, Bailey? I mean really, in your heart and in your head, what do you *really* want to come out of this?" His eyes had gone cold and distant, and I realized he was seriously asking me.

I swallowed hard and said, "I want them to hurt like I hurt. I don't want anyone dead, but I want them scared. I want them to stand there and watch their world burn just like I had to."

He hugged me close and kissed the side of my head, sighing out. "Consider it done, babe. Consider it done."

I held myself close to Rush's body under the sparkling summer sun and felt cold. Numb from the inside out. I didn't know or care what would happen to my brother. I didn't know or care what happened to Caleb, insofar that whatever did happen, I got my money out of it so I could start to figure out how to rebuild my life.

Rush plucked the thought right out of my head, or maybe just the worry that was likely on my face tipped him off to what I was thinking. He lay beside me and asked, "What did you want to be when you grew up, anyway?"

"Honestly?" I asked.

"No, lie to me. You know me and mine totally dig that," he said, and I could *hear* his eyes rolling. I laughed and he tickled me which only made me laugh harder, until suddenly he was on top of me, between my thighs and we were kissing and God, kissing Rush made so many things just not hurt anymore.

"You didn't answer the question," he murmured against my lips in a sing-song voice.

"I always wanted to teach kids, you know? How to ride, how to care for horses, that sort of thing."

"What, like have people pay to have their kids learn how to ride?"

"No, like a non-profit. Any kids, but yeah, maybe have people pay to fund that side of it somehow… Not super thrilled at the prospect, but maybe I could fund some of it with corporate retreats."

"What, like a B&B?"

"Yeah, why not?"

He tapped the tip of my nose with a fingertip. "You have the property, the house needs rebuilding, and eventually, when the legal bullshit is all settled, you'll have the money. Why don't you see if you can find some investors or some shit to get it started while you wait for the rest to come through?"

I let my head fall back to the blanket and let the wheels turn, thinking about it. "I mean, I could keep the main house as just ours and build some cottages in one or two of the paddocks. I mean, we've never needed that many."

Rush's expression changed, shuttering hard and I tipped my head questioningly. "What? What is it? What did I say?" I asked, alarmed at the sudden change in him.

"You mean that?" he asked, voice controlled and careful. I tried to think about what I'd just said, and it dawned on me; *I could keep the main house as just ours…* I thought about it, I mean really thought about the full implications behind those words and finally, I nodded carefully.

"Yeah, I mean it."

His mouth crushed over mine and I held his face between my hands. I know we were out in a public park where anyone could happen by, but I wanted him right then, so bad. I pulled back and said, "Take me home with you," breathless and wanting. He immediately got up and held a hand down to me. I took it and he hauled me to my feet. We folded up the blanket and stashed it back where it'd come from and made the ride back to the club.

He followed the curve of the track around to the building that held his room and we went in, skipping out on seeing or talking to anyone. Once inside his room, it was a flurry of hands removing clothing and passionate kissing.

Once both of us were out of clothes to remove, he lifted me and I gave a little leap, wrapping my legs around his hips. He sought blindly with his cock, eventually sliding right into me. I cried out into his mouth and he walked us up onto the bed so that he could get a better angle, more leverage, to make love to me the way I know we both wanted.

Hours. We spent *hours* wrapped up in one another until neither one of us could go another round, as much as we wanted to. It was evening by then, the room dark except for the golden glow of one lone bedside lamp. He kissed the back of my shoulder and I held his arms tightly around me.

"I love you, Bailey," he whispered, and I fell asleep, dreaming of what our life could be.

31

R ush...

"How's she doing?" Dragon asked when I dropped into the chair opposite his in the taproom.

I shook my head. "Asleep, for now, but pretty much as you'd expect, otherwise. Fuckin' heartbroken but she's tough. She's got some ideas, but that's not what I'm here about. This ain't a social call."

"Oh?" He looked at me over his glasses and set down his paper.

"I asked her what she wanted today, her response wasn't unreasonable. I'd like your blessing and the backing of the club to go get it."

Dragon set down the paper he was reading with a rustle. "Developer?" he asked.

I nodded. "We both know he ain't going to give us what we want."

"Still has until tomorrow to do it." He stared at me for several long heartbeats across the table and asked me, "What'd you have in mind?"

"An eye for an eye."

He raised an eyebrow. "Let me guess, you want Duracell's help with this one."

"I could tap Lucky, but this is more sophisticated than the kind of shit Lucky is used to pulling off. Lucky blows shit up, it's country style and gets messy. Cell does it, it's more controlled."

"Good point, what kind of shenanigans you wanting to get up to?"

"Like I said, an eye for an eye. He took Bailey's home from her, her livelihood…"

"Data!" Dragon called out.

"Yeah, P.?" Data rolled into view, looking back over his desk chair from inside the fishbowl.

"Find all of the GDG's holdings and projects," he said. Then addressed me when he said, "I think we'd all like to be involved in this one."

"What 'cha thinkin'?" I asked.

"Burn down the house, maybe blow up the car, but there are a lot of other ways to cost the man money that won't cause too much collateral damage to any innocents."

"What, like petty acts of vandalism to other properties?"

"Why not? Some sugar in the gas tank, some smashed windows and spray paint… make it look like kids did it… yeah, not bad. Could be some fun, too. Not a bad idea."

"No one would think a bunch of grown ass men pulled that shit off."

"Heat's already on from that stunt at his office. No sense in crankin' it any higher."

"Work smarter, not harder." I nodded.

"Go see who's around and might want in. Keep it off the airwaves."

"Thanks, D."

"She's my family by blood," he said with a shrug. "Tilly'd have my balls if I didn't do somethin'."

There was no fuckin' way I was going to tell Dragon that Tilly was gone, that she wasn't here anymore, and it'd been so many fuckin' *years* that he needed to let it go. There were just some things that were better left alone, and this was one of them. So, I did the only thing I could do. I nodded and got up from the table. I put my hand on his shoulder and gave it a squeeze before I left. A silent *I know* and *I'm here if ever…*

I went out back to where a few of the guys had a fire goin' and were chillin' around it, knocking back some beers after a long day. It was my luck that in addition to Trig and Reave, that Ghost, Rev, Thirteen, Blue, and Cell, were all out there.

I dropped onto one of the vacant swinging benches and Trig pulled a fresh bottle out of a cooler, handing it over wordlessly. I twisted off the top and took a drink, it was pretty good. The guys were all quiet, looking at me, and I finally grinned and said, "Who's up for a little mayhem?"

Laughter and a "Yeeeeah!" went up, someone clapped and said, "Alright now!" I laughed, too. I figured I wouldn't be turned down. It was getting boring around here.

"Where do we start?" Duracell asked, taking a drink of his beer.

"Data's running up a list of holdings and other shit this fucker has got. We ain't aimin' to kill anybody, but we damn sure wanna set a couple of fires, you in?"

"Dude's house?" he asked.

"Yeah, among other things."

Data came out to the fire, his hands stuffed in his pockets and said, "Piece of cake. He's got a house outside Lexington that he lives in with his wife, no kids, and the wife is with him at the hospital so if you're going to take it out, tonight would be a good bet. I tapped into their security feed and they don't even have a pet. Housekeeper's gone for the day –"

"No security?" Duracell asked.

"One guard at a gate shack."

"Good deal. Blue, you up for a little adventure?" Blue smiled at Duracell and nodded. Both of them stood up and Cell stretched. "Keep an eye on your local news," he said flicking his cigarette butt into the firepit.

He and Blue melted into the night beyond the flames and I had no doubt that Bailey's revenge would be played out, probably not just over the local news, but the national news as well. I looked to Data who shrugged.

"It'll be hard as fuck to trace back to us, this guy is dirty six ways to Sunday. You wouldn't believe the shit I turned up. He's got way more than Bailey and her mom pissed off at him. I'm surprised he hasn't had the lid blown off this shit long before we ever came along."

"So, spill it," Reaver called out across the fire. "Where we goin'?"

"He's got a development about twenty minutes from here..." Data said trailing off, he was tapping on his phone's screen and looked up. "Sorry was texting Blue the address."

"Completed?" Trig asked.

"Nope, still under construction. Got a bunch of earth moving equipment out there, foundations poured on a couple buildings, but that's about it."

"I'm down for a little sabotage tonight, how about you?" Reaver asked Trig.

"Seems to me, Rush ain't got much time, so he'd probably be best suited for this one. Sure he's going to want to be back before Bailey wakes up."

I nodded. "Shit, I'll go with you," Revelator said.

"Cool," Data said, "because an hour away there's another development, partially finished, that could use Lucky's attention. Again, no collateral damage, but it's probably right at the tipping point for going into the downhill slide into completion."

"Dude, if you can pull him off of Moira that'd be great." Reaver said, grinning. Trigger laughed and shook his head.

"Only thing Lucky likes more than pussy is blowing shit up, shouldn't be hard. I'll go get him." Trig killed the can of beer in his hand and crushed it.

"Guess it's you and me, Rev."

"And me," Thirteen said, getting up from where he was lying the length of one of the benches.

"Where the fuck your ol' ladies at, anyway?" I asked.

"Planning something for your girlfriend to take her mind off her troubles."

"Oh, fuck…" I muttered.

"Yeah, buddy! Welcome to our world," Revelator said clapping me on the back. I laughed.

"Come on, let's go before any of 'em get wise that we're up to something."

"Good idea. I've got two kids, Red would kill me if she knew I was up to anything that'd pull me away from family."

Thirteen was nodding. "No kids, but Dani's still got troubles sleeping."

We didn't say anything to that, what was there to say? You don't live in hell for *years* and come out unscathed. Dani did pretty good, but she was fragile from her time with the Suicide Cunts. I was pretty sure that the shit going on with Bailey was probably bringing up quite a bit for her, too.

"Best take a cage, not the bikes for this one," Revelator suggested.

Thirteen and I nodded, and I said, "Just let me finish my beer."

We drove out in my truck, about ten pounds of sugar in a plastic container in the back of it. Sunshine was going to be pissed we raided her kitchen but fuck it. This was for fun and a damn good cause.

We were laughing and joking the whole way there, Thirteen sitting shotgun while Rev sat in the bed keeping the sugar from spilling and talking to us through the back sliding window.

"They got any welding shit left out, I'm calling dibs," Thirteen said and Revelator came right back with, "Man, I am not hauling all that shit back to the truck. You can fuck that noise."

We laughed and pulled off to the side of the road about two minutes from the site. We got out of the truck and moved into the trees surrounding the place so we could scope it out. There was a temporary construction fence put up around the place which when we got around to the back side of it, we had no trouble untwisting the wires that held the chain link to one of the fence posts to let ourselves in.

It was dark and only a sliver of moon was out, so we had to bumble around a bit. We passed a flask between us, sippin' on some whiskey so if we did get snatched up, we might be able to get by with a misdemeanor drunk and disorderly or a simple trespass charge.

We were laughing and fuckin' cuttin' up trying to be quiet while still getting the job done. There was a backhoe and a bulldozer nearby that we had liberally dosed with sugar to the gas tanks when Rev asked, "You sure this is even going to work? I mean, I know it'd work on a car, but don't these things run on diesel?"

"Yes, it'll work, dumbass! I'm a mechanic, this'll fuck with the engine just like any car or truck." We did as much damage as we could to the site, but Data had been right. There wasn't much to fuck with at this one. We got the fuck out of there before anyone happened along and went back to the club.

When we walked through the front door, Dragon leaned back in his chair and asked, "Have fun?"

We all busted up laughing and I said, "See you guys, I'm goin' back to Bailey."

"Night, man, thanks for the trip, it was a riot."

Fun was over when I walked out the back door. Bailey was curled on one of the swinging benches, staring into the fire, expression somber.

No one else was out here, and I paused, watching the play of firelight against her pale skin. Her hair was loose and flowing around her face and she looked beautiful. Like some kind of angel sitting there in her satin night things. I went over to her and dropped onto the bench beside her.

"I woke up and you were gone," she said softly.

"Kind of hard to be two places at once," I said back and waited for her to flip out on me. I was surprised when she didn't. Instead she just kind of slouched over, laying her head against my shoulder, twining her arms around my bicep.

"Not gonna yell at me?" I asked with a wry smile.

"Not sure what kind of women you're used to dating, but you're not on a lead, Rush. You don't have to tell me where you go or everything you do. I get it. Some of it you can't."

"Still bothers you though, I can hear it in your voice."

"Well, yeah… I wake up in the middle of the night and my boyfriend is just gone, doing God knows what… just… just promise that if you ever want to cheat, that you'd tell me first before actually doing anything."

I put my arms around her then and she tipped on her side, laying her head in my lap. She looked fragile, all curled up on herself like that, staring into the flames.

"I'll never cheat, Bailey. That's one thing you *never* have to worry about from me. I know that kind of pain, and I wouldn't wish it on anybody else."

"He used to, you know? A lot. Mom would just make excuses and hide it. I could tell it hurt her, but she just let him. Saving face was more important. I think it was one of the reasons she hated Aunt Tillie."

"What the fuck did you just say?"

Shit.

Bailey sat up swiftly, Dray marching up the grass from the back door. Bailey was shaking her head.

"Dray, she was jealous. She always hated the fact that Dragon was faithful to your mother. That what they shared was *real*. She felt like your mother rubbed it in her face that she was free and that my mom was trapped in this loveless marriage with a man who couldn't even be faithful to her. My mom may have loved my dad, but I don't think my dad ever really appreciated or loved my mother... It just wasn't who he was."

Dray turned one of the lounge chairs around and dropped into it, facing Bailey. Bailey wiped at a tear and said, "How did we all just get *so fucked up?*"

Dray snorted. "I don't know, Bales. I wasn't really there. Not for my mom's lack of trying."

"I know, my mom has been *really* out of character lately. I don't know if it's because of Dad's heart attack or what."

Dray heaved a heavy sigh and said, "Bales, it's probably just all of it. You know that feeling you've got in the center of your chest? Like the whole world is flying the fuck apart and you're just doing everything you can to hold it together," he put his hands together like he was trying to hold something, spaces between his fingers. "but no matter how you try to hold on, shit just keeps escaping through your fingers and there's not a damn thing you can do except pretend you've got a handle on it, like everything is fine?"

"Yeah, how'd you know?" she asked.

"I may be younger than you by numbers, but I'm way older by experience," he said. "It was the same fuckin' thing for me when I was sixteen, watchin' my mom get killed. I still don't know why I'm alive, Bales. I'll never know why I didn't get hit... I just know that we've got one life and we can't spend it worrying about what this guy or that lady thinks about how we're living it. My mom knew that... Your mom is just now starting to catch on."

He leaned back heavily in his chair and stared his cousin down. She leaned back heavily in her seat, and were my feet not planted firmly on the ground, it probably would have set us to swinging. She dragged her eyes back up to Dray's and said, "What if I can't be like you, or Aunt Tillie?" She sniffed and took me by the hand, and I think, whispered her greatest fear, "What if this life you lead isn't for me?"

Dray smirked and shook his head. "You're listening, but you aren't *hearing* me, Bailey. You aren't supposed to live my life, or my mom's life. You're supposed to live *your* life."

I laced my fingers through hers and brought the back of her hand to my lips, pressing them against it softly. She looked at me and I murmured against it, "Baby, that's the thing about living this life. Our life is what *we* make it. Nobody else gets a say in how we do things, or where we go, or what we do. That's on *us*."

She laid back down, her head in my lap and stared past her cousin at the flickering firelight. We let her. I set us to gently rocking and we all just sat there, not saying another word. Sometimes you sit with people in your life and don't have to say anything. Sometimes, you get up from those times, and walk away feeling like it was the best conversation you ever had. It was like that for us that night, and when the fire burned too low to really see by, I picked Bailey up, and Dray held doors for us while I took my woman back to bed where we both belonged.

32

B ailey…

"Well, it ain't pretty, but it's totally doable," Shelly said, sitting back in her chair.

I sighed and pressed my fingertips into my eyes, rubbing. "I'm really starting to hate Blue Hills, which is miserable because I've always loved that place. I was always way more invested in it than any other person in my family, including my dad." I sighed and turned my head to stare out Shelly's office window. We'd just finished poring over the financials to see if I had enough to refund the money owed on incomplete contracts with the owners of the horses that had been housed at Blue Hills. Not all of them were as appreciative of the bait and switch to keep their animals safe during the crisis, either. A few of them threatened to sue until Marion Cranston stepped up and threatened to take offense.

That shut them up in an impressively short amount of time. God forbid anyone offends Mrs. Marion Cranston. Their reputation would take *years* to recover. I was beginning to severely doubt that my family name ever would.

"So please tell me you're saying that we can do it, *without* selling the farm. Because I don't want to have to sell it only for it to end up with the GDG, anyway."

Shelly laughed a little and said, "Don't you worry, I took that into account. No, when I say it's doable, I mean it's totally doable *but it ain't pretty.* It would literally leave you down to practically nothing in the business accounts you have access to, and your personal accounts to make it happen. The *good* news is –"

I stopped her, throwing up my hands and saying, "Ah, finally, there's some good news in here somewhere!"

She snorted and repeated herself, "The *good* news is, that once all the legal bullshit is dispensed with, you'll have enough for the renovations you want to make and to get Blue Hills up and running the way you want it."

"Yeah, that is good news, if it weren't for the fact that the legal battles are likely going to take years to complete."

"Not with what Data and I dug up," she sang out.

I let out an explosive sigh. "Lawyers, they get paid to move things along at the speed of snail."

Shelly laughed. "Won't argue with you there." She let out a gusty sigh of her own and said, "I know it's a lot of shit that's come down in a real short amount of time, and it feels like the whole world is fucking you raw, but this is it, I promise."

"God, so is this what the bottom feels like?"

"Yep, but I'm here to tell you, when you've hit bottom you've only got one direction left to go."

I smiled and nodded at Reaver's cousin. "It's just tough to stay positive right now."

"I totally get it, trust me."

A knock fell at Shelly's front door and she lit up. "Who's that?" I asked as she pushed herself up out of her chair.

"That," she said, "is plan B."

"Plan B?" I echoed, confused and got up to follow her. She went out to the kitchen and opened the door.

"Hi!" Ashton and Hayden called in unison.

"Shhh! Harmony is down for a nap," Shelly said, laughing.

"Oh, sorry!" Hayden whispered back.

"Dining room table," Shelly said. "More room to talk."

We went to the dining room table and sat. It seated six, so we all just sort of gathered around the middle. Shelly went back to her office and brought out her laptop.

"Okay, I called this little meeting because I've been doing some research and crunching the numbers and Ashton, I think I have a deal for you..."

An hour later we sat around the table in silence, Ashton saying, "Let me get this straight, you want me to buy into a horse farm."

I kept staring at Ashton and wondering why we were even having this conversation, I mean Hayden Michaels I understood because her family had money but Ashton Howard?

"What I'm proposing isn't so much a buy-in, as it is buying Bailey's brother *out*. The cost for renovations can be paid back in full as soon as the money comes up, and that would leave just interest on the loan which could be worked out over a matter of the first five years. All the facilities are in place for the most part, all you need is lodging for guests and to rebuild the house, right?"

"And horses... and probably the first year's operating costs –"

"Which Rush told me he already has covered," Shelly said.

"Wait, what?"

"He didn't tell you about that part?" Shelly asked.

I pushed back from the table. "No... no he didn't."

"While Mel's been on bedrest from having Chandler, she finally got around to uploading all the pictures she took of his furniture to a website so he could sell it. It's been well-received. He's got way more than what is at the club," Hayden said.

"The way it's going," Shelly said, "he says he can totally start funding your dream. That you guys would just need a little extra help getting it going sooner rather than later."

"And you have that kind of money?" I asked Ashton. She smiled and nodded.

"What can I say? Shelly is *really* good with money. The twelve million I received when my ex-husband died has grown and what it would take to get your retreat going isn't more than five hundred thousand or so."

"That's kind of a drop in the bucket for Ashton because I'm just that awesome."

"So, what do you say?" Hayden asked. "Think you and Ashton could partner up for a bit?"

"I still don't think I understand," I said. "What's in it for you?"

Ashton reached across the table and covered one of my hands with both of hers. "I get to watch someone's dreams come true, help one of the club's family, and help another one of the club members do so much more with himself than work on cars. What do you mean what's in it for me?"

"People just don't work like that," I said helplessly, tears springing to my eyes. I was just so overwhelmed by what they were saying, what they were proposing.

The girls laughed and Hayden leaned forward and said, "That's just it, we've been trying to tell you all this time, that's exactly how *our* people do."

"But you don't even know me!"

"We know Dragon and Dray, and we know Rush. Rush wouldn't love you if you weren't quality people, honey. It just wouldn't happen," Shelly said. Hayden got up and went into the kitchen and brought back some paper towels, handing them to me.

I laughed and dabbed at my eyes and blew my nose, "This is all happening so fast."

"Tends to be how things work around these guys," Hayden said smiling.

"Listen, real friends, people who genuinely love and care about you, they do everything in their power to make your life easier, not harder. That's the way things are supposed to work, Bailey... that's how you can tell when things are right. When things are *real*," Ashton said.

"Do you need a decision right now?" I asked and Ashton smiled, lighting up her strange golden eyes.

"No, honey. There's no expiration date on it either, you take your time. I was afraid that this may have been too early to really discuss, but it's there if you want it."

"Thank you," I said.

"Let me get us some lemonade," Hayden said and I nodded. I wanted to see Rush, to talk to him and get his take on things. To understand that yes, this really was for real.

33

R ush...

I was working on the damn front door I'd been building for Bailey before her fucking house went up. It felt good to be in my shop, but I was nervous today. Today was the day she'd gone to Shelly's, and the girls were going to tell her the plan I'd hatched to get her dream up and running sooner rather than later.

I decided I'd had enough of the garage now that I'd had a taste of something I'd meant to be doing all along. As much as I didn't want to turn my hobby of making things out of wood into a job, I didn't mind selling a bunch of shit I had stored here and out at Point Nowhere. It was just going to end up damaged if I didn't, and if selling it put me and Bailey closer to trying out a life together, then I was all for it. I think it was time for something new for the both of us.

I looked up from what I was doing and had to smile a little. "How long you been there?" I asked her. She was sitting on one of the high stools at the table in the corner of my shop I reserved for visitors.

"A while. I think I like watching you work," she said. "Something both captivating and soothing about it."

"Yeah?"

"Yeah."

She seemed off. A little sad, a lot reserved, and I worried about it. I couldn't fix the problem without knowing what it was, but I didn't think it was right to just come out and ask. Not this time. While it would have been fun under any other circumstances to rile her up and watch her go, I didn't think I'd get that particular reaction this time. It finally hit me what looked wrong about her. It was her eyelashes. They were sort of stuck together and I asked her, "You been crying?"

I dropped my chisel and carving knife and came around the door that was lying flat on the sawhorses so I could work on it. She nodded a bit tiredly and slipped off the stool, her arms coming up. I folded her into my chest and held on tight. Her arms went around my waist and she shook with these broken little sobs as she broke down all over again.

Too much, I thought to myself. *The meeting had been too much, way too soon.* The poor woman was in emotional overload, and I couldn't say I blamed her. Dad recently dead, brother in jail, a trusted family friend found stealing from her, mother pulling a complete one-eighty on the beliefs she'd held Bailey's entire life due to her own grief... House burning down, getting shot at – fuck. It wasn't exactly the lifestyles of the rich and famous shit that she was used to. It was *my* life, the one I wished like hell I could leave behind but when it turned back up like a bad penny, there I was in the thick of it again.

I wish I could say that I regretted it, but I couldn't. It'd brought Bailey right back to me when I thought I'd never see her again. It'd brought me right into her life to fix it for her the only way that I could, although I found myself wishing we ran like we used to. Had we operated like the old one-percent club we'd been, there would be a lot more bodies on the floor, sure, but Bailey's life may have ended up more intact than it was now.

Maybe it wasn't meant to be intact... the fucking voice of reason whispered out of a corner of my mind. *The knife goes through the fire so that it can become hardened steel.*

"Shh, I got yah," I soothed and waited out the storm, because what else could you do?

"I don't understand why anyone would want to do so much for me," she sobbed, and I chuckled and kissed the top of her hair.

"It's how we are, baby. We love fierce and we aren't afraid to live. People like us? We band together. We help each other. That's the way the world is supposed to work, isn't it?"

"It's the way it's *supposed* to work, but that doesn't mean that's the way it works, does that make sense?"

"Yeah, it does, but I guess that's part of what makes us rebels, isn't it?" She laughed, a choked broken sound and I smiled rocking her gently back and forth.

"I'm just so out of sorts," she said, adding, "I'm sorry."

"Nothing to apologize for, babe. Everybody gets overwhelmed sometimes."

"You don't."

I laughed. "Oh, trust me. I do. You should have seen the bitch fit I pitched when Nox hooked up with his girl and made her his ol' lady. Woo boy, not one of my finer moments." I smiled and said, "But you know what was?"

"What?"

I tipped her head back so I could look at her. "Falling in love with this beautiful woman right here." I bent my head and kissed her then, and her breath hitched.

Her lips were soft, and she'd replaced that lip balm that drove me crazy. The one that tasted like brown sugar. I almost wish she'd chased it with some bourbon like that first night. I drew back and asked, "You want it here or you want to go back to the room?"

She opened those big brown eyes, panting slightly and said, "Room, take me back to your room."

"You've got it, baby." I switched off equipment, hitting the button to close the bay doors. I grabbed her by the hand, pulling her out into the afternoon light before the door could come down and hinder our escape. She pressed close to me as we went into the building that housed my room and trailed up the hall. I stuck my key in the lock and we went in, shutting the door tightly behind us.

Bailey turned her face up to mine, and I bent and kissed her. Her fists knotted in the front of my cut and she pushed it back off my shoulders. I helped things along, piece by piece until we were both standing there naked as the day we were born, skins flushed with heat and the need to be a part of each other.

Her fingertips glided over my body, lingering over the spot on my ribs dedicated to the one percent diamond I had there. I asked her softly, "Too much?" needing to know if it was something she'd never be able to get over because that would suck. It would hurt worse than anything that'd gone before, and there wasn't anything I could do to change it. She smiled, shook her head, and reached up to bring my lips down to hers. I felt a knot of tension I hadn't realized I carried ease out of the center of my chest and out from between my shoulders. My spine loosening up with relief.

I hauled her fit body up against mine and deepened the kiss, letting my need for her shine through. She smiled against my lips and it was like a flower opening up to the sun, the change in her. I knew in that moment, that I somehow brought her joy. That being with me was the same as it was for me being with her. That we just needed to hold on to that. This attraction went way beyond just having the hots for each other. Some things were just fated to be, and we were one of them.

As much as we both liked it rough, I didn't want to go there with her right now. She was fragile, and I figured it was time to show her I had a few other tricks up my sleeve than just banging the shit out of her like some caveman. So, I got her up on the bed and laid her down on her stomach, taking my time to press my lips lightly to every square inch of her skin in these light little butterfly fart kisses until she was left gasping and giggling, her body wriggling at the tickling sensation.

Still, me being me, I pinned her fine ass to the top blanket. No matter how much she writhed, kicked, and begged me to do something else, I kept at it until *I* was satisfied. When I was? I flipped her on her back and did it all over again to the front of her body, that is, until I reached the juncture of her thighs… then my interest was captured with making her writhe due to an entirely different set of circumstances.

I rolled my eyes so I could watch her face as I kept her thighs open with the set of my shoulders. Bailey's eyes filled with the dark, hungry light of desire and her breath let out in a shuddering sigh at the first tentative touch of my tongue. I teased her opening with my fingertip and slid my middle finger easily inside her, stimulating her body with that come-hither motion, my knuckles pressed tightly to her outer lips. I lowered my mouth back down to her pussy and took that hard, little kernel of flesh into my mouth and sucked.

I felt her body tense, her hands gripping the covers to either side of her hips as she gave a slow, steady roll of them, lifting them unconsciously off the bed. I braced my free forearm across her hips and pressed her back down to the bed and I swear, the act of restraining her was enough to make her pussy pulse around my finger. It was erotic as hell how responsive her body was to what I liked, and not for the first time, I thought we were made for each other in more ways than one. I'd never been with a woman whose tastes complemented mine so fully.

"Stop, stop, stop!" she gasped and I leaned up. She arched an eyebrow and said, "I want to come with you inside me," and I had to smile. I liked the sound of that. I liked the sound of that a lot, and I wasn't about to deny a request like that, especially when I was so hard, I could crack rocks with it.

I climbed her body slowly, and pressed a few kisses to her skin, pausing to take one of her nipples into my mouth and suck on it, teasing it with my tongue while I watched her face. I adjusted my angle with one hand while I leaned on my forearm by her head with the other so I wouldn't crush her.

I pressed into her in one long, super slow, steady stroke and her eyes slipped shut, her breath escaping her in a long, satisfied, shuddering sigh. I held myself there, not daring to move just yet, and kissed her, holding her close in the warm cage of my body. Willing her to understand by touch alone just how much she'd come to mean to me with her willingness to adapt and keep going, her commitment to stay the course.

I loved these things about her, I loved her, and I really wanted her to stay the course with me and try on her dream for size. Was it scary? – As hell, but it was also the right thing to do. It was such a rush being with her, and I needed that in my life, to keep me steady and on course for walking this straight and narrow. Nothing was ever boring around Bailey Lynn Berling, and I really, *really* loved that about her.

She moved under me, her eyes closed, a look of concentration on her face, and I wanted to stay like this forever.

34

B ailey...

I WANTED RUSH, needed him like the very air I breathed but he was driving me all sorts of crazy and not necessarily in a good way right this minute. He moved in me, slowly and deliberately, and not at all with his usual fervor which set my nerves on edge. I was beginning to worry that something was wrong when he chuckled and bowed his head, sucking a nipple into his mouth. I arched, pressing more of my breast into his mouth and tensed down around his cock.

That felt good...

"Relax, baby," he growled against my chest, "I feel like a slow ride."

Oh, well, in that *case...*

I stretched my arms above my head and relaxed into his hold and let him take over. I adapted and decided that he could do whatever he wanted to my body, mostly because whatever he chose to do, I knew it was going to feel good. He always felt amazing.

He grinned down at me and murmured, "Wild ride or slow ride?"

"Whatever you want," I said back, voice low and husky and his face turned serious.

"I love you, Bailey Lynn."

"I love you, too, Logan."

He hooked an arm beneath my knee and folded it up to my chest, the angle he had me at making my pussy shallow, his slow driving thrusts feeling like they went impossibly deep. Some women, when their cervix was bumped by the head of a man's cock, they found it uncomfortable or painful, but not me. I couldn't get enough of the sensation. Loved it, wanted more – to the point I was willing to beg.

"God, like that, yeah just like that," I breathed, and Rush was always keen to give it to me just how I wanted.

"You like that?" he growled by my ear and I nodded.

"Yeah, I love that."

"Good."

He pressed himself tight to my body and ground against me, and *Oh, my God*, I liked that. It was like every time we made love, he found newer, deeper parts of me to touch and stroke. It drove me wild in ways I couldn't have even imagined existed.

"I want to watch you ride me," he whispered next to my ear and I nodded. Before I even knew what was happening, the world was spinning and I was straddling Rush, his dick still buried deep. I put my hands on his stomach, trailing fingertips over the curves and ridges of his muscles and used my legs to rise and fall, working his length in and out of me. His hands found my thighs, smoothing up and down them leaving heat and a tingling rush in their wake, a tingling rush that effervesced like champagne bubbles up into the rest of my body, causing my nipples to harden even further.

"Take your pleasure, babe. I wanna watch you do it. I wanna watch you make yourself come."

I felt the deep abiding ache of a building orgasm, and took my time nurturing it, grinding myself onto Rush's dick, gripping the ornate headboard as the passion between us simmered on low. I wanted to enjoy this feeling of hanging off the edge for as long as I could get away with it. It was that magic space between earth and sky, sleep and awake, pleasure and unimaginable bliss and I just wanted to discard all my worries and all my cares and just *live there* for a time.

Rush fostered and encouraged it, the words he murmured lost to me, so involved was I in concentrating on that feeling taking over my body, his cock just brushing that aching point inside me that fucking loved to be touched but rarely ever was. The golden glow suffused my being from my vagina out, crawling up through my body, leaving a faint, gentle blush of sensation everywhere it traveled even though nothing actually physically touched me there.

I tensed around him and cried out, riding on that very edge, about to come but suddenly it was so maddeningly unattainable. I needed that final spark, that last gentle nudge and I managed to focus on Rush's words then. "That's it, baby, you're almost there, now touch yourself."

My fingers drifted to the top of my sex and I found myself so incredibly wet and wanting. I barely pressed my fingertips into my clit and stiffened, my pussy seizing on that little touch and taking me the rest of the way. I arched, voice escaping my throat in a wailing moan despite the fact that I didn't remember giving voice to anything.

I crashed and was sucked under, rolled under again by the next pulsing wave when I tried to come up for air, and so completely consumed by Rush, I never wanted to take a breath without him being a part of it ever again.

I hadn't realized he'd rolled me physically as well as metaphorically until I came back to myself with him on top of me. He had one leg gathered up over one hip while he drove himself into me and I gasped. We stared into one another's eyes while he worked himself in and out of my body, taking his own satisfaction a moment or two after mine.

He shuddered above me and bowed his head, and I let my arms go around him, holding him tightly until the storm within us both settled. He gasped for breath in counterpoint to my own panting, and just managed to withdraw from me, vaulting one of my legs to collapse beside me. He gathered me close and kissed me, and we kept kissing until our breath returned to something closer to normal.

"Why didn't you take it, baby?"

The change in conversation was too rapid for me to follow and I closed my eyes and asked, "What do you mean?"

"The offer, me and the girls put together… helping you get your place up and running, why didn't you take it? What is there to think about?"

I lay my head back into the pillow of his shoulder and looked at him, committing every bit of his face to memory from his warm, golden brown eyes, to his sandy hair, close cut and barely brushing his forehead. From the light shadow of growth along his jaw and the grim set of his mouth as he waited for my answer. He was beautiful to me, but somehow, I thought he might get offended if I told him as much. That 'beautiful' might not be a descriptor he appreciated.

"I want it," I said and swallowed hard.

"So, take it; it's right there."

"That's the problem," I said nervously, scraping my bottom lip between my teeth. "Any time I've *really* wanted something, I've had to work for it, I've had to earn it, and nine times out of ten when I finally got there? It was either denied me, or like Blue Hills, was snatched completely out of my grip anyway. If something good is going to finally come my way, I want it to be you. I guess I'm scared, and overwhelmed, and I just don't know what to do…"

"Say yes," he said. "Stop letting these assholes tell you what you can and can't do. Stop coloring inside the lines and fucking *say* yes. Let a motherfucker come and try and take this from you. See what he gets."

I searched his grim face and said, "It was you, wasn't it? Or if it wasn't you, it was the club." I'd had the news messaged to me from several different sources about Giangiulio's house exploding in the wee hours due to a suspected gas-leak. *'Karma Hits Disreputable Developer'* was the going headline and the photos of his leveled house were displayed side by side with aerial shots of the burned-out shell that was mine.

"That's club business, baby. You know I can't and won't discuss it."

I closed my eyes and nodded, shivering a bit. Rush pulled the quilt at the bottom of the bed up over us both. He gathered me close and I cuddled into the cocoon of heat his body provided in the air conditioned hush of his room.

"So much is happening just so fast, do I have to decide right now?"

"No, baby, you don't. You can take as much time as you need with this."

I nodded and lay my head on his shoulder and picked at myself silently. *Why didn't I just say yes? What was holding me back?* I mean what I'd said had been true. I'd lost count of how many times I'd been promised something or other and had gotten my hopes up, only for funds and attention to be diverted to what the favored son wanted to do instead.

I thought Blue Hills had finally been something I could build and be proud of, but no, even that had been ruined for me by my brother. I wondered why he hated me so much, I mean he had *everything* he could ever want and God forbid I should *ever* complain about it... I just didn't know what the hell my problem was, other than I needed therapy, and likely a lot of it.

I drowsed peacefully in my lover's arms and he held me, no judgments, no recriminations, just held me and made sure I knew that whatever I decided, it was okay.

35

R ush...

"It's just an idea," she said to me, dropping into my lap. I looked up from the plans I was drawing up for a piece of furniture and put my arms around her waist.

I tipped my head to the side and said, "What is?"

"The corporate retreat, the bed-and-breakfast part of it, it was just an idea that I had, not a dream I was fully invested in and what's more, it's not *your* dream. I'm serious, Rush. What do *you* want?"

She straddled my hips and faced me, her fingertips lightly curling in the short hairs at the nape of my neck and I leaned back and looked her over. It'd been a few days of dealing with cleanup and shit over at Blue Hills. Storing things away and getting the stables and large barn ready to go dormant for a longer period than either one of us would have liked.

"I want a place that I can work on my furniture and be around horses. I like working with my hands." She wiggled her eyebrows at me and I laughed, and she smiled too. "But most of all, I don't give a fuck what

I'm doing as long as I'm with you and we're both some kind of happy and committed to doing it."

"I feel shitty for giving up on Blue Hills so easily, I was meant to deal with thoroughbreds, not yuppie corporate types. I mean, I would love to have a riding school, a place to introduce kids to the joy that is horses, but I went to school, got all of that education in hopes I'd be able to stay at Blue Hills, down on the ground and committed to making it the best damn racehorse farm and breeding facility Kentucky has ever seen."

"So, don't give up. Let's do it."

She looked thoughtful and said, "Do you think the offer will still stand if I don't do the riding school and B&B part of things?"

"Why can't you do both?"

"What?"

"Why not do a thoroughbred breeding program and a riding school? How many people do you think would pay to stay on a real working Kentucky racehorse farm? You said it yourself, Blue Hills is way bigger than it ever needed to be for just being a thoroughbred farm."

"No one is going to want a bunch of regular folks around their blue-blooded horses."

"Dude, what happens to a thoroughbred horse that doesn't work out for racing? I'm sure it's happened."

"Actually, you may be onto something, but I'm thinking more along the lines of retirees that aren't suited to breeding."

"What happens to them?"

"Slaughter, usually... It's always been a more than slightly depressing field to work in. A racehorse usually goes for a career of about seven years, but what about the next two decades? Some are bred, but some?"

"Some need to be retired to live out their days educating folks rather than just being slaughtered, I mean what the fuck? Shit, man… you're right, this ain't some dude ranch like back in Arizona, but at least they don't just go killin' horses when they outlive their usefulness."

"Okay, so what if we refocused a little…"

And just like that, she broke through whatever funk that'd been put on her and she started really dreaming her own dreams. We spent the rest of the night with my pad of paper and pencil thinking up ideas and going new directions with some of the space available at Blue Hills.

"We'd have to rename it," she said suddenly, and I looked at her.

"I'll leave that up to you, babe. If it were me it'd end up being something like Iron Horse or some shit and I don't think your hoity-toity rich crowd would take that seriously."

She laughed and said, "I don't think you're wrong about that."

"You think about talking to your mom's buddy? That Cranston lady?" I asked.

Bailey leaned back in her seat next to mine as we gently swung on one of the benches made for it around the cold firepit.

"It's not a bad idea," she said finally and nodded. "I think I could do that."

"Cool."

"Let me try my mother, see if she'd be willing to put us back in touch."

"Sure, sounds good. Or, you know, you could just call her."

Bailey gave me a shrewd look for a minute and said, "You're right. If this is going to be our dream and we're going to do it, *I* should be the one to call her.

"Now, *that's* my girl!" I crowed and she smiled.

"I think I'm going to miss staying here, though," she said with a sigh.

294

"Gonna take a good long while to rebuild the house."

Bailey's eyes grew distant for a moment and she said, "I think I might have just thought of a name for it."

"Yeah?"

"Yeah."

"Well, alright then. You going to tell me?"

"Not yet," she said with an impish grin. "I want to make sure it's really going to be a thing first."

"Oh, it's going to be a thing."

"That so, biker boy?" she said, and I loved it when she got sassy on me.

"You better believe it, rich bitch."

She laughed and leaned up to kiss me, and I kissed her back. Trig called out from the back door of the club, "We be interrupting anything heavy if we came out there and joined you?"

"Not at all!" Bailey called back.

He and Ashton moved up and took a swinging bench near ours, Ashton asking, "How's cleanup been going?"

"Almost done," Bailey said and I gave her a nudge. She rolled her eyes at me and I gave her a look that said I was going to fuck the shit out of her later for it. She rolled her eyes again and just sealed the deal on that one.

"So, Rush and I were just talking about what to do with Blue Hills, and I think I would kind of like to expand the idea I initially had for rebuilding, a little.

"Oh, yeah?" Ashton asked.

"Yeah…"

It was good, listening to them talk, hearing Bailey's voice grow animated and excited the more she laid things out to Ashton. It was even better watching Sunshine get all excited about giving horses a second chance rather than having them destroyed. Trig smiled at his woman indulgently and honestly, the laid-back brother could give a fuck what she did with her money as long as she was safe, happy, and he knew she would be provided for if anything happened to him. He'd said it often enough, anyhow.

Pretty soon plans were being made to move forward regardless of anyone else's involvement. Ashton made Trig call Reaver to see if his construction company was up to handling the building required and more.

I smiled like a loon, I couldn't help it. Bailey sure bounced back quickly, and I was glad for it. She was going to need every bit of that shit for the rough road of trials and court dates and shit ahead.

She turned to me, a fire in her eyes; some real excitement for a change and grabbed my hand. "We can turn the main garage by the house into a woodshop and park further down in what used to be the employee's garage."

I grinned and pointed out, "Still gonna have to have employees, babe." She frowned and I laughed at the cute expression on her face saying, "We got plenty of time to figure it out, don't worry."

"Promise?" she asked and I nodded.

"Promise."

EPILOGUE

Six months later...

B^{ailey...}

"Okay!" I cried and Rush and Trigger did the honors, pulling the sheet covering the sign at the entryway to the farm to reveal the new name and logo that Trigger had designed for us.

Phoenix Hills Equestrian Center arched in flames above a herd of stallions in racing formation, their silhouettes bursting into flames at the back as they streaked across the sign.

"Out of the ashes, let this place be reborn," Marion crowed and a cheer from not just the club, but the dedicated employees of when the place was Blue Hills went up. We toasted with champagne and laughed, most of us sniffling, it was freaking *cold* out here!

"Right, let's move this into the barn and try and get warmed up," Trig said and everyone started the trek up the driveway.

It was that time of year, and breeding practices were in full swing, Marion giving us the chance we needed to start anew. She loved the idea of utilizing the farm for not only its originally intended purpose, but as a means to educate and rescue horses that may be past their breeding prime but still had plenty of life left in them.

She and Ashton had both heavily invested in Phoenix Hills, yet I remained full owner. Well, at least everyone thought I did. I had a surprise for Rush.

The party wore on well into the night, and that was fine by me. We had a lot to celebrate. The house was rebuilt in the precise floor plan of the old, except the smaller barn that was attached, we didn't use as a barn anymore. We had converted it into Rush's woodshop instead. When the house was completed, he'd surprised me with a beautifully carved front door for it, and in fact, most of the furniture inside were his pieces. Hayden had had a field day with the decorating.

My mother had, surprisingly, been enthusiastic and proud of my accomplishments. Fully supporting my dream in every way that she could, while my brother? He was in disgrace and was just about to begin a prison sentence. Caleb was still fighting us out in court, but it was clear he was on the losing end of things.

I was cleaning up in our kitchen when Rush came up behind me and pulled me back into his chest, kissing the side of my neck.

"I have something I want to show you," I said and he groaned a little.

"Is it your tits? Please tell me it's your tits…"

"Even better," I whispered, and he said, "Really? Alright!"

"Come on, step into my office, biker boy," I turned in his arms and kissed him, and he smacked me on the ass. I jumped and let out a girlish yip.

"Lead the way, baby. I built that desk and I aim to fuck you over it."

"Ooooh, you're right we haven't done it in there!"

He trailed me into the office, and I picked up the manila file folder off the center of my blotter and handed it to him saying, "This is for you."

He frowned at it and flipped it open. It was so worth watching his brow, wrinkled with confusion, smooth into disbelief. His wide, golden brown eyes going molten with desire when he looked at me.

"You made me part owner of this place?"

"It's *ours*, not mine… so yeah."

"You're serious?"

"To borrow a phrase you guys like to use all the time, 'as a heart attack, baby.'"

"Oh, bitch. You better get naked."

"What, now?"

"Uh huh, *right now*."

He set the file folder down and came to me, pulling me into the circle of his arms and kissing me. I let my hands drift to his belt, and he moaned into my mouth. I don't think anything could be more perfect if I wanted it to. I squealed in glee as he lifted me and sat my ass on the edge of my desk.

"Oh, Christ, I love it when you make that sound," he growled against my mouth and I smiled.

"You're the only one that could ever make me make it," I whispered.

"I like that even better," he said.

"I love you, Rush."

"I love you, too, Bales."

"The forever kind of love?" I asked.

"Yep, the forever kind of love."

Perfect.

ALSO BY A.J. DOWNEY

Indigo Knights

1. Her Thin Blue Lifeline

2. His Cold Blue Command

3. A Low Blue Flame

4. His Wild Blue Rose

5. Her Pained Blue Silence

6. A Cold Blue Call

7. Her Reluctant Blue Cavalier

8. Forged Under Fire

9. Under A Blue Moon

10. Sound of Blue Thunder

Sacred Hearts MC Pacific Northwest

1. Over the High Side

2. Wind Therapy

3. Apex of the Curve

4. Low Sided

5. Eating Asphalt

6. Hammer Down

7. Only Fool Riding

The Voodoo Bastards MC

1. Bourbon & Blood

2. Whiskey Shivers

3. Moonshine Lullabies

4. Cognac Secrets

5. Tequila Damnation

Iron Wraiths MC

1. Original Syn

2. Love & Fear

3. The Hangman's Rope

Royal Bastard MC: St. Augustine Chapter

1. Iron Hearts

Paranormal Romance (with Ryan Kells)

1. I Am The Alpha

2. Omega's Run

3. Hunter's End

Indigo City Darker (with Jared KingPacal Lain)

1. Triple Threat

2. Double Shot

Standalones

Synchronicity

ABOUT A.J. DOWNEY

A.J. Downey is a Pacific Northwest girl living in an East Tennessee world who finds inspiration from her surroundings, through the people she meets, and likely as a byproduct of way too much caffeine. She specializes in real and relatable romance stories featuring that real-life kind of love that everyone craves.

Stalker Information:

Website
www.ajdowney.com

www.ingramcontent.com/pod-product-compliance
Lightning Source LLC
Chambersburg PA
CBHW070308280626
47159CB00017B/667